ISHTAR'S LEGACY

RACHEL SULLIVAN

CITY OWL
PRESS

ISHTAR'S LEGACY
Wild Women, Book 3

CITY OWL PRESS
www.cityowlpress.com

Cover Design by Mibl Art and Tina Moss. All stock photos licensed appropriately.

Edited by Heather McCorkle.

Map by Dani Woodruff.

For information on subsidiary rights, please contact the publisher at info@cityowlpress.com.

Print Edition ISBN: 978-1-949090-43-7

Digital Edition ISBN: 978-1-949090-44-4

Printed in the United States of America

To my readers.
I am truly thankful for you, and I hope you've enjoyed reading Faline's story as much as I've enjoyed telling it.

PRAISE FOR RACHEL SULLIVAN

"Strong characters. Smart writing. The most fun I've had between the pages in a long time! Sullivan's debut is not to be missed!" – *New York Times bestselling author, Wendy Higgins*

"Sullivan explodes onto the scene bringing her ideals of feminism and diversity with her. Strong female characters and world building collide leaving the reader breathless and eager for more." – *Samantha Heuwagen, Author of Dawn Among The Stars*

"A promising debut from Rachel Sullivan, Freyja's Daughter is an immersive urban fantasy novel with a satisfying feminist theme. Sullivan invokes a believable representation of mythological beings in a modern setting, and provides a contextually realistic interpretation of the lore surrounding them. Freyja's Daughter is a rare treat for urban fantasy fans." – *Caitlin Lyle Farley, Readers' Favorite 5 Starred Review*

"Freyja's Daughterhas strong female characters, captivating content, and Rachel Sullivan shows a talent for writing and content that I can totally see a fan base growing from. I am looking forward to more from this author." – *Tanja, KT Book Reviews*

"In this wickedly smart must-read debut novel, strong women warriors based on familiar mythologies and folktales band together to take down the patriarchy. Rachel Sullivan's compelling voice, unique worldbuilding, and enchanting characters makes her my newest one-click author." – *Asa Maria Bradley, Award-Winning Author and Double RITA Finalist of the Viking Warriors series*

"Freyja's Daughter, Sullivan's first book in her Wild Women's series, makes you want to binge the series all at once. Welcome to the entertaining, feminist, and inclusive world of Huldras, Mermaids,

Rusalki, and other mythical women—a world you won't want to leave."
– *Ivelisse Rodriguez, Author of Love War Stories*

"Freyja's Daughteris a fast-paced, thrilling tale of women reclaiming their power in a folkloric battle of the sexes. I can't wait to spend more time in Sullivan's exciting and enchanting world." – *Cass Morris, Authof of From Unseen Fire*

"The action in this book begins right away. Readers are pulled in through the first person point of view and are taken on the journey by Faline as she fights for her kind... For those who enjoy paranormal romance, this is a must read." – *InD'tale, Lynn-Alexandria McKendrick*

"Urban fantasy with good world-building...Faline's journey to self-realization and her growth as a leader of the various tribes - and carrying out a revolution - is well-developed in this book." – *Midwest Book Review*

Huldra—Forest women, able to cover their skin in bark and grow branches from their hands and feet, created by the Goddess Freyja.

<u>Washington Coterie</u>

- Faline

- Shawna

- Olivia

- Celeste

- Patricia

- Renee

- Abigale

- Naomi (missing)

Succubi—Empathic women, able to manipulate and absorb energy, created by the Goddess Lilith.

<u>Oregon Galere</u>

- Marie

- Heather (missing)

Mermaids—Aquatic women, able to shift their legs to a tail and cover their skin with scales, created by the Goddess Atargatis.

<u>California Shoal</u>

- ~~Gabrielle~~

- Azul

- Elaine

- Sarah

Harpies—Women able to sprout bird-like wings, feathers, and talons, created by the Goddess Inanna.

<u>North Carolina Flock</u>

- Eonza

- Salis

- Lapis

- Rose (missing)

Rusalki—Women tied to nature, able to read minds, practice divination, and cut lives short, created by the Goddess Mokosh.

<u>Maine Coven</u>

- Veronia

- Daphne

- ~~Azalea~~

- Drosera

- Aconitum (missing)

- Oleander (missing)

Nagin—Women represented by the cobra, able to use kundalini energy to manipulate the energy of a person from the inside, created by the Goddess Wadjet.

<u>United Kingdom</u>

- Anwen

- Berwyn

- Eta

Shé—Women able to change their lower half into a snake tale while in the water. On land they maintain their legs and can grow scales on their body for protection as they play their handmade instrument to change the energy, moods, and thoughts of others, created by the Goddess Nü Gua.

<u>China</u>

- Chen

- Fan

Echidna—Women able to change their lower half to a snake tail for

speed, defense, and squeezing their prey, created by the Snake Goddess of Crete, whose name is not uttered or known to outsiders.

<u>Crete</u>

- Calle

- Gerda

PREFACE

There once was a little girl, as rich and deep as the very earth itself. Within her heart, seeds were planted, and one by one these seeds took root. The little girl was not aware of the growth within her, for she did not know how to recognize such vines and leaves. Until one day, when she was much older, the vines burst from her fingertips with a power she never knew she possessed. And through these vines, seeds were planted into other hearts, until across the globe, the trees of change took root and grew to heal us all.

This was the last story Faline's mother whispered to her little girl, the last seed she tucked into her daughter's heart.
And the Hunters never saw it coming.

ONE

THE MOMENT I set foot in the waiting area outside the one-story Ashville Regional Airport in North Carolina, the soles of my feet tingled with the need to push roots into the east coast soil. Stars twinkled in the distance, peeking out between shifting winter clouds, their brightness muted by the city's light pollution. Above us, a sign clung to the cement outer walls, encased in lit bulbs.

Arrivals.

I'd walked through this relatively small airport, along the grounds of this part of the country, before. This time my heart quickened with a knowing. With the culmination of the past months, of the fighting and hiding and absolute hell, my body insisted that I rise like an ocean wave and crash onto the Hunters' shore, wiping them out for good.

Marcus grabbed my hand, pulling me from my battle fantasy and back into the moment.

"Where were you just now?" he asked with a twinkle of curiosity in his eyes and a smirk on his lips. We had unintentionally matched, both wearing bomber-style jackets and jeans with boots. Though, if you asked me, he wore it better.

"I think you already know the answer to that," I teased.

"I know I *know* the answer," he said, squeezing my hand, "but how does it look in your mind?"

I exhaled. My breath, visible in the winter night's frigid air, dissipated before I put words to the images in my mind. "I think you and Aleksander were on to something. I like the idea of blowing up the last two Hunter complexes. But this time with bigger explosions. I want the whole country to feel the fall of our oppressors."

I looked to my partner sister Shawna, who hooked her left arm into mine. Every huldra had a partner sister—another huldra born around the same time within her coterie, a best friend and sister to spend her life with. Shawna gave an approving nod.

We'd planned to drive rental vans to North Carolina, but decided it'd be smarter to fly instead. And my aunt Renee showed signs of travel fatigue not more than a day into our journey.

"Where are they?" my aunt grumbled. Her feet balanced on the edge of the sidewalk as she leaned into the road to peer left, in the direction our ride should have been visible from by now.

"Be patient," a nagin, Anwen, said. She stood tall, her long black and silver hair framing her dark skin and eyes. "They flew here on their own wings, not a machine's."

Renee ignored the British Wild Woman and silently continued toeing the edge of the sidewalk.

We hadn't wasted much time in Oregon after blowing up their Hunters' complex and then coming back to a Hunter ambush at our Airbnb. After collecting our things and trying to clean the place up as much as possible—though our new ally, the incubus Aleksander, was still going to owe repair charges, which we'd fully reimburse him for—we piled into our vehicles and made for the airport. We couldn't all get on the same flight headed to North Carolina—the flights were too full—so we had opted to use cash and buy tickets to leave the following afternoon. We'd rented hotel rooms under an incubus's name and Aleksander had his incubi bring the succubi's things to pick through at the hotel, deciding which items to leave behind and which to take with them on our little east coast excursion. Thankfully the incubus had brought us each fake identification cards as well, promising the cards had worked for other traveling supernaturals, but refused to tell us which and what kind.

The harpies had left Oregon right away, as soon as we'd made the decision to fly. Last we'd talked to them, from our hotel room right before we'd checked out and left for our flight, they were almost home and stopping at a rental car business to borrow a few passenger vans. Eonza assured us they'd be able to pick us up when our flight landed.

Yet, here we stood, a group of Wild Women, two incubi, and a Hunter. This airport looked nothing like SeaTac or some of the others I'd flown into. It exchanged the hustle and bustle of crowds I'd seen in the larger airports for handfuls of people strolling to cars parked in the distance, or waiting for a hotel shuttle. Sitting out here, our group probably looked like out-of-town visitors here for a super secret badass convention.

"I wish we could call them and see how far out they are," my sister, Celeste, complained.

The succubi leader, Marie, kissed Celeste's hand and smiled. "Leaving our phones behind was for the best, baby. Now we're untraceable."

"Hey, Aleksander," I said, turning to eye him as he sat away from us on a metal bench beneath the overhang as though it were his throne. He looked up from his hands with a questioning gaze. "Can you feel them approaching? What's your energy radius when it comes to that?"

Aleksander probably liked jetting off across the country less than my aunt Renee. But despite his best efforts, the incubus had locked onto me through the one-way incubus mate bond, and so wherever I went, he did too. Aleksander stood. The incubi leader reached over six-foot-two. A smile crept along his lips as he made his way toward us. His black wool overcoat barely shifted against his dark slacks. He looked like New York in North Carolina. He gave me a nod as he passed and said, "You should know better, Faline, than to ask a man his size, energy, or otherwise."

Marcus stifled a laugh.

I rolled my eyes.

Considering the circumstances—Marcus was my boyfriend and Aleksander claimed me as his future mate—the two men got along better than expected. They weren't friends by any stretch of the word, but I suspected both wanted to do right by me and each thought the other would eventually give up.

Aleksander stood to the left of my aunt Renee and relaxed his body, his arms falling to his sides. Renee took a few steps back from the curb and joined us in watching the incubus work. My skin tingled in pulses, as though I could feel his energy growing to encompass the surrounding area enough to sense if harpies were nearby. I peered at my sisters and aunts to see if they felt it too. If the sensations vibrated through them as well, they didn't show it.

The incubi leader spun on his heel and addressed his audience. "They will be here shortly." He casually returned to his throne of a bench, retrieved his carry-on, and made his way to stand patiently at the curb.

He couldn't have seen them when he'd made the announcement, because it was several minutes before the three blue passenger vans stopped at the curb and slid their side doors open.

"Thanks for picking us up," I said to Salis, a member of the harpy flock, as I filed into the van along with my coterie, Marcus, and Aleksander. My sensitive nose picked up the faint traces of the rental van's last occupants, and the rental company's inability to fully erase cigarette smoke.

Salis gave a nod, her tawny ponytail only moving enough across her shoulders to readjust the brown feather woven into a small strand of braid among her tresses. With one sharp movement of her lean neck, she turned back toward the road, hitting the gas the moment Aleksander shut the sliding van door. After exiting the airport traffic and making her way over to the carpool lane on the freeway, Salis spoke. "Once we near town, we will break off from the other vans. Each is going to a separate location."

"That won't work," Renee started in before I could ask Salis to explain her plan.

"We don't have cell phones to communicate with one another," Celeste clarified. She probably hadn't yet realized she wouldn't be sharing a bed with her lover Marie during this trip, let alone be unable to talk to the succubi leader.

Salis only stared forward through the windshield. Both my sister and my aunt had made statements, so in harpy fashion, our Wild cousin didn't respond. She probably assumed the huldra were talking amongst themselves. During my time with them I'd gathered, if nothing else, the harpies were pedantic.

I reworded my coterie's concerns and made sure to address the harpy. "Salis, they're worried they won't be able to stay connected to the other Wild Women groups, which is imperative to our mission here. Have you made provisions for this?"

I watched the harpy's expressionless face through the rearview mirror as she spoke.

"Each house has a landline," she said.

I figured the harpies would have already thought of everything we needed in the coming days. Unlike the Wild Women on this trip, other than my huldra coterie, they still had a group member missing. Only, we could all accurately guess where their mother was being held: in the North Carolina Hunter complex. The location of my mother's prison was a bit more difficult to pin down.

My mother had gone missing when I was a little girl. Up until recently, I'd always thought she'd been killed by jealous succubi, angry at her for mating with a human male their leader had claimed. Multiple times, Marie had assured me her predecessor, who'd trained her to be a succubi leader, never would have commanded such a thing be done. Succubi healed and helped, they did not hurt and murder.

Through my own bounty hunter research skills and Marcus's gathering of old police documents and Hunter intel, I now knew my mother had been taken by Hunters, along with a handful of other Wild Women, twenty years ago. According to the rusalki, the women taken at the time of my mother's disappearance had long since died, but my mother still lived.

When the Hunters recently abducted another collection of Wild Women—my partner sister Shawna being one of them—my hunt for the truth began. What I found were answers knotted in oppression masquerading as protection, lies about our kind costumed as history, and the trafficking of women whose humanity had been stripped away and replaced by objectification.

At first I only sought to get my sister back. It was the mermaids who had burned down the Washington Hunter complex. But their pyro tendencies lit a fire within me, an insatiable blaze to destroy each and every Hunter complex in the United States. Not only would I retrieve every Wild held in Hunter captivity, but I'd burn their prisons to the ground in the process.

"Where will we be staying, then, in relation to the succubi galere?" Celeste asked our harpy driver. If, earlier, she hadn't realized she wouldn't be sharing a bed with Marie, according to the need in her voice, she did now.

"Your coterie and the shé will stay in town; you'll be in the historical district," Salis answered in her regular emotionless tone. "The succubi galere will stay at a larger vacation home near the mountains. This will keep them away from the human emotions of the town's population, help them to gain their strength for the battles ahead."

Damn, the harpies' preparedness impressed me.

"The phone numbers to the other houses, where your comrades are staying, will be written beside the phone in the house where you'll be staying," Salis finished.

Salis exited the freeway and drove down what I remembered as one of the main roads in Burnsville, where I had once booked Gabrielle and I a room at a little motel she deemed beneath her. I smiled at the memory of bantering with the mermaid and wished, once again, that she'd trusted me enough to tell me why she'd felt the need to double-cross the Wild Women by working with the Hunters. I refused to believe she was mean spirited and wanted us to fail. But she would never be able to tell me. She was dead.

"Isn't that the motel?" Marcus whispered into my ear in a low voice as we passed the one-story brick motel lined with white doors and framed in off-white siding.

I suppressed an almost purring tone when I responded, "Yes, it is," with a smile and a wink. In one of those motel rooms, Marcus had admitted his real identity as an ex-Hunter. He'd confessed that he'd realized I was a Wild Woman. And best of all, within one of those floral-covered motel rooms, we'd made love for the first time.

If our fellow passengers knew what we referenced, they didn't make a show of it. This town held good memories as well as hard ones.

"So, Salis," I said, speaking louder and clearer to keep any possible questions about the importance of the motel at bay. "I'm curious, what was your thought process behind which houses you placed us in?" I realized my query could be seen as questioning her decision rather than seeking a deeper understanding of her strategy, so I clarified. "Your flock is quite strategic in all things, and I'm wondering which strategy is at play here."

Salis peered at me through the rearview mirror for a breath, her light eyes studying mine, then returned her gaze to the road. "I have already explained why I placed the succubi galere in the foothills of the mountain."

"True," I responded. "But why put us in the historical district? And where exactly did you place the foreign Wilds?"

"The shé, nagin, and echidna are on their way to a residential home in a newer community," Salis answered. "Not one owned by any of us, but rather an empty rental a business associate has agreed to allow us to access for the time being."

"And the one we're staying in isn't owned by you either?" I asked, trying to judge how easily the Hunters may or may not be able to find us.

"It is indirectly owned by us," she responded. "Passed to us through our flock's paternal grandparents but left in their family name."

She knew of her parental lineage? And had been given property through the father's line? Her statement brought up a slew of questions I promised myself to ask her later. Unlike my sisters and I, the harpy flock—Eonza, Salis, and Lapis—all had the same mother. Now, I wondered if they had the same father, too. They did bear a shocking resemblance to one another, which wasn't something you often found among Wild Women sisters. Did their father know he'd mated with a harpy? She'd said the house was from her parental grandparents, so I wasn't sure if that meant from her mother's grandfather or her grandfather.

After a few more turns our car slowed. Mature trees lined the quaint street, standing between the sidewalks and the well-kept traditionally built homes, spaced a comfortable distance apart. Salis pulled into the driveway of a house unseen from the road, with evergreen bushes acting as thick natural privacy fences. She parked in front of a brown detached garage trimmed with beige and merlot. The two-story home matched the garage, except for the dark red brick at its base, which not only covered the face of the porch in the front but wrapped around the sides of the house, maybe four feet between the ground and the light brown painted wood siding.

"It's a Craftsman home," Olivia said with awe. "I love this architectural style."

Olivia had a thing for houses, especially historical houses. Our coterie's research guru found the buildings in which history happened as interesting as the people who *made* history happen. Her afternoons of coming home from the library with new-to-her exciting facts about old things felt like another lifetime ago. Those days we weren't running from the Hunters—or to them—and we had time to pursue interests outside of scouting our next plan of attack. There weren't many historical homes open as museums in our area of Washington, but before life had gotten crazy, Olivia liked to take day trips to walk the creaky floors of houses of the past. Most of the time she'd brought Celeste with her, but sometimes Shawna and I joined too.

"Your coterie," Salis finally continued after turning off the ignition and twisting her tall, lean body in her seat to face me, "were chosen to stay in this home because its historical aspects could be of use to you."

"What does it have?" Olivia half-joked and probably half-hoped, "a secret room hidden behind a bookshelf?"

Shawna snickered.

"No," Salis said, unlatching her seatbelt and opening her driver's side door. "For a long while North Carolina was a dry state. As was this county. As such, my paternal ancestors were bootleggers."

Shawna quieted.

"We chose this house for you," Salis went on, dead serious, "because it contains a secret underground connected to cursed passageways."

TWO

IT DIDN'T TAKE much of an imagination to view the old house as more of a museum than a home. Not that I believed the harpies opened it to the public and charged admission to humans who wished to see sheet-covered furniture and dusty old clocks. With heavy curtains drawn and an obvious lack of plant life anywhere to be seen inside the home, our new musty surroundings felt cramped and depressing. Olivia, on the other hand, looked as though she was in heaven.

"Why are there so many clocks?" I asked absently, already irritated by the clicking sound each clock made every time a minute passed. No way could I sleep listening to minutes tick by.

Salis answered, pulling a sheet from a flower print couch with wooden armrests. "I suspect it had to do with the home owner's business below us."

We all stopped our wandering through the first floor to watch her, waiting for the next part of her story. Except, it never came. Salis continued pulling sheets from the chairs and tables and bundling them up to toss off into an empty corner. The wooden floorboard creaked as she made her way around the parlor.

"Care to elaborate?" Celeste prodded.

Salis finished exposing the furniture. She wiped her hands on her slacks. The same slacks she'd worn the day the harpies left Oregon to fly home. I doubted they'd had time to change before picking us up from the airport. Other than her clothing, she appeared bright and fresh, like she'd recently woken from a great sleep, not flown across the country. I highly doubted I'd look as good in the same circumstances.

"I'll do one better," Salis answered, making her way to a floor-to-ceiling hutch in the dining room. She opened the center drawer of the hutch, which sat at the half-way point, under the glass-encased shelves where I assumed precious glassware once lived. Palm up, Salis felt at the top of the opened drawer until her hand found purchase. She pulled her arm out just in time for the heavy piece of furniture to move aside and reveal a narrow wooden door.

Salis turned the knob as though she'd done it a thousand times before. "Follow me," she instructed.

"What happened to all the China from the cabinet?" Abigale remarked. "I would love to see the beautiful antiques."

"We boxed them up for safe keeping," Salis answered without turning around.

With the secrecy of such a place, the hidden lever and covered door, I would have expected more than the simple basement style stairs I traversed down. We moved single file, with Marcus in front of me and Shawna behind me. Marcus held his hand to the brick wall on our right. I saw just fine, but I held onto his waist at the ready to steady him in case his lack of night vision caused him to trip on some unseen thing. And also because his body felt like home to me and there was something about traveling to an underground place that made my skin crawl.

Maybe it had to do with the time I had been forced to wear a bag over my head to meet an incubi leader under the streets of Portland, where he not only proclaimed his lack of interest in helping the Wild Women obtain their deserved freedom, but also assured me that I too could hide like a sewage rat for the rest of my life.

Marcus would never ask me to hide my existence for the comfort of others. Not that Aleksander would ask that of me any longer. His footfalls sounded like he acted as caboose to our supernatural train headed for dank, musty surroundings. The incubi leader was now just as wanted as the rest of us. At least, we assumed so, since two Hunter leaders had to have seen him using his power of energy manipulation to fight and kill their kind as they left their men to die and retreated from the battle they'd begun in our Airbnb home.

I wondered if Aleksander still thought we didn't have it that bad.

Salis reached the bottom of the stairs first. Her steps echoed across brick as she walked to the far end of the room and lit two taper candles.

"No electricity?" Shawna asked, making her way around the room and running her fingers along the brick walls.

"My ancestors believed it to be an unnecessary risk," Salis answered, placing a box of matches between the two candles on an old dilapidated table.

The glow from the orange candlelight revealed a new layer to the room from the one I'd seen in the dark. Liquid splashes stained the wooden table. Gouges had been cut into the brick walls in no particular order, as though large metal things had smashed against brick over and over.

Oak barrels lay on their sides, scattered at the edges of the room. A copper barrel atop four legs with a pipe coming out the top stood upright in a corner. The damp air stank of vinegar and yeast. Glass jugs littered the floor, some filled with liquid resting in wooden boxes, others empty and broken on the brick ground.

"Your ancestors were moonshiners," Aleksander said with utmost admiration. "A difficult existence, but a noble calling indeed."

The secret basement was a good size, but it felt small and cramped with so many supernaturals poking around.

"Did you know any bootleggers back in the day?" Abigale asked Aleksander.

The incubus let out a deep, short laugh. "Know them? I was one."

It made sense. An incubus helping humans to access alcohol in a dry state and during prohibition. If the incubi wanted to have a good time, it helped if their human sexual interest was also enjoying themselves. Inhibition probably played a part too.

Aleksander's smile dropped and he shot me a look. "You find disgust in me so easily."

Ugh, I'd forgotten his ability to sense my energy, my emotions.

I fought back an eye roll and then felt a little guilty. "Sorry, I just pictured you making moonshine to help aide in your incubus efforts."

"You mean you assumed I needed alcohol to intoxicate human women to sleep with me?" he asked. "Do you think I'm some kind of monster?"

His question caught me off guard and I had to do a quick reevaluation of my unfair beliefs surrounding incubi. If they were the product of a night of passion between a succubus and a vampire, then their energy abilities were passed down from their maternal side. The succubi were not monsters. They did occasionally enjoy naked escapades with humans, giving them the best sex of their lives, but it was all very willing. So why would the same actions from an incubus make him a monster? Why was it okay for females but not males? It wasn't, and I'd been really sexist in thinking so, even subliminally. Part of me just really wanted to dislike this guy due to the whole "mate bond" thing he claimed to have with me.

"I'm sorry," I told Aleksander. "You're right. I shouldn't have assumed that."

"When I lay with a woman," he clarified, just to make sure I got the point, "I desire her to be in her right mind, without the influence of drugs or alcohol. It's not enjoyable if it's coerced, if she's not in full participation."

Salis raised her eyebrow at Aleksander's proclamation and I wondered if she were thinking about her sister, Eonza, who planned to bed the incubi leader sooner rather than later.

Awkwardness filled the basement almost as much as the scent of vinegar and yeast. After a couple minutes of silence, Salis graciously changed the subject. "I'll show you the rest of the house," she said, turning toward the stairs without blowing out the candles.

Our group followed her, but Marcus hung back. He grabbed my wrist as I began to leave and pulled me into his arms. The secret basement door closed, but from the sounds of it, they didn't cover the door with the hutch, thankfully.

"We're finally alone," Marcus whispered into my ear, his warm breath and the bass of his voice commanding all my thoughts to focus on him.

I gladly accepted and wrapped my hands around his back, pushing my body into his. His kisses started out sweet, soft, gentle. But they didn't stay that way for long. By the time his lips reached my neck they'd become hungry, demanding, and everything in me yearned to satiate him. Marcus went to work pulling my shirt off and once it was thrown onto the table, barely missing the lit candles, I grabbed the hem of his shirt and stretched it up over his pecs and shoulders until it joined mine amidst years' worth of dust.

His chiseled chest acted as the perfect canvas for the artful tattoos covering it. I pulled my head away from his just enough to take in the sight, the dagger and cross, the twists and twirls that started out thick and black and ended on pinpricks. The more I fell in love with Marcus Garcia, the more his tattoos reminded me less of his Hunter lineage and the more they belonged to him. They weren't Hunter tattoos. They were Marcus tattoos. That distinction made all the difference. The divot between his traps and his collar bone called to me and I gave them each a light kiss before shoving his thick body into the brick wall behind him, set on unlatching that belt of his.

Dust sprang from the motion and brick cracked behind him. We both snickered at our combined strength as we got back to kissing and touching, when something more than a crack sounded...and the wall moved.

We jumped away from the slowly shifting wall as a door-sized portion of it ground its way backwards.

Marcus and I shared a stare. "You think this is the cursed tunnel Salis so casually mentioned in the van?" he asked.

Curiosity rose in me, pushing aside my desire, for the moment. I grabbed our shirts from the table and tossed him his. Once fully clothed, I took a lit candle and pocketed the matches just in case, because seeing in the dark was easier with at least a little light. "I guess we're about to find out," I said.

Marcus reached for the other candle and gave a nod.

We passed through the opening into darkness. The square ends of bricks from the wall jutted out to meet the ends of bricks from the door when it closed, keeping the opening unseen. I made sure not to hit my head or any other body part as I passed through the threshold from brick flooring to stone and dirt.

Marcus and I didn't have to discuss the need for quietness, we already knew. While we didn't seem to be in immediate danger, it was always safest to assume we were. The Hunters would stop at nothing to find us. That included traipsing through old bootlegger tunnels—if they'd been able to find out about them. We crept single file down the tunnel, the curved walls maybe about three people apart and the rounded ceiling barely taller than Marcus. After a slight decline and a right turn, the air grew damper with the scent of mold and stagnant water. Old cobwebs littered the stone walls.

After walking for over five minutes in pure silence, without so much as a hint of another life form, other than spiders and rats, I figured it was safe to speak. "You think they used this tunnel to transport the moonshine?"

"Your guess is as good as mine," he answered, slowing to walk beside me rather than in front of me. He took my free hand in his. "I wish I could feel the energy down here for a better idea, though."

I hoped he wasn't attempting to resurrect the idea of allowing Aleksander to change him into an incubus.

I stopped and he turned to see why, still holding my hand.

"Maybe we should come back with Marie and Aleksander. What's the point of exploring a tunnel with nothing in it, nothing on the walls?" I answered my own question, thinking out loud. "I mean, we could see where it ends, that would give us some insight as to what it was used for. But if it's miles long, walking the whole thing is a lot of wasted time when we're supposed to be finishing the war I started."

"True." Marcus looked up at nothing, in thought. "This whole time I've been wondering if the place is cursed. How would we know?"

I cocked my head. "Wait, you believe in curses?"

He gave me a duh stare. "Faline, I'm a Hunter, supernatural warrior forged by monks, talking to a huldra, a folkloric protector of the forests created by the Goddess Freyja. Of course I believe in curses."

I studied the wall beside me. "Point taken," I uttered. "Well, if there is a curse there's nothing written about it on the walls—no warnings or anything. The whole curse thing could just be a figure of speech."

"So could Hunter," he added.

As he finished saying "Hunter" the light sound of pebbles being pushed around down the tunnel caught my attention.

I put my hand up and whispered, "I just heard something."

Marcus mouthed "What?" I shrugged my shoulders and listened for more. I couldn't be sure.

I closed my eyes to focus my heightened senses and lifted my nose to deeply inhale. The scent caught me off guard and slammed me with fear. Without an explanation, I grabbed Marcus's hand and turned on my heel, pulling him back toward the brick-lined basement opening. Our quick steps nearly glided over the stone, we were so quiet.

Once our shoes hit the brick and we were back in the moonshine basement, I searched the wall I'd slammed Marcus against to figure out how to close the damn secret door. Every brick looked like the other, none stood out as the one. I pressed my hand on each reddish square his back could have hit until one gave just slightly, pushing in. Slowly, the door eased shut, reuniting bricks until they once again melded into a seamless wall.

Only after we were alone again did Marcus ask, "What was that back there? One minute you were fine and the next you looked like you smelled a ghost."

I swallowed and exhaled. My fists clenched and unclenched. Tears sprang to my eyes. "I did," I said on shaky breath. "I smelled Gabrielle."

THREE

EVERYONE GATHERED around Marcus and I in the kitchen. Some sat at the small breakfast nook. Others leaned against the white and yellow tiled counter tops, obviously refurbished in the sixties some time. Celeste held the corded house phone Salis had told us about, its base attached to the wall between the refrigerator and the kitchen opening. She'd dialed the house where the succubi stayed and had Marie on the line. After grumbling about the old technology's lack of speakerphone capabilities, she held up the earpiece and pointed it at me.

I didn't want to say the same thing over and over again, and possibly leave out details in the process, so I'd waited until a harpy, the incubi leader, the succubi leader, and my coterie were within earshot to explain what Marcus and I had witnessed. I figured I'd call the foreign Wilds next.

"After you all left, Marcus and I stayed down in the basement to talk," I began.

Celeste snorted and I gave her a look.

"Marcus pressed a brick in the wall," I continued, "and a hidden door swung open, leading to a tunnel." My gaze found Salis. "Is that the cursed tunnel you were referring to?"

Salis gave no indication she heard me or even cared, until she opened her mouth, her expression still blank. "We have only heard stories. I wouldn't know."

"In the stories," Marcus asked her, "how was the tunnel cursed? Who put a curse on it?"

Salis finally raised an eyebrow. The small bit of facial expression showed me the large extent of her concern. "My foremothers died in that tunnel," she said and then pursed her lips. "It is a tunnel of hope and death."

I wanted to be sympathetic to the topic, but the questions spinning in my mind won out. "Wait," I said. "Hope and death? Your foremothers? Can you unpack that all?"

"My grandmother's father's father had used the tunnel to transport illegal alcohol," Salis explained. "When my grandmother's father fell in love with her mother, a harpy, our flock had been much larger in size, somewhere between the size of the huldra coterie and the succubi galere. They found a deep love in one another and he refused to stand by while she and her flock were tortured monthly by Hunters. He'd begged her to come live with him in this house, but she would not subject his family and their descendants to the Wild Women lifestyle of façade and oppression. After months of planning, he arranged for her and her flock to leave the continent with him accompanying them."

Salis paused from her story to add a current fact. "We can fly long distances as long as we're able to stop for breaks and food. Flying over the ocean does not enable breaks so easily and is something I've never heard of a harpy trying."

"Not even with the added energy of a succubus?" Marie asked through the phone.

Salis cocked her head in question. I repeated Marie's words for those who didn't have heightened hearing.

"No, we still wouldn't risk it," Salis answered before continuing with her story. "When it came time, the whole flock, along with my grandmother's father, rushed through the tunnel. It supposedly lets out in what used to be a carriage house. There they used to load the moonshine into a wagon, cover it up, and then transport it to its buyers. At that time, my mother's grandfather had wagons waiting for them with plenty of blankets to cover themselves. Men, friends of his, were waiting to drive the wagons to the docks where he and the flock would board a ship set for Europe." She paused. "They knew the chances that Hunters operated in Europe as well were high, but if they traveled as humans would, no one would know their true identities, including the European Hunters."

"But they never made it, did they?" I asked. This male ancestor of Salis and her sisters had tried to do what I was currently hoping to accomplish—save the Wild Women. I braced myself for the rest of her story, for the fate of the man who tried to do what was right and probably paid the ultimate price for his deeds.

Salis nodded. "There was a police raid at the carriage house. They had heard rumors of bootlegging from that building. While there, they noticed steps to the basement and the tunnel opening. The police inspected the tunnel and found the harpy flock, carrying bags of what the police believed to be outlawed liquor. They began shooting. My ancestors fought hard for their freedom, assuming the men were connected to the local Hunter authorities. When it was all over, only my grandmother's mother, pregnant with my grandmother, and one of her nieces had survived."

The harpy shook her head. "This is why I say the tunnel is cursed with hope and death."

This was why the harpy flock was so small. Maybe now they chose to keep their numbers down, but the murder of so many of their kind had to be the reason behind their decision. Fear pricked at me from all sides. Would we, in our own quest for freedom, suffer the same fate?

"How was his family able to continue transporting moonshine if the cops were onto them?" someone asked, but I couldn't be sure who with my thoughts too blurred by worry for what was to come.

"My grandmother's mother and her niece moved the bodies of the police to a separate location," Salis responded. "The tunnel was never again raided, to my knowledge."

"That explains why you smelled Gabrielle down there, Faline," Shawna interjected.

"How so?" I asked after taking way too long to process what she'd said.

"If Wilds died down there, their ghosts could inhabit the place," Shawna explained. "It'd make sense that another Wild ghost joined them."

I trudged through my memories of what the rusalki had told me under their lake in Maine. Had I asked about Gabrielle's ghost? Hadn't they mentioned communicating with her? Maybe it was the exhaustion or the sudden fear that we'd fail our mission to be rid of the Hunters just like the harpies' ancestors, but I couldn't remember that part of my underwater discussion with the rusalki.

I switched my thoughts to bounty hunter mode by default. "We should walk the whole tunnel and make sure it's not opened at the other end. I don't want any sneak attack surprises in this house, like in the last."

Everyone nodded in agreement.

"Marie, Aleksander?" I asked.

The two answered simultaneously, one through the phone and one in person, "Yes?"

"Will you accompany us, go ahead of us, to feel out the energy of the place? If it was ghosts I heard and smelled, you'd be able to sense them before I smelled them." I couldn't believe I was talking about hearing and smelling ghosts, but maybe it wasn't too farfetched.

Of course the two agreed, but we didn't get too far into setting a time before the front door opened without so much as a knock.

Being that the whole kitchen-full of beings were on edge with talk of Wild Women genocide and haunting ghosts, the comfortable entrance of Eonza and Lapis surprised us and caused a few screeches and startles.

When the crowd cleared and Eonza entered the kitchen in all her glory, followed protectively by her sister Lapis, we startled again, but for a very different reason.

Eonza stood, beaming with pride, tall and lean, and rubbing the large bump on her belly.

"Eonza," I uttered, looking from Aleksander to the harpy and back to Aleksander.

"Did you?" I asked the incubi leader.

"I didn't do that," he answered, motioning to Eonza's protruding, round belly.

Salis quickly moved to stand at the other side of her sister, both harpies seemingly protecting the one in the middle...and the unborn harpy she carried.

FOUR

"How did you get pregnant and start showing in the two days since I saw you, Eonza?"

The blonde harpy smiled widely at her accomplishment. "I found a male with which to mate before the rusalki called upon us to fly to Oregon. On the flight home I realized the mating had worked."

My aunt Renee, ever the nurse, stepped forward and looked at Eonza as though she were an experiment. "But how is that even possible? So soon."

Lapis answered, "We are not like you or humans. We do not carry our young in gestation. After successful copulation, we lay our egg seven to ten days later. We then incubate them for forty to forty-five days. Which reminds me," she said, turning to her sisters. "We need to get home and begin building the nest in preparation."

My mouth nearly dropped open.

"But it makes no sense, scientifically," Renee said, aghast.

Marie spoke up through the phone, knowing my aunt would be able to hear her. "None of us make sense, scientifically."

"How does this affect your flock's ability to fight alongside us in the coming weeks?" I asked, some part of my mind always on the mission at hand.

I realized how callous I sounded and added, "Congratulations, by the way. I know this is what your flock has been wanting."

Eonza actually smiled and her sisters nodded. If I had a diary, tonight's entry would be: Today I saw a harpy smile.

"Eonza cannot fight," Salis proclaimed. "Not until she lays her egg."

"But doesn't she have to incubate the egg after that?" Renee asked. "That'll take her out of fighting for over a month. We can't wait a month."

"We'll have to go ahead without her," Celeste said.

I looked to Aleksander to see if he showed any signs of feeling the amped-up energy in the room. Even I sensed the nervousness shared between the Wilds in the kitchen, and my abilities had nothing to do with energy work. The incubus stood tall and rigid, showing no signs of opinion or emotion.

"We each take turns with the egg," Lapis answered, defensively. "It increases the bonding effects, as we will all be this baby's mothers."

"Okay," I thought out loud. "So then when we're planning the attacks, we'll need to also take into consideration who will be with the egg and for how long." Wilds nodded and I continued. "You do realize this means that when we storm into the North Carolina Hunter complex, where your mother is probably being held, one of you will miss being there when she's released?"

The three harpies stared at me before turning to address one another with only their eyes. After a few moments, Lapis and Salis gave a short nod to their sisters and Lapis gave their answer to the rest of us. "Either Lapis or I will stay back during that attack. Eonza has already sacrificed so much for our flock by bringing forth this little one. She deserves to be there to rescue our mother."

"Okay," I said, glad to have that tiny piece planned out. I decided since we were at it, I may as well plan a little more. "I was thinking we'd strategize and train for a week. Then go north to rescue the rusalki sisters in captivity. We can save the North Carolina complex for last."

Eonza cocked her head. "Save my mother for last?"

Good point. But I knew she'd come around when I explained my reasoning. I leaned back onto the yellow fridge. "I've made mention that the Hunters are involved with human trafficking." I waited for signs the others in the room were following before I continued. "I've recently learned that they're funneling their victims through their North Carolina complex. I realize on the east coast we're dealing with older, more established brotherhoods, but the North Carolina complex has that plus visiting Hunters from other compounds. The Hunter I fought back in Oregon mentioned the complex being too full. I assume he meant it was full with victims they were trafficking, but it stands to reason they've also inherited a few Hunters from other states to help keep order and act as guards and protection from the outside until they get the women transported out of the country."

"So you're saying," Aleksander said, showing a hint of support with his slow nod and thoughtful eyes, "we won't be simply rescuing one Wild Woman from that complex, we'll be rescuing many human women as well?"

"Yes," I said. "Human women who are more than likely very close to eighteen, and the newer victims could still be heavily sedated. They'll be scared and lethargic. We'll need your energy skills as well as the succubi's."

"It would be an honor," he said, giving a slight bow, reminding me his real age did not match his appearance.

His show of chivalry went unnoticed by the others in the kitchen. I didn't think he cared.

"I can connect with a few guys in the brotherhood in Maine and we can start planning from there," Marcus offered. "Get a little information first."

I shook my head. "You've been outed, babe. That's not a trick you can pull from your hat anymore. The Hunters helped land you that job; I'm sure they've already taken it away. I bet your work has already left a message on your home answering machine telling you they've let you go with some poor excuse."

Marcus rubbed the stubble on his chin. "True. I should call my messages and check. Then I'll see if Rod has any connections. I don't think they know about him yet."

"So then, are we all in agreement that we visit the Maine complex first, and then the North Carolina one?" I asked.

Various forms of agreement met my question.

"Wait," Oliva chimed in. "When is your flock's next check-in?"

"We did it shortly before the rusalka came and told us to head to Oregon," Eonza answered. I swear her voice was lighter and happier, which tripped me out, if I had to be honest. "So not for another three weeks."

"How does that work with one of you having to stay at the nest with the egg?" Renee asked.

The harpies looked at one another, clearly realizing this difficulty for the first time. "I suppose," Lapis answered for her group, "we will have to have taken the complex down before then. Because sending word that one of us is nesting would cause the Hunters to possibly move the date up or change the rules altogether."

Something else we had to take into consideration. Another timeline we had to adhere to.

No one spoke for a breath or two, as though each person waited for the next roadblock to be announced on our path to freedom. Thankfully, we had the succubi along with the foreign Wilds this time. But without the mermaids, and missing a harpy member, we weren't operating under ideal conditions.

Aleksander straightened his blazer over his button-up shirt and exhaled loudly. "Well, now that that's taken care of, how about we go see what we can feel in that tunnel of yours?"

"I'll be right there," Marie said through the phone. She hung up.

Ready or not, it was time to go meet some possibly pissed off Wild ghosts.

* * *

Marie brought two of her succubus sisters with her and left the rest back at their temporary home to take a breather and enjoy the peace of their nature-filled surroundings. One of the two happened to be Heather, which meant her incubus mate, Mason, tagged along as well. Fine by me. The more energy workers we had, the better.

Although Celeste and the succubi leader were inseparable from the moment she walked into the house, once the brick wall door to the tunnel opened to expose its hidden contents, the succubus became all about business. Celeste hung back with me and our coterie, while Marcus, the two incubi, and the succubi forged ahead into darkness.

"The sadness here is palpable," Marie said quietly.

Aleksander grunted in agreement.

The tunnel felt more cramped than before as supernaturals crowded under the stone curved roof and between the narrow carved-out walls. I crept along behind the succubi and incubi, waiting for the scent of Gabrielle to smack me in the face again.

"Can you feel the difference between sadness and death?" I asked to whichever energy-sensing being cared to answer.

"Yes," a succubus said, the very serious blonde Wild with tattoos and a half shaved head. "Death doesn't feel sad, or of any emotion, really. At least not in and of itself. Death feels either entirely heavy or entirely weightless, depending on the circumstances surrounding the passing of the person. Emotions are layered."

"When we say sadness," Marie picked up where her sister left off, "picture a whole circle of swirling unmet desires and hopeless thoughts, with sadness being the outer shell. It's something like that. Much more layered than the word would suggest."

"Perfect way of explaining it," Aleksander complimented.

The succubus only nodded.

We walked for another ten minutes in silence, waiting for another comment on the energy or a new revelation.

And then it hit me. That scent. The salty sea smell of my fallen friend who ended up being a traitor to our kind. The mermaid who touched my life during a time when I was waking up to the reality that nothing was as it seemed; the mermaid who helped usher in my new skills and the old ways of accepting them.

"She's here," I whispered, stunned into stillness. "Gabrielle is here."

"There is death here, though it's old and faded," Aleksander started, turning to me with a raised eyebrow. "And also life, which feels more recent. But there are no spirits present."

"I disagree," Marie countered. Her sister grunted in approval. "No offense, Aleksander, but I'm not sure you've felt spirits other than those of incubi and humans."

Aleksander did not confirm or deny her assumption of him.

Marie went on, "There are certainly spirits here, but only wisps of their energy, as though they aren't stuck here, as though they come and go as they please, which makes me feel like they're older spirits, beings who passed some time ago. But I do not feel your mermaid spirit."

Marie closed her eyes and concentrated. "I think I am feeling what you're smelling, though." She turned toward the darkness ahead, with eyes still closed, and opened her arms wide. I assumed she was inviting the energy in, opening herself to feel it more deeply.

The echo of a pebble hitting the stone wall maybe a quarter of a mile deeper into the tunnel made us all jump. Marie twisted and ran to me. She gripped my upper arms and stared into my eyes. "I know this energy. I've felt it before," she said with a serious and somewhat shaky voice.

"What is it?" I asked, my mind blurring through possible supernaturals she could have encountered that I'd only heard about in my mother's stories or popular folklore.

"The mermaids," Marie said, turning to peer down the tunnel and then back at me. "The mermaids are back."

FIVE

"REALLY?" I asked the succubi leader in shock.

"Yes, living mermaids are here, underground, in this tunnel," Marie confirmed.

I peered at Marcus for all of a second before I let go of his hand and ran toward the scent, toward the mermaids. I couldn't be sure if I sped toward friends or foes, toward the Wilds who sold us out to the Hunters or the ones who had no idea their sisters were double-crossing us. And I didn't care. I pushed my boots into the stone and dirt, propelling myself forward. I heard the people I'd left behind shout my name, urging me to come back. But their requests only partially registered. And now I had to run even faster, in case the mermaids heard their shouts and tried to get away.

I had questions for them. I needed answers. They couldn't get away. Not again.

I followed the bend in the tunnel to the right, and soon after, to the left, until just as my legs couldn't carry me fast enough, they also couldn't stop quickly enough. I nearly pummeled into a small group of mermaids like a bowling ball into pins.

I caught myself before knocking over a red-haired Wild Woman. She instinctively held her arms out to protect herself from the incoming huldra. Recognition registered in her expression and the mermaid shifted her posture from preparing to push me off her to pulling me into an embrace.

"Faline!" Sarah exclaimed, squeezing me tightly before releasing me enough to look at my face. "It's so good to see you!"

Two smiling mermaids stood beside her, though none requested a hug from me. I didn't remember their names and I doubted they remembered me much other than the short time we trained together on my coterie's property. We hadn't even attacked the Washington Hunters' complex together; the mermaids insisted on accessing the complex through a creek, didn't show up until the very end of the fighting, and then lit the place on fire and hightailed it out of there.

We hadn't heard from them since the celebration ritual the night of the attack, and some assumed the worst, that the mermaids had abandoned us to our fate. The mermaids gained their freedom from American Hunters long ago, living off-grid on a remote island off the coast of California. Until the Hunters attacked their island. Still, it made sense that they'd be able to swim to a new land and live in peace and freedom, off the grid once again. And with the revelation from the foreign Wild Women about our continent being the last occupied by oppressive Hunters, it made sense that the mermaids would find a new place to call home.

"Where's Elaine?" I asked, secretly sniffing the air to detect any other mermaids nearby, just in case the Wilds I'd nearly run into weren't as friendly as they appeared.

Elaine was Sarah's partner. I'd met them during my short time on their island, before I attended their beach gathering where an elder explained my role in all of this, and I learned the truth of Wild Women for the first time since my mother's whispered bedtime stories when I was a child. Before the Hunters landed from helicopters onto the mermaid's island, wearing night vision goggles in a surprise attack. Before my first Hunter kill that night.

Together, Elaine and Sarah raised a little girl. Their little family lived in a room that shared a bathroom with the room I'd been shown to in the mermaid shoal's sprawling home. We'd met when we both tried to use the adjoining restroom at the same time. They'd asked to touch my bark and offered a feel of their scales in return. Despite my mistrust for mermaids as a whole, I held a fondness for Elaine and Sarah; the two who accepted my bark with awe rather than fright at a time when even I feared my inner huldra.

Sarah peered back down the tunnel before answering. "Ah, Elaine had to stay back at the house with our daughter. This isn't the safest place for a little one."

I rested my hands on my hips and looked around at the stone walls. "What is this place to you?" I asked. Maybe not the most eloquent of questions, but I figured she'd know what I was getting at.

"We've come back to rescue our sisters," Sarah explained with a smile and an upturn in her voice, almost as though she were sharing good news with me.

Her good news confused me. "Your sisters were captured?" The only captors I could think of were of the Hunter persuasion. Why would they need an old bootlegging tunnel extending from a basement to an old carriage house to rescue their sisters from a Hunter complex?

"No," she said with an even bigger smile as though she was about to gift me with a surprise. "For you! For all the American Wild Women."

I mulled over her words and her smile dropped. I hadn't given the response she'd hoped for. We could travel just as well on land. Why would we need a tunnel? Was she proposing we leave the states? Hide away like bottles of illegal alcohol in a car or van to a ship dock or airport?

"I'm confused," I admitted.

Her smile returned. "Oh, well, see, we did some research and learned that this tunnel used to be for bootleggers to transport moonshine."

"I know that part," I said. "I'm staying in the house where the moonshine was made." I didn't tell her who the house belonged to.

"Well," Sarah went on. "We spent time away and some of us just didn't feel right leaving our Wild Women sisters behind. We came up with a plan to sneak you through the tunnel and to a ship that'll take you to Greece. It's a beautiful area where Hunters don't have complexes and it's where we've started calling home. One of the islands off of Greece."

I nodded that I understood, but her plan still made no sense. "Why sneak through tunnels when we can drive around? We flew from the west coast to here, got out of the airport, and drove to the house we're staying in. No one stopped us."

Wait. How did they know we were all in the area? We'd just arrived.

"Just because you weren't stopped doesn't mean you weren't noticed," she responded. "It doesn't mean your presence hasn't already been reported to Hunter authorities. Our plan will keep anyone from knowing you've left."

"*Have* we been reported to the authorities?" I asked assertively.

Her demeanor changed from inviting to defensive. "How would we know?"

"That's a great question," I said. "How did you know all the American Wilds were in the area?" For a split moment I entertained the idea that a rusalka told them in a dream or something. But then I remembered the rusalki claimed they had no contact with the mermaids, and I believed them a hell of a whole lot more than I believed the mermaids.

Sarah peered at the wall before meeting my gaze. "We've been tracking you," she said quietly.

I rolled my head back, closed my eyes, took a cleansing breath, and rolled it forward to stare her in the eye. "For how long?"

"Mermaids were sent to your coterie's home as well as the succubi's home," Sarah explained. "They reported back that both were empty, called us from homes left unlocked and uncared for. We figured we were too late, but we decided to see if maybe we could find you at an east coast Wild Woman's home. Since the Oregon Hunter complex was leveled to the ground, we hoped you'd just moved eastward. Especially seeing as the east coast complexes are fully intact. First we tried the harpies, deciding to leave the place of our sister's death as a last resort. When the harpy home was empty too, we thought to leave, but then one of us spotted a van full of Wild Women, so we figured you all were hiding out here somewhere the Hunters wouldn't find you."

"Okay?"

She went on, "We moved quickly, searching through historical archives until we learned about this tunnel and decided to come down and check it out. And here we are." She paused and tried to gauge my blank expression. "It's not like we made this tunnel plan on the fly. Before we even returned to the states we came up with a few possible scenarios depending on where we found you."

Her plan didn't make the best sense, but part of me wanted to thank her for the thought. Another part wanted to ask her about Gabrielle's double-crossing and how the shoal felt about it after they'd had some time to let it sink in.

"Thank you for the thought," I started, thinking deeply on what to say next and how to phrase it.

Marcus and the others made their way around the bend in the tunnel and stood behind me. My coterie had to have heard the mermaid's plan.

"But we aren't going to run away from the only home we've ever known," I finished.

Sarah's face contorted like I'd just said the dumbest thing ever. "What kind of home is this that you have to hide in the homes of others?"

"That's only temporary," Shawna backed me up. She walked to stand beside me and link her arm in mine. "It's a means to an end."

I thought about the old grandmother trees the rusalka had told me about when she'd taught me to connect to the roots of plants to gain poison and energy from them. I thought of the park where she revealed the old ways my ancestors died, how they'd cross over from a huldra existence to that of a tree, opening the trunk to house them for eternity. I'd gone over this in my mind multiple times since then, puzzling the unsaid pieces together.

The huldra were protectoresses of the forests. If my ancestors encased themselves in trees, then really the huldra were protecting their ancestors, the wisdom of those women who'd gone before them, seeing as they could connect to the tree's roots to communicate with the tree and gain her wisdom. They had been protecting more than the forest. They had protected their way of life, their sacred circles of life and death and rebirth. The rusalka said I wouldn't find such trees in the states, but something in me said she was wrong. Whether we knew about it or not, and despite its difficulties and dark moments, our history was on this continent. Our home was here. Our grandmothers were buried here. We would not leave and allow the Hunters to win again.

"Sarah," I said feeling calmer, more resolute in my decision. "The Hunters have stolen what we hold dear. They've taken our history, our identity, and twisted those things into unrecognizable evil monstrosities. I will not also give them our homes, our land, the places of our grandmother's burials, our forest."

Shawna squeezed my arm in hers. "We will stay and fight them for it. For what is ours and should have always been ours."

Damn, my partner sister impressed me. Her strength and resilience. She inspired me.

"Help us," Patricia added quickly and almost in desperation. "Help us fight for the right to stay."

Sarah looked at her mermaid sisters before replying to my aunt's request. "I will have to talk it over with my sisters, both here and those back in Greece. We've already uprooted ourselves and built a home there. This continent is no longer our home to fight for."

I thought of the man who captained the small boat that took me to the mermaid's island. Gabrielle had later told me his ancestors were native to that island, and although they'd moved off the island for work, it had still been a place of great importance to them. She'd told me they were family to the mermaids.

"You don't have the same history in Greece," I reminded Sarah. "What will happen to San Miguel Island without the mermaids protecting it? What will happen to the sacred lands of your family when there are no longer surprise storms and heavy winds keeping the humans from visiting and building on that island?"

Sarah swallowed and gave one, stiff nod. My questions had hit a nerve. I figured this was a topic the mermaids worried about often. "I will bring this to my sisters," she said. "We will have an answer for you soon."

Marie pulled out a piece of paper from the small pocket of her tight-fitting red slacks. "Here's their phone number," she said, handing Sarah the paper. Sarah took it and thanked the succubus. But the succubus wasn't done. Marie caught Sarah's eyes and stared deeply into them. "We can be done with this once and for all. Think about that."

"I will," Sarah said, some of the indecision fading away from her face as her eyebrows and jaw relaxed.

The mermaids turned and continued down the tunnel in the direction they'd come from, the opposite direction of our moonshine basement. My group made our way back to the house. Marie and Celeste held hands, murmuring their thoughts about what'd just happened. Marcus wrapped an arm around my shoulder.

"Tell me a story, Faline," my aunt Renee requested from behind me.

I thought her request odd. "What kind of story?" I asked. "And why?"

"One of the stories your mother told," she said. "I know I used to scold you as a young girl when you repeated them; I did it for your own sake. I didn't want you telling them to the wrong person, so I figured if you weren't allowed to speak them at all, you wouldn't share them with anyone. But I could really use your mother's hopeful view of the world right now. I have none of my own to pull from."

Her words struck me with anger at being forced to suppress what little I had left of my mother, and with sadness at the decision she'd felt compelled to make. I thought of a bedtime story ready to be told as we made our way through the dark, dank tunnel.

"Before people honored gods and goddesses, they honored their ancestors," I said, thinking of the tiny crystal statue my mother carried of the Goddess Ishtar and how she used to let me hold it sometimes while she told her stories. "The greatest of the family line was their great mother, the woman who birthed their tribe. They believed pieces of her could be found in each mother who came after her. Her legacy passed down from womb to womb, heart to heart. Each of these great mothers, who birthed the people, who nourished them from the milk of her breast and who fulfilled them from the warmth of her arms, went on to be known as Goddesses, their souls continuing to nourish and guide their many children walking the earth."

My mother had once told me she carried a Goddess, other than Freyja, because Ishtar was one of the earliest great mothers and her legacy deserved to live on. I wished I had it with me now, but despite the many times I'd searched my tree home for the thing, I never found it.

I continued to the silent, listening crowd of supernaturals, "But other forces, those who didn't want the children of the earth to be protected, those who sought to enslave the children for their own greed and desire of power, took over the lands of the Goddesses. They created new myths to have the people recite, myths of how their Goddesses were raped and killed, or forced to be the daughter or lover of a more powerful, dominating God. They told the people lies that excused their use of domination and exploitation, placing the people's intuitive ways of love and acceptance as faulty. Soon the people wore the chains of duty and expectation, believing suppression of self and emotions to be holy."

"I don't think I like this story much," Olivia said. "It's depressing."

I smiled. I remembered feeling the exact same way as I lay in bed, a little girl gazing into the eyes of the Ishtar statue, small enough to fit in one of my hands, as I rubbed my fingers lightly over her wings. I couldn't understand how my mother could say such things with a smile and a glint of light in her eyes. But soon I learned the glint was hope, because her story took a turn.

"The great mother Ishtar has wings for a reason," I said, smiling as I connected my mother's story with what we were currently going through. "Those of her precise creation, Wild Women, have always been held in her bosom, and when they are ready to be nourished by her once again, she will flap her wings and rise, allowing them to rise with her."

Later, when I was a grown woman in search of my captured sister, I saw Ishtar again. Much larger, she stood carved into the cement wall of the main room in the harpies' home. Only, to them, she is known as Inanna. The carving had sparked long forgotten memories of my mother's stories.

"Does that mean we'll die and be reunited with the great mothers soon?" Oliva asked with the tightness of concern in her voice.

I considered my sister's question. I'd wondered the same thing a time or two, in all honesty. Especially after I'd seen the Inanna carving in the harpies' home and found out they'd worshipped her as the

Goddess who created them. Although, at the time, I'd kept the thoughts to myself, I'd wondered if that meant they'd lead us to freedom or to death. But today a new possible interpretation bloomed within my heart.

"I don't think so," I said as we neared the brick opening to the basement, the scent of yeast wafting toward us. "Eonza, a harpy, is bringing new life into the world soon, and if her mother is at the North Carolina Hunter complex, she'll be the last Wild we rescue. Along with her, we'll be setting human women free who will no doubt tell their stories against the Hunters. The brotherhood's shroud of secrecy will be torn from them, and their ways of manipulating the government from behind the scenes will come to an end. When the last Wild Woman is able to fly in freedom, a harpy, we will all rise with her."

"I take comfort in this story," Lapis commented. "Thank you for sharing it."

We entered the basement and I smiled in response. Marie and Aleksander returned the candles to their dusty table. The soft quiet of self-reflection rested over the group as we walked the steps up to the secret hutch door and the dining area of the old house. I wondered where my mother played into all of this. Would she be at the Maine complex? The North Carolina complex? The rusalka Drosera assured me she was still alive.

But Drosera never promised we'd survive the coming weeks. She gave no assurances to solidify my belief that my mother's story foretold the physical freedom of the Wild Women. What if it spoke of our spiritual freedom? The freedom of our souls leaving our bodies in death, rising up to be reunited with the great mothers?

I thought to share this little fact with the others. Lapis slid the hutch safely in place, covering the doorway to the basement. I almost opened my mouth to give another possible explanation to the story, when I looked up and Marie caught my eye. She gave the tiniest of head shakes and returned to her conversation with Celeste and Olivia.

Marie felt it too. Something huge was coming. Something that would determine the fate of all American Wild Women. Something she wanted me to keep to myself.

SIX

"YOU ARE IN GRAVE DANGER, wake up!"

My lids flung open and I jolted up in bed. Drosera stood at the bottom edge of the mattress, trained on Marcus and I. My sudden movement alarmed the ex-Hunter, who'd been sleeping soundly beside me. Within a breath he reached for his dagger on the side table and shot up to stab whoever dared to attack us in our sleep.

"Stop!" I hissed seconds before he bore his blade into the rusalka's chest.

She didn't flinch. He pulled back in an instant, but stood anyway, prepared.

"It's just Drosera," I said to calm him.

"Ah." He sat at the side edge of the bed and caught his breath. "Okay."

Drosera stood in darkness, the light of the half-moon barely filtering through the bedroom window, not touching her directly. I'd seen her kind in the moonlight, their skin seemed to glow. Tonight, though, I couldn't even make out the hue of her auburn hair and green eyes. She wore what looked and smelled like two pieces of deer pelt. Her top had no distinct shape; the animal skin looked as though it'd been cut with a dull knife and tied under her armpit to cover her breasts. The deer fur skirt hung at her hips and extended to her upper thighs.

"What kind of danger are we in?" I asked, my heart still thrumming from being woken up in such a creepy way.

"A journalist threatens to reveal the harpies," she said in her wispy voice. "As we speak he is gathering evidence of their existence."

"Why?" I asked. But I immediately realized that was a stupid question. Because he was a journalist, it was his job. That's why.

She answered anyway. "He believes he can win a Pulitzer for his efforts," she said.

I considered her warning for half a second before my first thought escaped my mouth. "By the time he goes public, we'll probably already have taken down the remaining Hunter complexes. I don't see the problem. Living out in the open may feel freeing."

"Whether or not it is freeing makes no difference," she said, peering around the room as though she were looking for something. I didn't risk asking what she looked for. Rusalka had a way of talking in circles, so when they were actually speaking in a straight line, a person would be smart to keep their mouth shut or risk letting the conversation spiral out of comprehension.

"You are not the only Wild Women in the world," she continued. "Others who live happily do not wish their peace to be disturbed."

I sat up taller and threw my covers off to swing myself over the side of the bed and let my legs dangle. My first instinct was to complain about the fact that even if we became free from the Hunters, we were still not truly free if women from the other side of the world had the power to dictate how we lived. But then I thought of it from their perspective. Maybe a small part of me could see why rocking the boat could scare some Wilds. I remembered the Hunters' warnings to us during our monthly lessons. One of their reasons for us attending check-ins was to make sure we didn't use our abilities, because once we started, we wouldn't have the control to stop and eventually humans would notice. Humans feared what they couldn't understand, and in their minds they'd only understand us after they've dissected us and studied us in cages.

But that brought me back to my original thought: how free could we be if at the end of all the fighting, we were still hiding?

Either way, I didn't have the right to make such a decision for every Wild Woman in the world.

"Okay," I finally said, deciding to back down this time. We could deal with the idea of outing our kind once the Hunters were taken care of. Maybe certain groups would opt to reveal their existence and others wouldn't. "If the journalist reveals that just the harpies exist, because he couldn't know of the other types of Wild Women, then why are you worried about the others being upset?"

Drosera stared at me before speaking into my mind. *No one is perfect.*

I stared back in awe. Not because of her oddly cloaked statement, but because she'd talked in my mind! She hadn't done that since her sister Azalea died.

"You did it!" I said, excitedly. I almost bound to her and wrapped her up in a hug, but I couldn't be sure how she'd take that and I still feared those birch scissors she and her sisters carried around, able to cut life down with one snip of a strand of hair.

She barely nodded, but a hint of a smile lifted her lips. "Our abilities are slowly returning."

"Well I'm happy for you," Marcus said with a warmth and genuineness that almost choked me up. "It's a huge step in your grieving process and you should be proud of where you're at in your healing."

Drosera's smile dropped and she peered at her toes. "It has not been easy," she admitted. She looked up and met Marcus's gaze in the dark room. "Death is nothing more than a transition, than a life changing its form." She cleared her throat. "But such a change aches down to the marrow of your bones and touches every part of your soul."

Marcus swallowed and nodded. The moonlight caught his glistening eyes. "I don't remember my mother, but just knowing I'll never experience the cadence of her voice or what it feels like to hug her cracks my heart in two."

I watched my boyfriend, sitting there in his boxer briefs, his huge body weighing his side of the bed down, and my heart broke for him. I'd been so focused on learning whether or not my mother was alive, and figuring out how to get her, that I'd forgotten to ask Marcus how this was affecting him —all this talk of mothers and the upcoming motherhood of a harpy.

"Drosera," I said, thinking out loud. "Would you be able to find out if Marcus's mother is alive?"

The two turned from one another to look at me. Marcus waved his hand in the air. "Don't worry about that," he said, dismissing my idea. "You shouldn't use precious woman-power to locate a ghost. You don't have time for that right now."

"No we don't," Drosera agreed.

I refused to accept that as an answer. "Then afterwards," I stated unwaveringly. "After this is all done and over with, we will find your mother's grave." And if we found no grave, maybe I could convince him to ask the rusalki to help us find her alive.

"I'd like that," he responded, his brows slightly furrowed as he fought back emotions I doubted even he understood. The loss of our mothers at a young age, and the weeds of unfamiliar feelings such a loss seeded, was something we had in common.

I pressed a gentle hand to his bare back. He leaned in to kiss me on the forehead.

The rusalka cut in without so much as an apology. "If the other Wild Women learn of this journalist, they will expect you to take care of him."

"And if I don't?" I asked, a little perturbed at her interruption and the fact that strangers expected things of me.

"Many value their anonymity," Drosera said in a serious tone. "And as I told you, they are not perfect. Like many, they could be pushed to the point of killing for their way of life."

"That's ridiculous!" I accidently yelled.

"Is it?" Drosera sharply answered right away. "Is that not what you're doing?"

"I'm killing for my right to be free," I countered. "Huge difference."

"Is that not what they would also be doing?" she asked. "Killing for what they deem their freedom to be? Freedom from being known."

Shit, she had a point.

I exhaled. "So you're saying if I don't get this journalist under control I'll make enemies of a bunch of Wilds who are well versed in their abilities and not afraid to use them?"

"Yes," Drosera answered.

She peered at the door as though she had done what she'd come for and anticipated walking out of here and disappearing into thin air. She may have been done, but I wasn't.

"Before you leave," I said quickly to gain her attention. "I wanted to let you know where we're at with our plans to attack the Hunter complexes."

Drosera's gaze rested on me again and she shifted her weight from one leg to the other. Her brown animal skin skirt moved down her hip, exposing more of her lean lower abdomen muscles. "You have chosen to end the Maine complex first," she stated.

Oh yeah, if she was able to speak into my mind again she was also able to hear my thoughts. Still, I decided to say my next question to keep Marcus in the loop. "Is this a wise decision? Will we survive?" I asked with a little more desperation than I realized I felt.

Drosera cocked her head and studied me. "The trees have lost their leaves for the winter," she started. "Who can say, once their inner work and self-reflection is complete for the season, and they begin to blossom leaves once again, which branches will be most plentiful and which branches will produce little to no leaves?"

"Are you saying you don't know?" Marcus surmised, and I could have laughed and kissed him for it because I'd done the same thing when I'd first started dealing with odd Wilds. I also winced a little, worried that his interruption of the rusalka meant we'd never learn the meaning to her parable.

Her gaze shifted from me to the ex-Hunter. She narrowed her eyes and I wondered if he felt the massaging fingertips on his brain, a side effect of having your mind read by a rusalka.

"As you are not a tree woman I should not expect you to understand," she said to Marcus in a way that lacked the tone of belittlement, but also didn't exude acceptance. "The huldra is a tree with many branches. Where she flows her energy, those branches will produce leaves. Where the energy is blocked, those branches will not produce leaves and they will eventually die, grow brittle, and break. She chooses which branches receive her energy and which do not. In one form or another, we each choose our own destiny, so it is not for me to divulge one's future when what I see is merely one possibility of many."

I must have caught onto rusalki language because her meaning made complete sense, not that I liked it much. "What she's saying," I explained to Marcus, and also to get confirmation from Drosera, "is that my decisions and where I place my energy will affect whether we win or lose."

"Not only your decisions," she corrected. "But the decisions of everyone involved. Each of your choices, the choices of all of you, weaves together into a tapestry that will soon become history. I can see a few possible outcomes, but one changed decision can bring forth a whole new set of possible outcomes."

With that taken care of, or rather not taken care of, I asked the rusalki another question, one that was more reality than spiritual. Hopefully one she could answer. "Will your coven be well enough to help us in Maine?"

Her expression relaxed a little. "Ah," she said as though she were sighing away the weight of my last question. "Yes, and we've devised a plan with which to take them by surprise."

Though my heart pounded with excitement over this, I waited, but when she failed to expound, I prodded. "What is it?" I could really use a little good news. A dash of hope right now could go a long way.

"Our plan is in the beginning stages and not yet ready to reveal," she said. "We must first get their permission."

"Whose permission?" I asked.

"I would rather not say."

"Have we met them?" Marcus chimed in.

She seemed to think on that for a second. "No, I don't believe you have."

"Are they other Wild Women?" I asked, as though Marcus and I took turns playing twenty questions.

"Hm," Drosera said, tapping her chin. "I suppose they were, once."

Images of my tree foremothers popped into my mind, the elder huldra as they passed over by stepping into the trunk of a tree where they'd begin the final phase of their life journey. I yearned to know what my mother knew of this practice, to ask her how she'd learned of it if American huldra had never done it. And I yearned to travel to Nordic places, to the woods there, and grow my roots deep enough to connect with the roots of my ancestors, to absorb whatever wisdom they were kind enough to share.

"Are they tree women?" I asked, hopeful the answer would be yes.

"That is enough," Drosera answered with a sway of her hand. "It is time that I return to planning with my sisters."

"What time is it?" I asked.

Marcus tapped the screen of his throw-away phone on the bedside table. It lit the room in a muted blue. "Three in the morning."

I stretched my arms and stood. "Considering the news, I guess it's also time to gather the coterie and pay a visit to Eonza, find out more about this gem of a man she chose to make a baby with. Then a few of us can go to wherever he lives for a house call." I threw my robe around my bare arms and tied the waist portion. "Maybe Marie can work her magic and make him forget he'd ever met a harpy." I pictured the scene playing out and thought of how amazingly shitty our luck had been with our latest bright ideas—Eonza's being one of them. I hoped making a baby with a journalist wasn't one of those choices Drosera had referred to, but I could almost bet it was. "It'll either work like a charm or fail miserably and out yet another group of Wild Women."

If this journalist outed us, dealing with the Hunters would be like a walk in the park on a gorgeously rainy day compared to the wrath of angry Wild Women.

SEVEN

I PUT a fresh pot of coffee on and made my way upstairs to wake my coterie as the coffee brewed. If I was going to pull them out of their warm beds before the sun even thought about coming up, the least I could do was present them with a steaming cup of coffee for their efforts. After making my rounds I made my way back to the kitchen and set out mugs, creamer, and a spoon for quick and easy access.

The old wooden stairs creaked as huldra made their way to the kitchen, no doubt following their noses to the nearly full coffee pot.

"Good morning," Aleksander greeted me, looking way too awake in his silk pajamas. He bypassed the morning drink of choice and made his way to a chair beside the kitchen table. "Why the early morning meeting?"

I hadn't woken him up. "It's not a meeting," I assured him. "So you're not missing out on anything if you want to go back to bed."

"I would rather stay with my housemates," he said with a wink. Way too awake...

I leaned against the tiled countertop and took a sip of warm liquid. After relishing in the bitter taste of earth, and then taking another two sips, I answered the incubus. "Drosera visited me. Apparently Eonza forgot to mention that she made her baby with a journalist. One who's set on winning the Pulitzer for outing her kind."

That woke them all up.

"So we need to deal with this little snafu sooner rather than later," I continued. I fielded questions much like the ones I asked Drosera, but by the bottom of my first cup of coffee, we all agreed we needed to silence the journalist. We weren't entirely sure on the specifics of how, but we hoped the harpies could help us come up with that part.

The harpies had already returned the rental passenger vans, and we didn't want them to come pick us up anyway. So we traveled old school style—on foot. Oddly enough, Lapis had left their location on the notepad beside the phone at the old house, but not a phone number. They were staying in the same one-story hotel I'd arranged for Gabrielle and me what seemed like a lifetime ago. The one Gabrielle had passed on, where I ended up sharing a bed with Marcus for the first time. Ah, memories.

We weren't staying too far from the motel, and an early morning walk got my blood flowing more than I'd anticipated. I missed my home, my property, the woods. I missed the quiet loudness of nature, the serene commotion. Walking hand-in-hand with Marcus, huddled in my coterie, I took in a snippet of what I'd missed so much. In the wee hours of the morning, before most humans woke from their beds, only the sounds of small animals rustled through the bushes of front yards and wind blew through the leaves of trees surrounding us. And it was glorious.

The heaviness of my newest task to deal with the journalist rose from my shoulders as we left the older residential area of town and quickly ended up in the older business side of town. We passed brick buildings containing shops and doctor and dental offices, all closed up tight for the night with only dim outdoor lights shining over their entrances.

I smiled and inhaled, squeezing Marcus's hand. As impossible as life felt at times, it was as though nature sent us little gifts of hope for a better tomorrow in the form of a sunrise or birdsong.

Or a tree in an alleyway?

I paused and squinted my eyes, peering deeper into the dark alley between two brick two-story buildings claiming to house medical and insurance offices. The tree moved and I froze.

"Someone is watching us," I whispered under my breath, only loud enough for my coterie to hear. It's not that I didn't want to alert the men too, but I also didn't want to be heard by whoever stood in the alley.

"You think it's the journalist?" Marcus asked with the same whisper.

I inhaled deeply again, irritated that I'd been too caught up in the scent of morning that I'd missed the non-human female watching us.

"No," I answered. "She's not human either."

I thought it over for all of two seconds before I said, "I'm going to see what's up."

I unclasped Marcus's hand and stood taller, squaring my shoulders as I walked assertively over to our audience. She smelled like no other Wild I'd ever met before. As I got within one hundred feet of her, she turned and ran the other direction.

And so I chased her. Maybe it wasn't the brightest idea, running into an alley in the middle of the night to chase a supernatural woman. But both the huldra and the bounty hunter in me wouldn't have it any other way.

When she picked up her pace, I yelled, "Wait! Stop!"

Yelling in the middle of the night for humans to hear was also not the best idea. And it's not like she listened either. She turned the corner behind the building to our left and lost me. When I made it to the corner, I caught no sight of her and only the faintness of her scent still lingered in the damp early morning air.

"Dammit!" I huffed under my breath. I balled my fist and struck the wet brick wall.

The others of my group came running around the corner, asking if I was all right. No, I was pissed.

"Did you get a good whiff of her?" My aunt Patricia asked as we got back onto the sidewalk toward the motel.

I shrugged. "Apparently not good enough."

"Which type of Wild Woman did she smell like?" Shawna asked.

"Maybe the echidna were out for a morning walk and didn't want us to know."

I stomped from the sidewalk onto the blacktop parking lot of the motel. Gone were the reminiscent feelings of the last time I walked into this motel, or the simple pleasures I found in the nature around me.

I stood outside of room number three and knocked loudly. "She didn't smell like any Wild Woman I've ever met," I grumbled as I waited for a harpy to answer my knock.

I knocked again.

Finally Lapis drew back a floral print curtain and peeked out the front window at us. The chain on the door slid and the door opened. The three harpies shared a king size bed, and with Lapis out from under the covers, her two sisters sat up and leaned against the wooden headboard.

Lapis clicked on a bedside lamp and sat at the edge of the bed.

I waited for everyone to crowd into the small room, and the door to close, before I spoke.

Aunt Renee replaced the chain lock at the top of the door.

As I woke my coterie this morning, and on my walk to the motel, I'd gone over a rough outline of how I'd gently bring up the topic of Eonza's poor choice of a mate. Each and every one of those words had flown out the proverbial window the moment I caught a non-human woman spying on us.

I stood at the foot of the bed, dead straight with Eonza, and looked the harpy in the eyes.

"So, Eonza, you decided to make a baby with an attention-hungry journalist, huh?" I said in not the nicest of tones.

She opened her mouth to speak, and then shut it again. Lapis answered for her instead. "We did not fully research the male before they mated. It was an opportunity that presented itself and so she took it."

"And then?" I asked, wanting more than the obvious.

"And then," Lapis continued, defensively, "he saw her wings."

I jumped back in shock. "What the fuck, Eonza?"

Both Lapis and Salis stood on the bed between Eonza and me in a jolt. Wings burst from their naked backs and talons exploded from their fingers and toes. Within a heartbeat the two harpies were ready to defend their sister and their newest unborn flock member.

Tension filled the room and my sisters and aunts rushed to flank me, each growing vines from her fingers and crouching low enough to prepare for an aerial attack. Marcus breathed down my back and I felt his right arm brush against me as it moved for his dagger.

"How dare you come into our resting chambers demanding to know flock business," Salis seethed, her wings outstretched.

The harpies, standing above us battle-ready, were a terrifying sight. I could imagine the scare Eonza gave the journalist with only her wings showing. No wonder he wanted to out her kind. Other than being internationally recognized, he'd also be regaining a smidge of the dignity he probably felt he lost when he no doubt wetted himself.

But this wasn't just flock business.

"Flock business, my ass," I retorted, holding my ground. "When Wild Women start showing up to stalk us, this moves out of the realm of flock business and into the realm of American Wild Women livelihood."

Lapis's blue wings relaxed and the tips fell to the mattress. "What kind of Wild Women?" she asked.

Salis folded her light brown wings and pulled them snug against her back. Her talons slowly retracted.

"I have no clue," I answered, a little less seething and a little more irritated. "Not one I've ever smelled before."

Lapis and Salis sat at the foot of the bed and I took a few steps back. My coterie relaxed too, pulling their vines into their fingers and spreading out away from me to sit on the table and chairs, or lean against the back wall. Marcus and Shawna stayed close.

"Drosera came to me this morning," I continued. "She said that if we don't stop the journalist from revealing your kind, the other Wild Women of the world will take action...against him and then against us." I narrowed my eyes. "Please tell me he has no proof, that whatever he's planning on writing has no evidence to back it up."

Lapis raised her chin and held my gaze. "He took a picture with his phone."

I closed my eyes to calm myself enough in the time it took me to slowly inhale and exhale.

"What would Drosera have us do, then?" Eonza spoke up.

"The only way to effectively shut him up is to kill him," my aunt Renee suggested.

We all turned to her, shocked at the ease in which she delivered a damning verdict.

"My sisters and I will not take any part in killing an innocent man," Eonza declared.

"Neither will I," I agreed. The human male hadn't tried to hurt or kill us. At least that hadn't seemed to have been his intention.

"I won't," Marcus said.

"Nor will I," Aleksander added.

"Okay," I said, my hands out in front of me. "We aren't going to kill the guy. Next option?"

"We can ask the mermaids if they know anything about the new Wild Women in town when they call as they've promised," Olivia offered.

Celeste cut her partner sister off. "The succubi," she said.

Olivia looked at Celeste with scrunched eyebrows. "The mermaids will tell us the new Wild Women are succubi? That makes no sense, sister."

Celeste widened her eyes and gave her partner sister a second to think about what she'd just said.

"Oh," Olivia uttered, giving her sister a nod of approval. "The succubi can wipe the guy's memories of Eonza's wings. Smart."

"Yeah, that'll work," I added, remembering I'd had that idea while talking to Drosera. Stress and lack of sleep really left me feeling like a dull knife among daggers. "That should work."

When I'd first met Marie she'd been sitting on her red couch with a human man who wore only boxers. I had interrupted their night of fun by barging in, asking the whereabouts of my sister, Shawna. When Marie spoke about Wild Women in front of the human, I'd been shocked until she'd explained he would only remember that night as a hazy dream of ultimate pleasure.

The succubi had the ability to manipulate energy, which included sexual energy. Seeing as we were all energy, succubi could redesign memories as well as render a person motionless. This was why my aunt Renee had blamed the succubi for whispering into the minds of the men who took Shawna, and the man who'd tried to attack me in the Bellevue hotel bedroom—the man I accidentally killed. Of course my aunt had been wrong. The succubi didn't aim to hurt, they aimed to help, using their abilities to heal humans and bring them joy as well as pleasure. But either way, they were capable.

Which meant a couple hours between a succubus and the journalist would end in smiles on both their faces. The succubus would have a good time and get to use her energy abilities for good, and the journalist would have the best romp of his life—no offense to Eonza—and be left without his memory of Eonza's wings. Sure, he'd also never end up winning a Pulitzer or some other prestigious award for reporting about Wild Women, but he also wouldn't out a group of Wilds and in turn feel the wrath of those of them from different lands with a lifestyle to protect.

"I believe that'll work," Eonza said. She stretched her neck and arms as though she were just rising from bed. "I'm famished." She peered at the clock on the bedside table. "There's a coffee place opening soon. We should get breakfast."

Having experienced the highs and lows of an emotional roller coaster, all before the sun came up, my group, fueled with nothing but coffee, supported Eonza's plan.

I wondered, though, as we walked out into the crisp early morning air, which Wild Women were following us. How many were there, lurking in the shadows? And most importantly, would we be able to fight them off if we failed to stop the journalist in time?

EIGHT

By EARLY AFTERNOON, my coterie, Marcus, Aleksander, Marie, and two of her succubus sisters walked the bustling streets of Charlotte, North Carolina with a mission: Enter the building of the Charlotte Tribune, find Brice Smith's office, and redesign his memory of Eonza and her wings.

Earlier that morning, over a mocha and a blueberry scone, I listened as Eonza told the story behind her and the journalist's moments of baby-making. From the way she'd explained it, no passion entered the picture, but if she had lost control and released her wings, there had to be at least a little unbridled pleasure involved. Clearly, she'd left the good parts out of her retelling. I'd never say as much to her face, though, with those talons of hers.

The journalist, Brice, had been in the Mt. Mitchell area for a weekend nature retreat where he occupied a rental cabin along with seven others. Brice didn't say much about why he came, other than he needed a break from everything. He'd been hiking alone in the woods when the harpies spotted him from a treetop. Lapis and Salis flew home in a hurry to leave Eonza alone with the unsuspecting male.

According to Eonza, they mated right there in the woods. She'd left out the part where she flashed her wings, and only mentioned them going their separate ways and her flying home when she knew he wouldn't see her.

Soon, none of that would matter.

"Hey, does the idea of changing someone's memory of an event feel a little off to you?" Marcus whispered into my ear as we ascended the cement steps toward the glass front doors of a twenty-story building.

It was something I'd thought about on our drive to the city. "I guess if he was a doting father, excited to meet his baby, yeah, I'd feel bad erasing his memories leading to his upcoming fatherhood," I said. "But he's not. He has no idea she's pregnant, and he's putting his career over the livelihood of a living being."

We passed the guard at the front desk on the main floor and within seconds Marie and her sisters spun their energetic abilities. The beefy guard waved us by with a goofy grin plastered across his face. I didn't want to know what the succubi had made him feel. We crammed into the elevator and Marie pressed the button to the eleventh floor, where the guard had told her we'd find Brice.

"True," Marcus said, once the elevator began rising. "If the harpies were found out, I know of a few government agencies who'd stop at nothing to get their scientists' hands on them. Wings and talons on soldiers would be helpful weapons."

I shivered at the idea, one I hadn't thought of and one that made me better understand why the unknown Wild Women were so set against allowing word to leak out. If the world knew even one kind of Wild Woman existed, they'd begin to believe the other folklore as well. It could lead to a worldwide hunt, each country searching for supernatural women in hopes of creating the biggest and baddest war machine. My stomach turned at the thought.

A few Wilds in the elevator with us shifted in place, clearly uncomfortable with Marcus's revelation. When the elevator doors opened on the eleventh floor we all exited with a stronger sense of mission to our task. Rows of cubicles greeted us along with sounds of fingers tapping keyboards and cell phones vibrating on desks. Flat screen TVs hung from each of the four walls, all on different news channels, the sound muted and the newscasters' words dictated in quick moving letters at the bottom of the screens.

Despite the group of ten supernatural beings wandering onto their work floor, no humans seemed to notice our presence. I looked to Aleksander who wore a glassy expression as he focused on the buzz of the room and its human inhabitants. The incubus was hard at work keeping us energetically invisible.

Marie popped her head around the gray half wall of the first cubicle closest to us and asked the human for Brice's office. With her question answered, she turned toward us and began walking to the left. We followed, passing rows of cubicles, until we reached the far wall lined with offices. Each office had a wall of windows separating the room from the larger portion of the eleventh floor. We found Brice's office as the second to the last on the left. "Smith" had been etched in block font on his glass door.

"Wait out here. We'll only be a few minutes," Marie said as she started to open the office door to let one of her two succubus sisters walk in with her.

Through the windows, a man who looked to be in his forties peered up from his laptop and watched our group outside his office. His overgrown beard stubble and bloodshot eyes told me he'd been pushing tirelessly to get his Pulitzer story out to the public. I wondered if he was working on it at this exact moment. How close had we come to being dissected and our DNA studied to build super warriors?

"No," Marie's other sister said, grabbing her arm. "Let me help do it." They exchanged a knowing look, and Marie gave a nod. She stepped back to stand beside Celeste as the blonde, tattooed succubus entered Brice's office alongside a second succubus.

A tired smile rose to Brice's lips as they walked from window to window, closing the blinds to shut out the world and give them the privacy they would need.

"You look exhausted," I heard the blonde say quietly in a poor-you voice.

"I am," Brice said with a sigh. "I've been trying to put a huge story to bed so it can go to print tonight."

"Oh?" she said, even quieter.

He started to reply, but a moan replaced his words.

Okay, I'd heard enough. I didn't care to listen to what was to come...or who was about to come.

I hurried away from the office and toward a mess of newspapers strewn atop a long table backed up against a wall beneath one of the flat screen TV's. I decided to read to occupy my mind because Goddess knew, if I heard another moan I'd...I didn't know what I'd do, but I didn't want to find out either.

The others seemed to feel the same as they made their way over to me and the table of newspapers, and grabbed something to read, something to distract themselves. Aleksander was probably used to hearing the sex noises of others. It probably didn't bother him in the slightest. But he joined us nonetheless. I assumed he kept close to maintain the energy of disinterest around us to the humans in the office.

Shawna shoved the front page of a local newspaper in my face. "Look," she exclaimed and she shook the paper so much I couldn't read the print. "Another teenage girl, a self-proclaimed wiccan, has gone missing."

I snatched the paper and steadied it enough to read. "Holy shit," I said on an exhale.

Marcus stood behind me and read the headline story over my shoulder. "This is the Hunters' doing. Look how the story is spun to make the victim look evil, like her disappearance was somehow her own fault by toying with the occult."

"Are you saying a Hunter wrote this article?" Renee said, stretching her neck to see what we were reading.

"Either that, or a Hunter is the editor of this newspaper," he answered, still reading over my shoulder.

"That's not a newspaper from this company, is it?" Renee asked.

"No," I said quickly to quiet what I knew was a worry inside her that would soon take over if not squashed right away. "This isn't the Charlotte Tribune."

As long as we weren't in the presence of a Hunter, other than Marcus of course, I didn't care where this man worked. I had no intention on finding his office. Why hunt one Hunter when I could hunt a whole complex of them and rescue the innocent women they were collecting in the process? Still, my blood boiled by the time I finished reading the article and handed it off to the next huldra who wanted a look.

Shawna gently touched my arm. "We'll get them," she assured me. "We'll save the girls."

"The article said her friends reported that she'd texted them to say she was heading out to a private ritual on someone's property, but they didn't say who," I explained to my partner sister. "We know who. They're making it out to look like she'd been involved with some private cult that meets to sacrifice dogs and cats. It's ridiculous." How the Hunters spun a story about a wiccan woman rubbed raw the justice-seeking part of me, not to mention my huldra side. It was as though at every turn the Hunters created lies to suppress powerful women who held a kind of magic the brotherhood couldn't access.

"We know the truth, though," she said with a kind smile. "Just like we aren't evil demon beings who lure men into the woods to eat, she's not evil either. Hers is just a religion like every other religion."

"Not according to the Hunters," Marcus corrected.

"Well," Shawna said in a less gentle and comforting tone. "The Hunters are close-minded and think anyone who doesn't believe how they believe is wrong and on the path to hell. They're bullies."

My gaze caught the flat screen hanging on the wall across from us and I drowned out the conversation between Marcus and Shawna about the atrocities committed by the Hunters in the name of correct belief systems. "Breaking News," flashed across the screen as a female reporter stood at the edge of a forest, a fire blazing behind her. Her words streamed across the bottom of the screen, telling of the odd timing of a local forest fire in Maine—odd for the time of year. She went on to talk about how local firefighters were struggling to keep the fire from spreading to the populated regions.

"As far as the unpopulated area behind me," the reporter said, motioning to the burning trees, "we're still awaiting word from the new owners of the land, a private commercial real estate investment cooperation, as to how they'll move forward in containing the fire. I'm told they're currently in talks with Greenville's fire marshal."

"How much you want to bet that new real estate investment

cooperation is led by Hunters?" I asked no one in particular, as we stayed glued to the television.

"They're probably trying to convince the fire marshal to hold off, to let a portion burn because they're planning to develop it anyhow," Marcus answered.

The reporter went on to speculate the fire's cause—teens getting high while camping in the woods behind her.

I hadn't realized Olivia watched the broadcast too, until she groaned and said, "Must they demonize everything? In that one statement they've made a whole generation and a plant out to be culprits."

"Those trees look familiar," I noted. "I think..." I studied the backdrop, up in blazes. "I think that's where the rusalki live."

Marcus and Shawna stopped talking and shifted their gazes to the flat screen.

"Oh shit, they're doing it," Marcus muttered, shock painted along his wide, focused eyes.

"Doing what?" I asked.

He didn't look at me to respond. "You know how I told you I thought they were staging little attacks here and there to see how you all would react in different situations, different scenarios?"

"Yeah," I said. "You told me that's what they were doing when they landed on the mermaid's island and when they invaded my coterie's property and the Airbnb in Oregon."

"I also said that once they collected enough data they'd strike for real." Marcus paused and swallowed. "Faline, this is it. They're striking now, and they won't stop until every last one of you is captured. I know it. I can feel it in my bones."

I backed away until my butt hit the table of newspapers. My heart thrummed and my throat went dry. This was it. Their big push. They must have found what they needed to complete their plans to do with us what they'd been working on for the last twenty years or more. I had hoped to attack their remaining two complexes, to win the two remaining battles. But the Hunters, they were clearly done with battles; they had just started a war.

NINE

Marie paused abruptly and turned toward the direction of Brice's office moments before I heard his door softly open and shut. Relief washed through me when two succubi came around the corner with smiles plastered to their faces. At least the Brice issue had been handled. One less fire to put out.

I cringed. Now we had a real fire to deal with. One our team didn't start.

No words were exchanged between the succubi and us. They simply joined our group huddled around the newspaper table. Those of us who were still holding any papers dropped them back onto the pile and made our way to the stairs. I doubted any of us had the ability to contain the anxious energy pinging around inside us. From the change in her expression, I assumed the blonde succubus, who didn't know about the fire in the rusalki's woods or the news article, felt our anxiety and knew something was up.

We made it down the many flights of stairs in the cement stairwell, to the first floor, and out of the building before a succubus spoke up. "Brice no longer believes the wings he saw on Eonza were real," she updated us. "Hopefully, the replacement memory we gave him will stick." Her eyebrows scrunched in a concerned look to her leader, Marie. "What's wrong?"

Marie exhaled and shook her head slowly. "We can't be sure, but Faline thinks the Maine forest on fire is where the rusalki live."

"We *can* be sure," I corrected. "The newswoman said she was standing in front of the forest surrounding Moosehead Lake. That's where the rusalki are."

Marie turned to address me. "That area is huge, according to the maps."

How'd she know? Did she actually research the rusalki?

Marie rolled her eyes. "I can feel your distrust rising. Yes, we've done a little digging into each of the Wild Women groups we have agreed to fight alongside. It would be stupid not to."

"It's not distrust," I clarified.

"Then what would you call it?" she asked in the same tone a mother would question her child with crumbs on her shirt, claiming to not have eaten the missing cookie.

Cars and busses barreled past us as we stood on the sidewalk in front of the multi-leveled business building. The mid-morning sun hid behind thick, grey clouds, casting a muted darkness onto our surroundings.

"I'd call it questioning," I answered.

"Same difference," Marie said, turning toward her succubus sisters to ask for particulars in their completed mission of placing new memories in the journalist's mind to push the old ones containing Eonza's wings out.

A horn honked. The scent of a hotdog cart caught my attention and my stomach growled, despite our coffee house breakfast. I patted my pants pocket for my cell, to check the time, and remembered I hadn't picked up a new burner phone.

"Help them," a disembodied voice called to me on the autumn breeze.

I spun on my heel, searching nearby crowds for the person who uttered the words.

A cold hand rested on my right shoulder. "My sisters, they need your help," the voice said again, this time centimeters from my ear.

I froze in place, my arm hairs standing on end. Were the harpy ghosts real? Had they escaped the underground tunnel system to find me?

I slowly reached my hand out to grab Shawna's arm and squeeze. She paused in the middle of her conversation with Marcus and Oliva. "What's up?" she asked in a tone way more lighthearted than the situation called for.

"There's. Someone. Standing. Behind. Me," I said.

"No there's not," Shawna responded.

"It's a spirit," Marie said. She closed her eyes, inhaled deeply, and exhaled slowly. "A rusalka spirit, from the feel of her."

My fear dissipated. Within a breath I went from scared shitless of the unseen to almost crying with the opportunity to communicate with the rusalka who helped to save my sister. It had to be her, the only rusalka who'd died and would know to contact me. "Azalea?"

"Yes," the voice answered. "Please, they need you."

I hushed the few conversations still buzzing among my group of supernaturals. When I had their attention, I said, "We need to get to Maine, ASAP."

"The fires?" Renee asked.

Azalea answered into my ear, "Our forest is burning, our home."

"But they're safe in the lake, aren't they?" I asked the rusalka out loud.

"They pull from the Great Mother," she explained, "from the forest and the lake, to create their dome under the water. Without the power of the trees, the dome will collapse."

I reiterated her words to the group.

"Can't they just zap themselves out of there?" Olivia asked.

Good point.

"They call upon Mokosh for their abilities," Azalea's spirit explained. "Mokosh lives in the dirt, in the trees, in the water, in the ferns, and animals. The trees are dying rapidly, the animals have fled, the plants fear for their lives. None have energy to spare to aide my sisters."

I had so many questions. How was Azalea able to visit me? Was I able to hear ghosts now, or just her? And why couldn't the others hear her? I suspected it had everything to do with her and not much to do with me or any new abilities.

But one image roared through my mind—the blazing fire flames I'd seen on the screen. The orange flames licking up and down tree trunks, burning my favorite parts of nature to ash. We didn't have time to postulate as to how a spirit came through to the living. We had Wild Women to save.

* * *

I sat in the back row of the mini-van as Aleksander sped down the freeway away from the airport and toward Moose Lake. This time we didn't bother with luggage, or lodging, or even letting the foreign Wild Women know what we were up to. After a two-and-a-half-hour flight that Aleksander was kind enough to cover for all of us, we'd taken an Uber straight from the sidewalk in front of the Charlotte Tribune headquarters to the Charlotte Douglas International Airport.

We saw the smoke of the forest fire from the plane before we began our descent. The view only intensified our need to be there already.

"Has she come back?" Renee asked, wringing her hands. "Has Azalea given you an update?"

Marie and I shook our heads at the same time.

None of the car rentals within the airport carried an available passenger van, so Aleksander had opted for the next best thing. Of course, there weren't enough seatbelts for all of us, but desperate times... Squishing in among sisters and friends was nothing compared to what the rusalki were dealing with at the moment.

"The mermaids will meet us there," Patricia said to calm her sister. "They may be there already, helping. Everything will be okay."

When we had returned back to the old moonshine house after breakfast, before heading to Charlotte, Sarah called to give us her number. She hadn't clearly said the mermaids would help us in our war against the Hunters, but we'd figured giving us her number was a good start to the discussion. On our way to the airport Aleksander let me use his phone to call Sarah and let her know the rusalki were in trouble. She said she'd call back and within minutes she called to let me know a few sisters of hers were in the Nova Scotia area and would swim over.

"I just...I just can't help but think," Renee said with a shaky voice. "What if the Hunters had burned down our woods, our home, when they'd descended on our property?"

I shook with worry and anger and fear. Was nothing sacred to the Hunters? Not even nature? I almost scoffed at my own question. Wild Women were of nature, created by Goddesses, and we were nowhere near sacred to the brotherhood. We were the opposite, animals filled with evil intent. In an effort to destroy us, they were killing off plants, trees, and animals.

Anger won out, and my huldra stirred to the surface, ready to enact a punishment worthy of the crimes committed.

"How far?" I half-asked, half-growled.

Aleksander stumbled over his answer and cleared his throat to begin again. "The GPS says we're close. Maybe another ten minutes or so."

Marcus squeezed my hand to calm me, but my huldra didn't much appreciate the gesture. Comfort was not what I wanted right now. I gave him the side-eye and he released my hand.

Shawna, who sat on the floor between me and the row in front of us, rubbed my shins with both hands.

None of the others in this vehicle knew the reality of an uncontrollable Wild Woman. None, other than Shawna. The others had had the privilege of inviting their inner Wild to come out through practices and meditation. They were able to gently coax theirs out. They didn't understand the effects of having their Wild's first full reveal to be one of trauma, of being drugged and having to fight for your life. My inner huldra and I were connecting better—I was able to stay present when she emerged—but it still often felt as though she and I were two separate beings working to coexist in the same body. And when I couldn't control my huldra, it felt as though I couldn't control myself. I hated not being able to control my own thoughts and desires. And if I were honest with myself, I loathed the fact that my power had been first forced *from* me rather than eased out *by* me.

The Hunters had just about taken everything from me. And now they were attempting to finish the job. Fury pulsed within me and my vision blurred. Shawna rubbed my shins more vigorously.

"Marie," Aleksander called from the driver's seat. "You want to deal with that for me? I am too busy making sure we aren't noticed by law enforcement to calm her uncomfortably erratic energy."

Marie didn't waste time in answering. She turned from the front row of seats and glared straight into my eyes.

"Don't," I heard myself beg before a cloud of relaxation settled over me.

Aleksander pulled off the highway and located a back road to take toward the fire. The flames lit the night sky with an eerily orange hue. The mini-van made its way from the dirt road into an opening among the trees lining the forest. The moment the car stopped, the cloud of relaxation lifted and my huldra stirred to attention.

"Cover your noses," my Aunt Patricia shouted as the side van door slid open with force then stopped with a jolt.

"And if you feel depleted of oxygen," I said as I sprang from the van and surveyed the land before me. "Try to grow your roots deep enough to attach to a plant's. They may be willing to share."

I pushed off to bolt into the woods when Marcus grabbed my forearm to stop me. I spun around and glared at him. My huldra did not want to be held back from saving her friends.

"Don't go alone," Marcus said. "Please. The Hunters could be out there, waiting."

"The Hunters are here," Aleksander said, his eyes closed and body facing the heart of the forest. "But they are heading toward the water, toward the lake."

"The lake is this way," I shouted so everyone could hear over the roar of the hungry fire. "Follow me!"

I raced past trees into the thick smoke. Ferns smacked my legs. Already the air seemed void of enough oxygen, so I pulled my shirt up to cover my nose and mouth and pushed forward. My eyes burned and watered. Intense heat from what felt like an oven all around me caused sweat to pour from my brow. I wiped the back of my hands across my eyes and searched through the smoke for hints that I was headed in the right direction. Seeing in the dark was not an issue, it was the smoke that kept my line of sight from being visible. The faint scent of water lingered in the air and I trusted it enough to run in the direction it came from. If the Hunters were nearing the water, odds were I'd find the rusalki there too.

My huldra vibrated along my surface but allowed me to keep the reigns and stay in control. I followed the hint of moisture in an otherwise parched setting—the normal wetness held by a Maine forest in the winter devoured by the heat of flames. The footfalls and panting of my group told me they followed close behind. My ears caught the snapping of burning branches and the crackling of dead leaves being consumed by the orange glow.

The lake was near. I could feel it. I picked up my pace...and ran right over the edge of land and into the water. With a shock, I scurried to climb back over the short drop-off and onto the muddy shore. I sat, sopping wet, hidden by smoke and branches, searching for a trace of Hunters within the water, hoping a head would pop up out of the surface so I could jump on top of it and dig my roots into the lake floor to drown him.

I unlaced and pulled my boots off in a hurry, throwing them haphazardly to the side. Marcus, Shawna, and Aleksander stopped short behind me before falling into the water from the land ledge. I didn't turn to look at them, but their silence told me everything I needed to know. They too were studying the water for any sign of movement. And then the movement came.

The head of a male peeked out of the lake top. I stood to dive in after him, but Aleksander grabbed my arm right before I jumped. I turned to glare and fight him off me, when he motioned his head toward the water. I followed his gaze to see the Hunter's head lean back so that his mouth could inhale oxygen. Instead he belted out a scream before being pulled back under. A tail fin thrashed the water, creating bubbles around the man as he sank from view.

Aleksander must have felt the presence of the mermaids.

They'd beaten us here. And despite the bad dealings between the mermaids and the rusalki, the mermaids were out for blood.

Another Hunter surfaced and kicked his legs like his life depended on it, swimming toward the shore. A sleek scuba mask wrapped around his face, but inner condensation kept me from seeing his eyes. His wetsuit-covered arms shoved him forward. The Hunter's strength proved no match for the mermaid's water prowess. A green scaled arm shot up from the water beside him, nails latching into his back, tearing at his wetsuit. The mask muffled his scream as he twisted himself to fight off his water predator.

"They're coming," Aleksander whispered loud enough for Marcus to hear. The incubus turned toward the tree line behind us and raised his arms, at the ready.

Marcus instinctively reached for his dagger but came up short. "Fuck," he grumbled under his breath.

Shawna and I stood behind the two men, no longer watching the water, but close enough to jump in if needed. The first Hunter crept from the smoke, between evergreens, like a shadow becoming whole. Three more followed, their daggers raised for attack.

I thought to call out for my coterie, but their own shouts suddenly rang through the forest. "Mother?" Shawna yelled, turning on her heels to try to get a better idea of which direction to run. "Mother!"

Two more Hunters closed in on us from the right side, the side Shawna and I decided the shouts of our coterie came from. The smoke must have kept them from following us. Each Hunter wore black cargo pants, black boots, and black zipped-up jackets with black beanies. Empty dagger holsters hung from their hips.

The thick air around us tingled with the flow of energy. Droplets of sweat tricked down the back of Aleksander's neck. He was keeping the Hunters at bay, but for how long?

All six Hunters stared at us, antsy to attack, as though an invisible bubble kept them from coming any closer, as though they waited for the bubble to burst.

"How much longer can you hold them?" I asked Aleksander quietly enough to hopefully keep our enemies from hearing my exact words.

"Minutes," he responded in a strained voice. "And I can't fight them all at once either. This is depleting me too much." He stiffened his stance. "You have one minute to come up with a plan of attack."

"We'll rush the four in front of us and you two rush the two to our right," Marcus said to Shawna and me with hurried words. "Once you've taken them out, find your coterie. Does that work?"

Shawna nodded.

"Yeah," I said. I turned to my partner sister. "Take your shoes off."

She looked down at her tennis shoes. "Oh yeah." She pulled them from her feet and flung them, along with her socks, to rest beside mine.

"Ready?" Aleksander grunted the words out.

"We are," I answered, ready to launch myself at the Hunter to my right. Shawna flexed her fingers and cracked her neck.

Aleksander warned us, "The energy shield is coming down in five... four...three...two..."

War cries of more than five women sounded from behind the Hunters, muffled at first, but growing in clarity and riotous. The four Hunters in front of us turned to view their incoming attackers.

"One!" Aleksander yelled. He and Marcus ran for the four Hunters whose backs were now turned toward the supernatural males, only to stop short as two burst into flames and screamed out in pain.

Aleksander turned to run back toward the lake and warn us in the process. "Get out of their way!"

"Whose way?" I yelled back, an arm's length from my target.

A Hunter swiped his dagger at me and I ducked out of the way. I splayed my fingers and shot vines from my fingertips to tangle and restrict his fighting arm.

"Theirs!" Marcus shouted, pointing to the women's silhouettes as they moved through the haze, each carrying fire in her hands.

TEN

TECHNICALLY, the enemy of my enemy should be my friend. But a cliché saying was nowhere near enough to answer whether these fire-wielding women were friends or foes. And I didn't want to wait to find out. A ball of flames hit the man I fought on the shoulder. I quickly pulled my vines from his arm and backed up. I grabbed Shawna's hand and ran to jump with her into the lake. We'd swim to our coterie. Mermaids we knew were a safer bet than fire-throwing women we didn't know.

Before we swam up the lake, I treaded water and called to Marcus and Aleksander to join us. A ball of fire shot past Marcus's ear, barely missing his hair, and landed in the water, extinguishing on impact.

No way would I allow these women to hurt my man. I struggled to get up the slippery lake edge and onto land, when Marcus jumped into the water, followed by Aleksander.

"Swim between the two of us," I shouted to Marcus and Aleksander, trying to be heard above the women's battle cries and the Hunters' screams of agony. "Hopefully the mermaids will know not to mess with you."

I had no way of knowing whether or not the Wilds in the water knew Marcus, and I doubted they knew Aleksander. I couldn't risk losing the man I loved and my ally, the other man who claimed to love me. Haze settled over the lake, bringing with it an eerie glow. We swam as quickly as possible to get the men to safer land and away from both the fire women and the water women.

When the fire women's voices quieted with distance, and the shouts of my coterie became clearer, we veered toward the shore nearest our people. Our feet touched the squishy lake bottom and we ran up the shore, water streaming down our soaked bodies.

An inhuman screech bellowed from below the surface of the lake and we all instinctively turned to see where exactly it came from. A yellow and orange scaled tail cut through the lake top and smacked back down, sending waves rippling. Blood bubbled to the surface as all traces of the mermaid disappeared beneath the water. The men ran faster toward dry land.

"Your coterie is this way," Aleksander yelled, waving his arms to the right.

Shawna and I met up with the men on the shore and sped through the forest at their pace. Depleted from using his energy manipulation abilities during the drive and against the Hunters, the incubi leader ran slower than usual.

I saw my sisters' and aunts' silhouettes fighting larger shapes before I could make out their faces. With two Wilds for every Hunter, my sisters and friends were crushing the enemy in a way that relit the ember of hope I held for our kind winning the war for our freedom.

With vines spurting from her fingertips, Shawna bolted to her mother and Patricia. She whipped her mother's and aunt's attacker in the face before wrapping her vines around his neck. Her mother, Abigale, and Patricia each grabbed one of the Hunter's arms, holding them down from slashing Shawna's vines. Together they brought the Hunter to his knees until he was blue in the face and toppled over from affixation.

I sprinted to the Hunter held face down in the dirt by Marie and her succubi's energy influence. He struggled to push himself up, his forearms beneath his chest, pressing into the leaf-littered ground beneath him.

He tried to put up a fight when I wrangled his dagger from his hand, but it was as though he hadn't the energy left to hold it any longer. The succubi had rendered him speechless, so he only watched me yank the dagger from his weak grip. His eyes widened when I lifted his head from the dirt and moved his dagger under his neck, ready to end him.

It wasn't anger or hatred that flashed through his eyes, but something else. Almost as though he begged me to let him be done with this all. In a way, I related.

He mouthed something to me before I pressed the dagger's blade against his neck enough to ease blood from his skin.

"Marie," I called out. "Let him speak for a second."

She narrowed her eyes but gave a stiff nod.

Sound sprang from the Hunter's moving lips. "Find my brothers," he whispered in a raspy voice, no doubt depleted from fighting against succubi energy in the smoke. "They want to help you."

"Hunters want to help us?" I asked, confused and weary of another trap set by the Hunters to ensnare my Wild sisters and me.

"They've left the brotherhood," he coughed out. "Braver than me."

Marcus's words flowed through my mind. He'd once spoken of Hunters who would one day see enough atrocities committed by their brothers that they'd denounce the organization they'd known their whole life and work to clear their consciences by righting the wrongs of their fathers. At my feet, I believed, lay a Hunter ready to clear his conscience.

"You can still leave them," I encouraged the Hunter amidst fighting, weakened battle cries, and screaming. "I know a couple ex-Hunters who can help you."

For less than a second, the Hunter gave me a smile, his eyes lighting up with what looked to me like thankfulness. "I'm not brave enough," he whispered before butting his forehead into the dirt and catching his neck on his dagger's blade. He choked on his blood as the red liquid pooled between his chin and the ground. His body went slack.

I dropped the dagger and backed away, still crouched low to the ground.

"Marcus," I called out, sounding about as frantic as I felt.

The ex-Hunter left the incubus to help Olivia and Celeste finish off their combatant and ran to my side. He crouched down to my level and touched his hand to my cheek.

"What happened?" he asked softly. "What did he do?" He lifted my chin and then searched my hands and arms. "Did he hurt you?"

I shook my head. "He said he wanted to leave the brotherhood, but he was too weak." I paused. "And then he killed himself."

Marcus's shoulders slumped, and for the first time, he gazed down at the dead Hunter with sympathy. "He was done fighting against himself for the sake of the brotherhood," he said with a sigh. He gently eased the blade from under his brother's neck and wiped the blood from the metal. "The oppression of the Hunters hurts more than the Wild Women."

"He was like you," I uttered, the thought being the only one swirling in my mind, cluttering and confusing my prior beliefs about Hunters. Marcus and Rod weren't the only sane needles in the Hunter haystack. Marcus had told me this was the case, but I hadn't fully understood until this moment. "He was like you and now he's dead because of it."

Marcus wrapped his arm around my shoulders and pulled me to his chest. The base in his voice vibrated against my cheek. "There's many more out there like him, Rod, and me."

"He said he had brothers who left the brotherhood and want to help us." I spoke into Marcus's muscular chest.

"We'll find them," he assured me. "Aleksander and I have already started discussing how to locate the rogue Hunters."

I nodded, and for the first time since hearing the dead Hunter's words of redemption, I noticed the fighting had stopped. My coterie, Aleksander, and the succubi stood around us, watching and listening. I peered up at them and gave Marcus a squeeze of a hug before standing. He stood with me, his arm wrapped around my waist.

"Don't move," said a woman's voice from the beyond the haze. "Release the female and we'll think about not blowing a hole through you."

"I think they may be talking to you, Marcus," Aleksander said through unmoving lips.

"I have to move to release her," Marcus replied to Aleksander, before freezing again.

One woman, flanked by six others, emerged from the cloud of brown and gray smoke. All stood with palms up, cradling flames of various colors and shapes within their hands. They looked alike, with dark sun-kissed skin and long black hair.

The woman who looked to be the leader couldn't have been younger than forty years old. She wore a floral print halter top and cut-off jean shorts. Her bare feet walked along the earth leaving singe marks in their wake. The fire she carried burned red hot and circled in on itself like an ever moving ball of flames.

"If we had known you Hunters were still active in your oppression of Wild Women," the leader said, "we would have come a long time ago."

I moved in front of Marcus and shielded him with my left arm. "Where do you come from?" I asked.

She regarded me with suspicion. "Why do you protect the Hunter? I feel your Wild fire burning within. Have you sided with your oppressor?"

"My name is Faline Frey," I started. "And I am a huldra of the Washington coterie. This ex-Hunter is my mate." After the words left my mouth I realized I probably shouldn't have started with exposing my connection to Marcus. The feud between Wild Women and Hunters was old, worldwide, and well established. Introducing myself as the mate of our enemy was a bonehead thing to do. But I'd meant to express my claim on him—that not only was this fire woman in American Wild Women territory, but she was threatening my mate. Something she should rethink.

"There is no such thing as an *ex*-Hunter," she proclaimed. Her sisters cheered at her announcement as though she spoke Goddess's truth.

"Well," I said, thinking of not only Marcus and Rod, but also of the Hunter whom I'd just watched slit his neck on his own dagger. "That's where you're wrong. I know this because I'm standing beside one and I've met others."

Also probably not the best first impression, so I continued with a softer, less disrupting statement. "I understand why you'd think that, though. I used to be of the same opinion not very long ago." I looked at Marcus and kept my gaze too high to catch a glimpse of the dead Hunter who'd wanted out of the brotherhood. "But personal experience has taught me otherwise."

The leader of the fire women studied me for a few breaths before she relaxed her stance. She pointed to Aleksander. "You are no Hunter. This is not your battle to fight."

He answered as though she'd asked a question, which I suppose she could have been leading to. "You are correct, ma'am. I am an incubus and do not wish to fight you either."

"An incubus," she said as though she were trying the word on her tongue for the first time. "I've heard of your kind but have never met one." The flames in her palms extinguished, as did those of the woman flanking her. Suddenly the night felt much darker, though a forest fire roared less than a mile behind them. "What is your name, incubus?"

Aleksander took a step toward the woman but didn't reach his hand out to shake hers. Good call. I made a mental note to refrain from automatically shaking her hand if the moment we formally introduced ourselves—rather than me stating my name and her correcting me—felt like it needed a physical greeting.

"My name is Aleksander," he said. "Aleksander Berg. I am the leader of an incubi hoard in Portland, Oregon. And you must be a Wild Woman of..." He paused to study her. "Of the volcano Goddess Pele. You wouldn't happen to be alae?"

He could have just spoken in another language for all of what I understood of his statement about her kind and goddess. Wait. I had heard of Pele. "You're from Hawaii?" I blurted out. "But that means you're American Wild Women. Why have I never heard of you?"

She gave me a look of impudence before answering. "I am Ailani, the high chief of my people, the alae; humble servant of Pele. We have no Hunters on our islands. They tried to join the other white men in colonizing our land, but our alae ancestors would have no part of their ways and they ran them out with the help of our friends, the mo'o sisters."

Okay, so clearly we'd gotten off on the wrong foot. I needed to right things before they went any further. She and her sisters were American Wild Women; this was huge. They were more our distant relatives than the nagin, shé, or the echidna. These women were from American soil. They had more stakes in this revolution.

"We are also driving the Hunters out," I said. "My coterie and the other Wild groups of this country. We've ruined two Hunter complexes and we have plans to ruin the last two before the month is over. We are appreciative of your help tonight."

As though on cue, the three rusalki, sopping wet and naked as the day they were born, walked from the lake and onto the shore. I'd expected their skin to glow in the moonlight, but with the amount of smoke blocking the moon, their skin didn't so much as glimmer. They slowed their pace when they noticed the alae watching them. Drosera pulled birch scissors from her knotted hair.

Three mermaids I'd never met, but who looked familiar, exited the lake after the rusalki, naked and strewn with lake weeds.

A new kind of stand-off started. The exhausted mermaids and rusalki locked eyes with the alae. One alae on the left side of their leader lit a little flame in the center of her right palm as though she were preparing for things to get ugly.

"There, there," a woman's voice said in a Spanish accent as a delicate hand breeched the smoky haze and patted the shoulder of the alae holding fire. "This night has already turned out to be quite the disaster. Let's not make things worse."

The alae extinguished her fire and lowered her head. Although her body language made her out to be submissive to the new woman entering our space, her leader, Ailani, held her ground. "Conchita," she said, staring into the woman's eyes. "We were merely making introductions."

Conchita smirked and gave a slight nod. She made her way over to me and put her hand out. I hesitated.

"I am not a fire woman," she laughed. "I am the opposite, in fact."

ELEVEN

EACH TIME a new type of Wild Woman was introduced to me I ran through a mental debate, first scolding myself for not spending more time researching folkloric women who were possibly walking the earth, and then blaming my lifelong education of Hunter-skewed Wild facts. Of course, I could have dug into our kind after I flipped the bird to the whole Hunter establishment, but starting a revolution leaves little time for much else.

"Are you a water woman?" a mermaid asked.

I didn't pretend to know what Conchita was, but I also decided not to appear ignorant. I let the mermaid's questions shed light on the dark-haired woman standing before us with the confidence of a war general and the grace of a woman who knows her place...is at the top.

Conchita inhaled deeply and answered the mermaid on a smiling exhale. "Yes, I am a xana, created by the Goddess Danu. We are more commonly known as a type of water nymph." She narrowed her eyes and studied Marcus for a quick second before returning a soft gaze to the mermaid. "We hail from Spain."

I answered the water nymph's offer of a handshake. "Thank you for being here," I said. "But I am unsure why Wild Women from Spain would make an appearance, unless the rusalki asked you here." I thought better of that statement once it left my lips. The xana woman had to have come from Spain before the Hunters set the fire to the rusalki's woods. She arrived too quickly. She would have already been around.

Conchita released my hand and took a step back, closer to the fire women than me and my exhausted group of either drenched or sweaty supernaturals. She wore dress slacks and a button-up silk shirt. Her thick black hair cascaded down her shoulders to reach her elbows. She looked as though she had stepped out of a fashion magazine, not out of the smoky haze of a forest fire. She indicated the alae behind her with the sweep of her hand. "The alae are the closest Wild Women, and the least likely to be overcome by the Hunters, so we sent them to keep an eye on the journalist issue."

I had to stop her there. "Why not just contact us and see if we were handling it, which we were."

Conchita cocked her head and narrowed a gaze at me. "We couldn't be sure you were trustworthy enough to contact, to allow knowledge of our existence." She blinked and her shoulders relaxed before she went on. "You were raised under the tutelage of Hunters."

Yet another group of Wild Women who'd failed to step in and help us. I wondered if she'd give the same reason as the others. I was too irritated to find out. I nearly shook my head and suppressed a sigh. If Eonza had only waited to be impregnated, none of this Brice crap would be happening and we'd be able to focus on the bigger issues at hand...like not being taken out by the Hunters. But no amount of frustration would change our current circumstances, so I pushed it from my mind and tried to look at the positive. Now we had more possible Wild Women to join our fight. I just had to convince them it was a fight worth their effort. "Well, I appreciate you being here," I said to both Conchita and the alae standing behind her.

"I was sent to check up on things, as a delegate, one could say." Conchita bowed her head for a moment. When she raised her eyes, they fell back onto Marcus. This time, though, she seemed to scrutinize him.

"A delegate?" I asked, partly to find out why she considered herself an ambassador when none of the other foreign Wilds had, and partly to get her to stop looking at Marcus in such an unnerving way. Did she agree with the alae that he was a Hunter, still very much a part of the brotherhood?

Ailani, the chief fire woman, answered. "The xana are leaders of all free Wild Women." Her voice dripped with admiration. "Their leader, Avera, is the reason they are free."

"Wait," I countered. "I thought you said your kind is free because you ran the Hunters out." Maybe standing in the burning forest wasn't the best time and place for a Wild political history lesson, but I'd learned to take the opportunities whenever they presented themselves. Discovering our hidden history helped me to unravel possible scenarios for our future.

Conchita touched Ailani lovingly as though to say she had this one.

"The xana came to the Iberian Peninsula with the Celts in the early days," Conchita said. "We thrived there until the Romans descended upon our ways. Not too long after the Romans, came the first Hunters. They built their first complex in Spain and operated it under the guise of a monastery. The xana were the first Wild Women to be oppressed by the Hunters, the first of many." She ran her fingers through her hair and smiled as her eyes went distant in far off thought. "We were also the first to overthrow them and continue to overthrow their attempts at uprisings in other lands."

"How'd your kind do it?" I asked, my voice now dripping with adoration.

"Which time?" she said with a laugh.

"Will you come back to where we're staying, as our guest?" I offered. "I'd love to hear the details of every single time your kind overthrew them. I'm sure it'll help us in our efforts."

"You are the leader of the American Wild Women under Hunter rule?" Conchita asked matter-of-factly.

I turned to look at my group of rusalki, mermaids, succubi, huldra, an ex-Hunter, and an incubus. "I suppose I incited the revolution," I answered, still uncomfortable with the idea of being a leader of any sort.

Marcus spoke up. "She rallied her people together, stood up against the Hunters' oppression in a way that inspired others to do the same, helped her kind to learn how to wield their own abilities, and has been a key part in planning each and every attack. Her actions have even inspired Hunters to leave the brotherhood. So yes, Faline Frey of the Washington huldra coterie is our leader."

The adoration in his voice... I could have pounced on the man right then and there, surrounded by Wild Women and a blazing fire. Instead I gave him "eyes" and mouthed "later."

Conchita offered his frankness a different type of response. She took four steps and stood an arm's length in front of him. She looked my ex-Hunter up and down until she reached his face and seemed to study his eyes and nose. "Did your love for the huldra Faline inspire you to leave the brotherhood?" she asked, her head tilted in curiosity.

Conchita's head reached the height of Marcus's chin. He inhaled and leaned down a little to look her in the eye. "No," he answered. "I left the brotherhood before meeting Faline."

"Why is that?" Conchita asked.

"Why do you want to know?" Marcus responded, clearly uncomfortable giving personal information to a stranger, whether she was on our team or not. I didn't blame him. He hadn't exactly had the easiest time with my fellow Wild Women.

"Because," she stated bluntly. "You look *very* familiar."

"Trust me," Marcus said. "We haven't met before."

"Oh," she said with a nod, backing up. "I am not suggesting we have."

"Then what are you suggesting?" I asked.

Why couldn't anything ever be easy? Yet again we were in a two steps forward, one step back situation. The xana had just agreed to come to our place and help me figure out how to defeat the Hunters the way her kind had. So of course a difficulty would find its way to my plan in the form of some sort of bad blood or disagreement between my boyfriend and the holder of important information.

I looked to the alae to see if one had a flame at the ready as tension began to build between Marcus and me and the xana. No flames danced in alae palms, so I figured maybe the tension came from only my side of things. I was just sick and tired of watching Marcus be questioned after all he'd done for us. All he'd done for me.

Conchita gave a warm and inviting smile. "I am suggesting that I have met a family member of his. An ancestor."

* * *

"Is it possible Conchita was referring to another Hunter?" I asked Marcus as we sat in our hotel room in a town called Augusta, Maine.

The Maine Hunter complex was situated on a plot of land outside of city limits. We couldn't keep the forest and the rusalki's home safe from their fires, but we could bring fire to their complex.

First, we needed some rest.

Marcus leaned across the bed and stretched. Topless, his pec muscles pulled and his abs tightened. I had to focus to keep my train of thought when all I wanted to do was climb aboard him and go for a ride. The constant danger and impending battle kicked my survival instincts into high gear; chief among them was mating. I supposed my huldra had a little to do with that.

"I don't know how long xana live," he answered, following a yawn. "I know my father is from Spain, so she may have met him in his younger years, or my grandfather."

I nodded in thought. "Yeah, but why would they stand out to her in particular? Why would *you* stand out to her?"

He shrugged and from my vantage point, standing at the side of the bed above him, I got to see his more obscure muscles in action. If I were the salivating type, I'd have dripped drool on his chest.

"I've heard of the xana, though," he said. "Of course, in our stories they're more Hunter home wreckers than Wild Women liberators. Go figure."

"Well, hell," I laughed, crawling onto the king-sized bed to lie beside him. "If any Wilds are in the stories of your people it means they're pretty awesome."

"True," he said, his voice deepening and vibrating into the side of my neck. He turned to press his lips below my ear. "True. The fact that huldra are included in our stories is proof."

The smile in his eyes faded to reveal a serious depth. "Do you know how amazing you are?" Marcus asked.

I stuttered over my answer, part of me wanting to joke and part of me wanting to graciously accept his compliment. He continued before I chose a response.

"The very thought of you fills me with hope—hope for my life, hope for the world, hope for the sake of hope," he said, his voice a low rumble. "Everything you are is everything I love about you, and if I lost you..."

I rolled to my side and then onto the sexy ex-Hunter. "That goes both ways, you know," I said, leaning forward to thread my fingers through his hair. "You've broken so many of my assumptions and helped me to believe both freedom and happiness are available to me. If you get yourself hurt tomorrow, I'll never forgive you."

Marcus chuckled, lightening the mood just enough for me to break our intense eye contact to straddle him and unbuckle his belt. I did need to stay focused on the reason we were even in Maine. But didn't we also say we needed to rest before lighting the Maine Hunter complex on fire? And what better way to induce a restful sleep than to ride the pleasure train?

I didn't waste time or words asking Marcus if he agreed. The way he gripped the sides of my hips and the hunger in his darkening eyes held all the consent I needed.

* * *

We'd only gotten about five hours of sleep, or maybe an hour of play and four hours of sleep, before meeting up with the others in the empty hotel lobby. The sun hadn't come up yet and the free continental breakfast hadn't been set out in the lobby-turned-dining area. We sat on chairs pulled to the couches for our makeshift meeting. The hotel's kitchen bustled with the sounds of food sizzling and dishes washing. I caught scents of sausage, bacon, eggs, and baked goods being prepped and cooked, and my stomach begged for a sampling. With the human kitchen staff out of earshot, we supernaturals worked to plan our next attack.

"I just don't know," Renee commented for the third time, despite the presence of our new pyro allies. "We blew up that last complex.

You don't think this one will be fortified for a fire or something similar? We kind of have an MO now, I'd think."

"Mom," Olivia groaned. "It's not like we have a ton of alternatives for the picking. In fact, we have barely anything at our disposal. But we do have fire-wielding Wild Women."

Celeste spoke up. "Honestly, I'm kind of excited to watch them do their thing."

Ailani grinned. "You won't be disappointed."

The three rusalki, who had opted to sleep somewhere outside, triggered the hotel's automatic double doors and made their way to us. The moment I noticed them, I nearly clapped with excitement to see how the one human in the lobby reacted. I couldn't think of a single instance in which I'd been out in public with a rusalka. I watched the hotel attendant at the front desk watch the rusalki, his eyes wide. I waited for him to remind the barely dressed women of the hotel's no shirt, no shoes, no entrance policy, stated clearly on the outside doors, but he didn't utter a peep. He only gawked. A little anti-climactic, but still entertaining.

That's when I noticed Aleksander and Marie focusing their attention, and no doubt their energy manipulation skills, on the lone attendant. Okay, his lack of reaction made more sense now.

Normally energy-wielders started the fun, but not this time.

The rusalki appeared more worn than usual. Their bare feet were caked in soot and partially burned branches stuck out from their knotted hair. Bags hung under their eyes. Splatters of blood stained patches of their nature-made clothing. When they made their way to our group, I offered them each a seat, but they shook their heads, preferring to stand.

"What can you tell us about your local Hunter complex?" I asked.

I fought from holding my nose in their presence. Gone were the aromas of a delicious breakfast spread. These women brought in with them an odor of burnt dead things and algae.

Drosera closed her eyes and exhaled. "They have our sisters, and they are both alive."

"Whoa," Celeste gasped. "How'd you find that out? When did you find that out?" She paused and clarified her remark. "We know they're likely at that complex, but last I heard you couldn't be sure. Something with how they were able to block your mind reading."

Drosera gave a slow nod. "The Hunters who attacked our forest last night had visited the Maine complex beforehand. Not all were stationed there. But a handful had seen our sisters and knew of their whereabouts."

"Then we'll plan on hitting that portion of the complex first. Where are they?" I asked.

Another rusalka, Vernonia, answered me. "The complex is small, smallest of all the American complexes. It is also the oldest." Her hazel eyes lacked their usual sparkle. Her dark brown hair held more twigs and moss in its knots than her sisters'.

"Is it made of brick or wood?" Ailani asked.

"Wood," Vernonia answered, dully.

Ailani and her alae sisters grinned wickedly. "Old wood burns the brightest," one of them said to another.

"And quickest," another alae added.

Vernonia finished answering my question. "My captured sisters are highly sedated. They will not be able to help themselves to freedom. They will not be able to recognize us when we enter their minds." Pain flickered across her expression. I wondered how many times she and her coven had tried to make contact with their missing sisters since learning of their whereabouts last night.

"Are they being held in a cabin attic?" Shawna asked, her voice filled with empathy.

Vernonia's hard eyes softened when she regarded my partner sister. "They are not." She paused before continuing. "The Hunters are holding them in an above ground prison cell made of cement."

My breath hitched. I didn't know if the alae and Conchita understood how closely connected the rusalki were to Mother Nature, their Goddess Mokosh. It's why they slept in burrowed out holes in the dirt, why they mourned under water. It's why they only wore animal skins and covers offered by their plant friends, why they killed with birch scissors and ate only what their Great Mother gifted them. Once, when she was alive, Azalea had told me that these things are the umbilical cord connecting them to Mokosh, the one who gives us all life and is the source of their abilities. I suspected they were able to pop in and out of a place with simply a thought due to that strong connection. They were of nature. And the Hunters had gone to extra efforts to make sure two rusalki's umbilical cords were severed by essentially placing them in a cement box. I doubted they'd even put a plant in their confinement.

"What?" Ailani asked after my breath hitched.

"What the Hunters are doing to their sisters is nothing short of torture," I responded. "I'm sorry," I said to the rusalki coven.

"Well," the alae chief said. "We'll just have to torture them back."

"With fire," Renee added blandly, clearly unimpressed with the fiery direction of our planning.

"Don't worry," Conchita, the xana, spoke up to reassure my aunt and anyone else who failed to vocalize their trepidations. "The alae are highly tactical."

My mind whirled with that one statement. If the alae were American Wild Women and highly tactical and free, why didn't they try to help us? The foreign Wilds had mentioned not knowing we were here, or that we were oppressed. But surely the alae knew something about our situation.

They operate on a different thought process, Drosera said into my mind. A tingling sensation across my scalp accompanied her words.

I gazed at the rusalka. *And what's that?* I responded wordlessly. *They can't be bothered with outsiders?*

No, Drosera answered. *They prefer to keep alae dealings to themselves; island happenings belong to the islanders and nobody else. As a people, they've had enough of others who think they know better coming in and trying to erase their ways, their sacred things. They do not wish to do the same to others.*

Suddenly, I felt like an ass.

Conchita looked to the alae chief, Ailani. "How are you thinking of attacking?"

Ailani took turns making eye contact with everyone listening before she spoke. "We'll use the smoke screen tactic, I think." She looked to her sisters who excitedly nodded in agreement. "Are there woods around this complex?"

"Yes," Drosera said. "The complex sits on twenty acres of land.

They use much of it for outdoor training and initiations. The main building is smaller than the others we've seen. The cement block holding our sisters is behind the main building."

"Perfect," Ailani said.

Drosera seemed to know Ailani meant no offense in her delight.

"So here's what I'm thinking," Ailani continued. She rested her hands on her knees and looked off up to the right before her gaze found mine. "Our limited resources won't be a hindrance. We'll collect tires and gasoline. That shouldn't take too long. Wait. How far away is their complex?"

Drosera answered, "We never drive there. We do not know."

She tilted her head in question, so I stepped in. "The rusalki don't need to drive; they transport themselves in a more...unique way."

"You would call it teleportation," Drosera admitted.

"Wow," Ailani exclaimed. "Okay then. Can someone figure out how long it'll take us to drive there?"

An alae got up to approach the front desk person, her linen pants, short-sleeved shirt, and sandals a stark contrast to the human's winter layers. I heard her ask about using their business center, and he showed her around the corner.

"So we'll try to make it there by sunrise," Ailani went on, talking as though this was absolutely in her wheelhouse. "When first light dawns, we'll fill the insides of rubber car tires with gas-soaked cloths and light the fabric, letting the tires roll between their main building and the woods. First, though, we'll start a small, contained fire in their woods." She paused to add a commentary to her own plan. "I know it's not the best thing for the environment, to burn gasoline and rubber, but desperate times call for us to be even more desperate. So when they see the smoke from the tires, they'll think it's from the fire and run to stop it. We'll be waiting between the smoke screen and the flames. Hopefully, they'll send most of their Hunters to combat the fires and out to the woods to search for the rusalki, who they'll assume started it as retaliation."

Celeste finished voicing Ailani's plan with a smile. "But instead, they'll find us."

TWELVE

It took us twenty minutes to procure tires and gasoline. It took us another thirty minutes to drive from the hotel to the woods outside the Maine Hunters' complex. So, our desire to attack as dawn broke wasn't exactly staying on schedule.

In the early morning hours, as the sun peeked over the mountains, huldra, alae, a succubus, a xana, an ex-Hunter, an incubus, and rusalki tromped through the wet forest littered with orange and brown fallen leaves decomposing into the dirt floor. The small complex sat nestled on a clearing in the center of a forest. We positioned ourselves at six different points, each with a gas-filled tire and an alae to lite that tire. To Marcus's great irritation, Aleksander refused to not be in my group. I refused to not be in Shawna's group, so together, Shawna, Marcus, Alexsander, an alae named Laia, and I stood, waiting for the signal. A light drizzle fell from the sky and I hoped it wouldn't ruin our smoke screens before we had a chance to take advantage of them.

My scalp tingled and I instinctively reached up to itch it as my gaze bounced to Drosera, who stared intently at me.

The succubus has a message for you, Drosera spoke in my head.

I looked to where Marie stood, waiting, with Celeste and Olivia.

No, the succubus back in harpy territory, she corrected my assumption.

Oh, I answered in my thoughts. *Heather?*

My gaze turned to Drosera who gave a nod. *Her joining a Wiccan forum proved successful. She has been invited to take part in a private ritual. Tonight.*

I gave a nod back. *Good. Thank you. So you've established a line of communication with her, then, to keep track of her just in case?*

I didn't know exactly how the rusalka mind-reading thing worked, and I doubted I'd understand fully if one tried to explain it to me. But not having had time to pick up a new batch of burner phones, knowing we had a connection to our sisters back in North Carolina eased some of my burden.

Drosera gave a quick, tight smile. *We have been keeping watch on those we left behind.* She turned to face the cement block holding her captured sisters and the feeling of rusalki fingers kneading through my thoughts disappeared.

Good. So things were going according to plan. With any luck we'd be home tonight in time to be Heather's back-up and expose the human trafficking ring in North Carolina. I made a mental note to call in some sort of tip-off to the local police station before heading out to the woods where Heather was told the ritual would take place. If the cops arrested those there hoping to kidnap Heather, there'd be fewer Hunters at the North Carolina complex for us to fight when we rescued the harpies and my mothers and burned the place to the ground.

For now, though, I needed to focus on the task at hand: burning the Maine Hunter complex to the ground.

I stood barefoot, my feet apart just enough to hold a firm stance. I held my hands out in front of me, my fingertips buzzing with the need to sprout vines, my palms eager to push branches from my bones. Shawna stood to my right, in a similar position, and Marcus to my left. Aleksander insisted on standing in front of me, for protection he'd explained, but neither Marcus nor I would have it. So after some debate, the incubi leader stood in front of the space between Shawna and me.

A breeze ruffled my hair from behind and brought with it the scent of a dead buckthorn bush up in flames. I flexed my fingers in anticipation.

"You ready?" Marcus whispered to me.

I nodded, still staring forward, before I spoke. "I am."

"Faline," he said, his voice strong, gentle, and full of requests that I be safe.

I looked at him. His eyes held worry for me and I knew it wasn't because he thought I was incapable. He'd told me the opposite on more than one occasion. But, each time we fought, each time we went into battle and came out alive and together, we knew that odds were mounting up against such an ending for our next battle.

"We'll end up together," I whispered back, the statement playing on repeat in my mind as a source of comfort. *We'll always end up together.*

I wanted to kiss away the creases between his brows, assure him that we'd both be fine.

But Conchita's bird call rang through the woods and everything happened so quickly.

Laia touched her fiery palm to the gasoline inside the tire and the thing pummeled out thick, rubber-scented smoke. With precision and force, she shoved the smoldering tire to our left and jumped back as another smoking tire came at us from the right, creating a wall thick with dark smoke.

I coughed and almost turned my head to gasp a gulp of cleaner air when the calls of Hunters rang out from the complex and their emergency siren screeched through the morning.

"Here they come, here they come, here they come," Shawna said, just loud enough for me to hear.

My huldra shook within me at the ready, excited more so by my partner sister's excitement.

Shouted directives from the Hunters in charge to their men grew closer until only smoke separated them from us.

We shouted no battle cries this time. We did not yell or even speak loudly. With stealth, we quickly took down the first two Hunters who entered our domain and waited for more.

And more did come.

The Maine Hunter complex may have been the smallest in the United States, but they definitely had a surplus of Hunters. Man after man, dressed in black cargo pants and a black long sleeve shirt, came running into the woods and was met by one of us, wielding our goddess-given abilities to our advantage.

The silence of our sneak attack gave way to Hunters radioing for backup and yelling at those behind them that it was a trap. We took that as our cue to move forward, outside of the dissipating smoke screen and onto the complex property. But when we moved past the smoke and into the clearing, all I saw was chaos. We weren't fighting in an enclosed building like the main building of Washington's Hunter complex or the Airbnb house we'd stayed at in Oregon. Pockets of battles spread out in the large clearing, against the main building, in the woods, outside a small cabin.

It felt wrong. It all felt wrong.

"Marcus!" I shouted. "Something isn't right. We're too spread out."

In the distance, I noticed Conchita pulling a stream of water from the morning dew on the plants below her and pressing her right hand to the lock on the door to the cement block, holding it there. The rusalki stood guard around her. One Hunter took notice and ran at them, his dagger drawn. Drosera pulled her birch scissors from her hair, up in a knot atop her head, and shoved them out in front of her. The Hunter stopped short and waved his dagger at her scissors, clearly afraid to get within snipping distance. Suddenly, he stood rigidly still and opened his hand, allowing his dagger to drop to the dirt. With soldier-like steps he walked to Drosera and leaned forward, presenting her with his blond high-and-tight head. Calmly, she pressed the birch scissors to his scalp and snipped. The Hunter dropped dead at her feet.

Conchita got the door open and they rushed into the cement box.

"They're in!" I yelled to anyone who could hear.

"Awesome!" Shawna yelled back while thrusting her branches through a Hunter's chest. She gave me an evil grin as she helped him to the ground.

Three Hunters came out the side of the main building and set their sights on me. In addition to their regular black uniforms, each wore a black sleeveless vest on top of their long sleeve shirts. Pins and medals decorated their vests, catching the light and glimmering when they walked.

"I think we've got some top brass coming our way at two o'clock," I yelled.

Laia was busy torching a Hunter, but Aleksander, Marcus, and Shawna huddled in with me, our backs to each other.

"I've never seen them before," Marcus said as the men got closer.

"They're coming this way, for us," Shawna exclaimed to our little group.

"Not for much longer," Aleksander said. "I'll take care of them."

The incubus lowered his head slightly to focus his energy on the group of three higher ranking Hunters. The Hunter in the middle tripped over his own foot as though it had gone to sleep. The Hunter to his right lifted his hand.

Two shots fired and Aleksander's back hit mine with a hurtling force as he fell backwards, shoving me forward. His body landed on me, trapping me between him and the ground. Shawna closed the gap and vines burst from her fingertips, long and leafy, moving sporadically as though she were trying to confuse the shooter as to where to shoot next.

The Hunter in the middle of the three-man group regained his gait and they picked up their pace.

I worked to carefully push the tall, muscular incubus off of me without hurting him further and pushing him closer to death. When I finally rolled him to his back, I crouched over him and checked his pulse in his neck. Aleksander's lips lifted only slightly as he gave a half grin.

"It feels good," he said on a scratchy voice. "To have you this close to my lips, touching me."

"I don't know how this works," I said hurriedly, looking him over. Blood pooled on the right side of his stomach, drenching his button-up. "Do you need to take energy from me to heal? To live?"

He coughed a laugh. "You want to have sex with me right here and now?" He cleared his throat and pressed a hand over his gunshot wound. "Agh." He inhaled deeply. "I suppose it makes sense, you being a huldra, that you'd want to seal our mate bond in the forest." He coughed again. "Timing stinks, though."

"I'm being serious, Alek." I wiped his hair off his forehead. "What do you need?"

"Faline! Look out!" Marcus yelled, caught on the winning end of hand-to-hand combat with a Hunter.

I looked up just in time to see the middle Hunter pointing his handgun at me. I tucked and rolled to the right and heard a bullet whizzing past my head.

"Not her!" the Hunter on the right commanded.

I didn't have time. If I wanted any of us to live, I'd have to help Aleksander later. I spun up onto my feet and ran to stand with Shawna and Marcus as the high-ranking Hunters neared us and the tree line. The three of us took our stances, Shawna and I with thick, deadly branches growing and Marcus with his dagger ready, his most recent foe dead at his feet.

When the three high-ranking Hunters got within six feet of us, the one on the right gave another command. "Leave the leader alive. Kill the rest."

Without warning, Marcus ran at the men, swiping his dagger through the air. He plummeted it into the chest of the center Hunter. The Hunter engaged his ex-brother in hand-to-hand combat. Shawna and I ran forward to fight the other two. She reached them before me and wrapped the vines from her left hand around the Hunter's neck while shoving vines from her right hand into his throat with a warrior's scream. I reached the Hunter with the gun and tried to pull the weapon from him with my vines. He slashed through them with his dagger, sending burning pain through my hands and arms. The vines growing from my feet wrapped around his ankles and I kicked my right foot backwards, sending him off kilter. He fell backwards and shot his gun as he went down.

Shawna's agonizing scream pierced my huldra's rage. I stopped and turned to my partner sister. It all happened so slowly, as though someone had pressed a slow-motion button and I could do nothing to move faster, to get to my sister any quicker. The shooter scrambled to his feet as Marcus gave a hefty shove to his attacker and ran to Shawna.

I made it to her before he could, though I didn't know how—it all seemed a blur. She fell into my arms and I almost dropped from the sudden weight. I refused to lay her on the ground and hover over her as I had Aleksander. I refused to let her fall.

"Shawna! Shawna! Stay with me," I begged. "Please. Marcus!"

Marcus caught us both up in his arms, helping me stand by carrying some of Shawna's weight. My legs shook with shock.

Blood pulsed from my sister's left shoulder. "It's just a shoulder wound," I assured her and myself. "No major organs. You'll be okay."

"I think," she ground the words out through pain. "I think the bullets are made with bloodstone. It hurts like a motherfucker."

"Grab her," the middle Hunter told the others. Marcus and I looked up, away from Shawna, to the three Hunters. Marcus released his hold on us and I leaned to the side before righting my stance enough to hold my sister up. He spun around to fight off his ex-brothers.

Arms grabbed for me, and I clung to Shawna tighter. I wouldn't let them separate us. No, not again. I screamed into the woods, to the trees, to anyone who would help us, who would help my sister. Arms wrapped around my waist and heaved me backwards. Still, I wouldn't let my sister go. Marcus left the Hunter he'd been fighting and stabbed my attacker in the side with his dagger as he punched the man in the face. I pulled from my attacker's grip and turned to choke him with my vines.

One shot rang out so loudly, everything else rang around me with a muffled hum.

Marcus dropped.

I screamed. My huldra wailed.

Arms grabbed at me again and another set of hands pulled Shawna from my arms to dump her in the dirt.

I fought for my life. I fought for my sister's and my lover's lives. My huldra thrashed and bit for freedom. The taste of copper filled my mouth as I spit out a chunk of flesh and went in for another.

Something scorching hot pierced my side and then something

heavy and burning was draped over me, rendering me motionless, weak. Hunters hauled me away from Shawna and Marcus, away from the complex, and deeper into the forest, away from the fire and the fighting.

I opened my mouth, but nothing came out. And soon, even opening my mouth grew too difficult.

THIRTEEN

I SNIFFED the air to ensure I was alone before peeking my eyes open. I half expected to find myself in a boxed cement holding cell with the two captured rusalki sisters. What I found appeared to be a room twenty stories up in a city full of high rises. The sheer drapes pulled shut left little to my imagination about my outdoor surroundings.

The Hunters were nothing if not clever. Trap the rusalki in a cement box to keep them shielded from their Great Mother. Trap a huldra, who grows vines, high enough up in a city to keep her from accessing the ground and planting roots beneath the building. I'd never tried to break through layers of concrete with the vines from my feet, though I figured I could if I had to. But twenty stories worth? Yeah, that wasn't going to happen.

I sat up slowly, waiting for a cocktail of drugs to hit my head and swirl my thoughts. Nothing happened, outside of the scorching pain in my side each time I used my ab muscles. Trying not to move my torso, I peered around my bed and then to my arms. No green liquid-filled IV bag, no IV stand at all. But damn my thigh ached. I leaned forward in the twin bed and the pain in my side made me immediately wish I hadn't. I held my core perfectly still as I rubbed my right thigh and winced from the soreness of touching it. Another scorching pain shot up from my right side and I lifted my shirt to see what the hell hurt so badly. I peeled away a rectangular strip of fresh gauze framed by medical tape. A small patch of blood covered the inside center of the bandage.

I touched the slit made into my side and sucked in a breath. Recollection hit me like a Mac truck and made my head swim worse than any drugs could ever do. I sprang from the bed. My dirty bare feet hit the floor shortly before my knees followed, my whole body screaming in pain.

The wound in my side had been made by a Hunter's dagger…when they took me…and left Shawna, Marcus, and Aleksander to die.

"Shit," I cursed quietly so no one would hear me as I worked to pull myself up and make my way to the window overlooking a city. The dagger went through muscle, core muscle my body used for basically every movement, which meant just walking burned like a scalding knife.

The room I was being held in looked like any other master bedroom, with a door open to an en suite bathroom, night stands on each side of the bed, a black six-drawer dresser, and various pieces of framed art sprinkling the walls, all of skylines and architecture. Whoever lived in this place didn't have much of an appreciation for nature.

Who was I kidding? A Hunter lived here. I stood as pain ricocheted through my core and legs. I wanted to snoop through the room before someone heard my rustling and came to shoot me up with some of their famous Hunter drugs, enough to knock a Wild out for days. I couldn't defend myself in such a weak state. I needed help in the form of something sharp.

I slowly winced my way to the bathroom and searched through the drawers under the sink for scissors or a razor or even a pair of tweezers. All I found was Q-tips, towels, and travel size bottles of shampoo, conditioner, and body wash. Oh, and my pathetic reflection in the mirror. Dark half-moon bags hung under my bloodshot eyes. My auburn hair held knots at the back of my head like a crown of matted hair. Dirt smeared along my jaw line and elbows. My lips were cracked and bleeding. I stared at the faucet a moment before realizing how thirsty I was. I turned the knob and scooped water from my hand into my mouth, the movement of bending over the sink shooting burning agony through my abs. The water still ran as I braced my arms on each side of the sink and sucked in enough air to help me push myself to standing again. The sudden need to pee forced me over to the toilet where once more I pushed through the pain to sit and then stand again.

Well, if my captors hadn't heard me falling out of bed, they definitely heard the toilet flushing. I tried to push past the throbbing in my abs to hurry back to bed and realized I should have checked the bedroom doorknob first, before looking out the window and searching the bathroom. I'd not finished climbing into bed when the sound of keys jingled outside the door and the knob turned. Okay, so I had assumed right, it had been locked.

A woman, standing around five and a half feet with mousy brown hair pinned up in a bun entered the room. Clarisse.

I groaned. "Ugh, I should have known you'd be involved in this."

She held a folded red blanket in her arms as though she held the ceremonial pillow a queen's crown rested upon. "Now that you're up it's time to move you," she said as though nothing were out of the ordinary; as though I weren't being held against my will.

I thought to ask if this was how they transported their human trafficking victims but decided against letting her know I knew about their latest attempts to sell young Wiccan women. Not when we were so close to exposing them.

If there was any of *us* left.

The alae had planned to torch the complex. I hoped the Hunters didn't detain them first. I hoped my loved ones got out of there before the place went up in flames.

Wait. Heather. She was supposed to have met up with a person we believed was a Hunter or Hunter's daughter masquerading as a Wiccan to collect what they deemed as throwaway women to sell to the highest bidder. How long had I been here? Oh, Goddess, I hoped Heather was okay. Her incubus boyfriend, Mason, probably would have accompanied her, but I doubted the two of them could outfight a group of Hunters.

"Where are you moving me to?" I asked as Clarisse hesitantly eased toward me and then quickly threw the blanket she'd been carrying over my shoulders like someone who'd throw a net over a wild animal.

"Ah," I groaned, the weight of the blanket uncharacteristically... exhausting. "What is this?"

I shrugged to try to push the thing from my back, but my ab muscles shot another burst of hot pain through my body.

Clarisse jumped back. When I ground out a sound of pain from the movement, she quickly reached forward and clasped what looked like the two corners of the blanket around my neck. She jumped back again.

I looked down. It wasn't a blanket, but a shawl of sorts. I lifted a heavy arm to rip it off of me.

"It's no use," Clarisse said. "The clasp is locked and neither of us have the key. Plus, they've embedded tiny red stones all through the shawl. That's the red sparkles you see in the pattern." She tilted her head. "Oh, you can't see them. They're on your back." She shrugged her shoulders and lifted an eyebrow. "Well, I guess you should have changed me and made me one of you when you had the chance, huh?"

The sadistic woman was referring to the day Marcus, Azalea, and I rescued Shawna. Clarisse had been in the attic when my inner huldra broke free and tore apart the huge Hunter holding my sister captive. Clarisse had admitted to being part of the human trafficking ring, taking the blame for organizing it, and begged me to make her a Wild Woman. Little did she know, it didn't work like that. Not that I would have "changed" her even if it did work the way she believed.

She'd killed the rusalka Azalea that day and I'd sworn to her that the rusalki would make her pay for her crimes against their coven. Yet here we were, me being held captive and Clarisse still alive. With the help of her Hunter family, she'd officially skipped bail shortly before I'd picked up Samuel Woodry from Pike Place Market in Seattle.

I closed my eyes, took a breath, and opened them again. I was in no place to make Clarisse even more of an enemy. I had to play nice, as much as it disturbed me. "Can you tell me where they're taking me?" I asked semi-politely.

Clarisse turned to me as she placed her hand on the bedroom doorknob. "I'm not authorized to give you that sort of information." She opened the door and walked out.

Within minutes of her closing the door behind her, it opened again and four armed Hunters entered the room wearing what looked like nylon breastplates with bloodstones stitched into a dagger pattern on their chests. The Hunter organization had been getting more and more creative at using Wild Women's kryptonite, the red bloodstone. Of course, it didn't work nearly as well on post-menopausal Wilds. Too bad menopause was nothing more than a far-off reality for me.

With bloodstone draped across my shoulders and on the Hunters, I was rendered helpless. My vines and branches couldn't grow; it subdued my huldra in lethargy. Not that I'd felt her much when I'd woken up here, but now I knew for sure I couldn't rely on help from her. Two Hunters stood at the foot of the bed and the other two each took a side.

"Stand," the two at the foot of the bed ordered.

I tried, but my side wound burned with searing pain and my right thigh ached too deeply to use the muscle. The movement from before had been too much. The Hunters at my sides grabbed my biceps and heaved me up, dragged me across the bed, and stood me before the other two.

I screamed out in agony.

"Let's go," one of the Hunters said as they heaved me forward, dragging the tops of my feet across the wooden floor when I failed to move them quick enough to walk on my own.

They hauled me through the otherwise empty penthouse, void of furniture and decorations, and into a private elevator. After a short ride up, the elevator doors opened, greeting us with a gust of wind and the whirring sound of a black helicopter ready for takeoff. They loaded me into the thing and squished in beside me. Clarisse sat inside waiting, her headset over her ears. Once the Hunters holding me situated themselves, their headsets in place and safety belts on, the helicopter lifted off the launch pad and flew out of the city they'd been holding me in.

I fought my growing exhaustion to stay present, to watch the helicopter's route as it flew over farmland and forests. I accidentally nodded off a couple times, but finally woke with the jolt of the helicopter's rails hitting the ground. The Hunters' lips moved, speaking into their headsets, but seeing as I didn't have a headset and my huldra abilities were on the fritz, I couldn't hear what they were saying.

I studied my surroundings. Turned out, I hadn't needed to keep an eye on the route we took in case I needed to tell the rusalki where I was, or in case I had the opportunity to escape. I knew exactly where the Hunters had taken me.

The three higher ranking Hunters who'd seized me at the Maine complex waited a distance away from the helicopter with serious expressions and arms at their sides as though they stood at attention. They kept the same formation they'd had last time I saw them.

A Hunter from inside the helicopter flung the door open and another pressed his hand into my back, shoving me out and onto the ground. I rolled to my back, grabbing the throbbing pain in my side, holding in a shout. Hunter boots made their way near my face and I stiffened, preparing to be kicked in the face. They heaved me up from the ground and forced me forward, toward the three higher-ranking Hunters.

"Hello, huldra eight-two-zero-one-three," the middle Hunter said after blowing a puff of cigar smoke into my face.

I coughed, which sent scorching pain through my abs. Goddess, I hated muscle wounds.

He flicked ash from the end of his cigar and seemed to study it. "Don't mind this," he said, bringing the thing to his lips again. "We're just celebrating the successful capture of the leader of the little revolution you've started."

The two Hunters beside him gave deep laughs and puffed their cigars.

Dicks.

"Take her to her room," he said as he and the two others turned and walked toward a large curved-top wooden door outside what looked to be a huge circular brick building.

He paused and didn't bother to turn to face me. "Oh, and welcome to the North Carolina Hunters' complex." He coughed out a laugh and continued walking.

FOURTEEN

CAPTAIN DICKWAD HAD CALLED the space I now stood in my room, but it felt more like a cell to me. Either the Hunters were getting cocky or they knew I had no chance at escaping, because they hadn't even bothered to put a bag over my head as they had led me into a monastery-looking building and up a couple flights of stairs to what looked like old servants' quarters, down a dank hall, and into this cramped space. Did monasteries have servants' quarters? Maybe this was the area for lower ranking monks. Did monks have rank?

If I lifted my arms out to the side, each would touch a wall, but my side wound urged me not to try.

Once the Hunters had brought me into my room, Clarisse brandished a key, removed my bloodstone shawl, and closed the door behind her. We'd shared no words.

Now I breathed in the damp moldy scent of my quarters and wished I'd at least tried to ask her a couple questions. I carefully lay on the smaller-than-twin bed and rested my hands out in front of me, willing vines grow from my fingers. My fingertips tingled and tiny buds pushed up from under my skin, like little bubbles, only to sink back into my fingers. I curled into the fetal position, holding my side wound for at least a small amount of comfort.

I couldn't help but think about everyone I'd left behind at the Maine complex. My walk here without a bag over my head reminded me of the first time I'd visited the incubus with Marie in his underground home. I hoped Aleksander was okay. The moist smell of the bedcovering reminded me of the bootleg basement under the harpies' secret home. Had the mermaids in the tunnel agreed to help yet?

And of course, I couldn't get Shawna and Marcus out of my head. I sent a little prayer up to Freyja, begging her to keep my partner sister and the love of my life safe from harm. From the tiny bed, I watched the sun set through a small window encased in iron bars and drifted off to a restless sleep.

* * *

I woke up to the sounds of birds chirping and a girl screaming to be let go. Forgetting my current lack of well-being, I jumped from the bed and threw myself against the door to break it down...and flopped off the wooden thing like a tennis ball on a brick wall. The agony of the impact, let alone the movement of bouncing off it, made my vision go a little dark.

Nursing my pride and my side, I hobbled back to bed. That had been right up there with one of my stupidest moments.

As though someone stood on the other side of the door and realized, from all the clatter, that their abductee had awoken, the door unlocked and Clarisse waltzed in with a tray holding a plate of toast and a bowl of applesauce. She set the tray on the nightstand beside the bed and unfolded the red shawl from under the tray.

I let out a groan. "Where are you taking me now?"

"Again," she stated dryly, as though she blamed me for this fact, "I'm not authorized to share that with you." She paused and changed her tone. "But you're not going anywhere until you eat. You missed dinner last night. They won't allow you to miss a second meal."

I started to ask her why, but figured she wasn't authorized to tell me.

I considered the food a moment. They weren't administering drugs intravenously, but that didn't mean they wouldn't put something in my food. Except, I didn't feel drugged, just weak. And anyway, if they wanted me drugged, they'd drug me. Not a whole lot I could do about that at the moment. I slowly spooned apple sauce into my mouth as Clarisse watched. After I finished the last bite of dry toast, she held out the shawl.

"All right, time to go," she said, as though I were a dog waiting for her to put my collar on.

I only sat on the bed and stared at her.

She sighed. "Don't make me call in one of the guys outside this door," she said. "I promise you'll still have this thing locked onto you, but your walk won't be nearly as pleasant once it's done."

For fuck's sake. How had my life gone so fast from organizing battle plans to taking orders from Clarisse? I exhaled, stood slowly while placing pressure on my right side, and turned to show her my back. The moment the red shawl rested upon my shoulders my lids felt heavy and I wanted to crumble onto the bed. Before I turned to face her and walk out of the room, I peered down at my hands and tried to grow vines. My fingers only shook with effort.

Someone on the other side of the door pounded on it twice.

"We have to go," Clarisse urged.

We made our way out of the dark, cramped portion of the building, through an entry area with plush couches, full of natural light spilling in through stained glass windows from the top of the great door to the ceiling. We passed the tiled entry, void of any living beings, and made our way down a wider, more decorated hall. Clarisse stepped aside when she brought me to another door, and two Hunters took three steps to stand at each side of me.

"Come in," a familiar voice called, despite the Hunters' lack of knocking on the door.

The two Hunters escorted me into an office and shut the door while Clarisse waited outside. If this guy was here, Marcus's father couldn't be far.

"Please," John said, waving to the empty chair before his desk as though I were a business associate of his and not his captive. "Have a seat."

I didn't need my huldra abilities to smell the strong cologne he wore, no doubt a habit from working with huldra who could smell the scent of his emotions.

John. The male who had vowed to protect the Washington huldra coterie as the leader of the Washington Hunter complex, who'd looked me in the eyes and spilled poisonous lies from his mouth as though he were a mama bird feeding her young. And we had eaten those lies up as though our lives depended on it.

I seethed with something stronger than anger. Hate. Malice. The desire to see him, above anyone else, the slow victim of my huldra's worst torture.

I refused to sit in his presence, but it only took one nod from him and the two Hunters shoved my shoulders down, forcing me to take a seat. I balled my fists at the pain in my side and thigh, but I wouldn't give him the satisfaction of hearing me cry or seeing me shudder.

I stared daggers at the man.

"Thank you," he said as though I'd had any choice in the matter.

Plaques and ribbons, all with some sort of dagger insignia, littered the office walls. This couldn't be his office; it had to belong to the silver-haired man in most of the photos who looked very much like the Hunter who'd shot Marcus and Shawna in Maine. I eyed the most prominently displayed name on the plaques and awards, set on burning it into my memory. Joseph Alexander had most certainly made my slow-torture list.

John noticed my wandering eyes and said, "Yes, old Joe's been kind enough to let me use his office for the time being." He stretched and leaned back in his swivel office chair. "I thought we could use someplace private to talk."

I almost rolled my eyes, but I didn't even want to give him that. I kept my expression blank.

"You are a prisoner in our home, so to say," John started. His hair had a little more salt than when I asked him for help in finding Shawna at the Washington complex and he'd denied my request with some bullshit about her being in succubus territory. Then he'd told me his job was to protect us from ourselves.

Goddess, I wanted to strangle him where he sat.

"If you play nice, once we're done taming this little uprising you've caused, you will be promoted to a guest in our home." He spoke in that casual friendly way he used to talk to us when we came in for our monthly check-ins and when he taught his version of Wild Women history—*his* story. "You have become quite the commodity, and I'd hate to see one of my men end your life. It'd be a waste. And if I dislike anything, it's waste."

John stood and scooted his chair in under the desk. "Have I made myself clear?"

I stared forward.

I noticed him making a motion from my peripheral view. The Hunter to my right grabbed my chin in his calloused hand and forced my head to nod. When he pulled his hand away he wiped it on his black cargo pants.

"Good, good," John said, as though he hadn't just forced my fake compliance. "You can go now. You look like you could use some fresh air."

The two Hunters pulled me from the chair and walked me down the hall and out a side door into an enclosed area. They released me but didn't remove my burdensome shawl. They turned and shut the door behind them, leaving me alone in what looked to be a courtyard of sorts, if courtyards included twenty-foot tall chain-link fencing with barbed wire at the top, a few planters of weeds, a human-sized cage, and one lone red maple tree.

I hated the way I felt without access to my huldra, vulnerable, weak, and utterly incapable. I'd been around bloodstone before—rescued my sister from a room at the end of a bloodstone filled hall; helped the succubi escape from a prison cell covered in bloodstone. But I'd never had the stuff draped over my body.

I made my way over to the maple tree, with its thick, old trunk and exposed roots peeking up through the dirt. I ran a hand along its smooth bark and pressed my cheek to the trunk. Which had come first, I wondered, the tree or the monastery. And had this building started as a monastery? Did it include underground passageways as Aleksander had mentioned traditional monasteries had? I needed to find someone here willing to talk, someone who wouldn't just parrot how they were not authorized to tell me things.

I racked my brain for Hunter facts Marcus had told me. They couldn't be alone with females, which probably had something to do with why they sent Clarisse in to cover me with my shawl before they entered the room to escort me out. Clarisse also wasn't allowed to be alone with a male, due to her being engaged, which from the ring I saw on her finger, was still a thing.

I paused and remembered more recent discussions I'd shared with Marcus. This was the complex where the Hunters were holding the women they were trafficking out of the country. But where were they keeping them? I held to the tree but took in my surroundings. The grounds appeared well-maintained, outside the current courtyard I stood in, and quiet. No sign of groups of drugged-up young women waiting to be transported.

Goddess, I hoped I didn't find Heather here. I would never forgive myself for asking her to be bait. Though—the thought gave me a shred of hope—whichever Hunter tried to detain her would assume she was human and would be unprepared for an energy-controlling succubus.

The door from the hallway to the courtyard opened again and a tall, lean woman who looked to be in her fifties slowly made her way out, a Hunter on each side of her holding what looked like wrist shackles imbedded with bloodstone. She eyed me as they walked her to the cage, escorted her inside, closed the cage door, and unlocked her shackles as she held her arms through an opening. Once they removed her shackles she pulled her arms into herself and rubbed her wrists vigorously.

We stared at one another as the Hunters exited the courtyard. The moment the door to the building shut, I hurried over to the cage as quickly as my side would let me and stopped before I got within reaching distance. She looked familiar, not like I knew her, but as though she looked like someone I knew.

"You're a harpy, aren't you?" I blurted, assuming they'd placed her in a cage so she couldn't fly away.

The woman sized me up with a sharp gaze. It was her, I was sure of it. Goddess, her mannerisms were just like her daughters'.

When she didn't answer I kept going. "I know your daughters, Eonza, Lapis, and Salis. You must be Rose."

The woman lifted her left eyebrow but gave no other indication as to her thoughts or feelings.

"Eonza is pregnant and due to birth the egg any day now," I whispered, nearing the cage.

The woman's hard expression dropped as she cradled her face into her hands. Her shoulders fell forward and her chest heaved with silent cries. I wanted so badly to wrap my arm around her, to comfort her. All I had, though, were my words. "She's healthy and safe. All three of your daughters are."

The harpy, Rose, looked up at me. Her blue eyes now bloodshot from crying. "They haven't been taken?" she asked in a small voice.

I shook my head. "No, they're hiding in a motel, last I heard. They'd put us in empty homes unconnected to any Wild Woman names."

She gave a faint smile. "My girls are very intelligent."

Damn straight they were. Except for the whole journalist Brice snafu, which didn't need to be brought up at the moment.

"They told me they'd taken my girls also, to different complexes, separated them," she said, her voice growing in strength.

I shook my head. "They lied. What's new?"

"So then, I assume you have not come to rescue me. What are you?" she asked, looking me over for a sign as to which Wild group I heralded from.

I shook my head. "My name is Faline. I'm a huldra," I said, finding an ounce of joy by just conversing with another Wild, by being able to proudly state my name and kind. Then there was the fact that if their mother was alive, my mother really might be too.

Rose tilted her head in a quick, sharp movement like a bird in thought.

"What?" I asked. "Did they tell you lies about me too?"

"From the Washington huldra coterie?" she asked.

"Yes, that's where I'm from. The only huldra in the United States," I confirmed. "Why?"

She gazed into my eyes a moment and neared the cage. "Because," she whispered under her breath, "I've met your mother. Naomi, she's here."

FIFTEEN

"MY MOTHER?" I breathed the words, clinging to the harpy's cage. "She's alive?"

My head started to spin and I realized I had been holding my breath. I inhaled deeply, my wide eyes locked on Rose.

"She is," she answered with a nod. "Though I doubt they will allow both of you air time at once."

"Air time?" I asked.

"Yes." She cleared her throat. "It's why they bring us out here, to breathe fresh air. They believe the oxygen keeps us healthy, more able to reproduce."

My head spun again, but for a different reason. I knew they'd taken Shawna and other Wild Women with hopes of creating a Wild/Hunter hybrid. But Rose's explanation made it more real. "Have they been trying to procreate with you and my mother?" I asked, a new anger rising within me.

"They have," she said, her eyes cast down. "Though with us they have not been successful. She tells me they've tried different methods through the years, and she believes they've been effective, though she refused to say how she knows that."

I had so many questions about their breeding program, if I could call it that, but none rang louder in my mind than the fact that my mother was alive. "How does my mother look?" I asked, knowing full well I had little to compare Rose's analysis with, seeing as the Hunters took my mother when I was only seven. "Does she have a schedule? When she comes out here?"

Rose's chest moved like she'd silently chuckled. "They don't afford us schedules. I suspect they think it gives us an upper hand, makes them more predictable. And she looks good. She misses you."

I felt like a little girl in my aunt's lap, hoping to pry a story out of her about my mother, something to keep me warm at night. "She does?" I heard myself say in that little girl voice.

Rose's smile warmed—the smile of a mother who knows a hurting little one when she sees her. She leaned in, closer to the metal cage. "When I first arrived I only plotted to escape. But after my faulty plans failed me," she tapped the cage, "your mother lifted my spirits by talking with me about that which we are most proud of, our daughters."

A tear welled in my eyes. "How?" I asked. "How could she have been here so long and still be able to raise your spirits? A newcomer?"

Rose took a slow breath. "It's that tree." She motioned with her head to the single old tree in the courtyard. "During her years with the Hunters, she had been moved from complex to complex. But she's been here the longest, long enough, according to her, to get acquainted with what she deems as her plant family. She spends her outdoor time with the tree, says its wisdom lifts her spirits." Rose shrugged.

"We have to escape; we have to get her out." My arms ached with emptiness, now that the rusalka's promise of my mother's life had been confirmed. Knowing she was here, so close to me, in the same building...my heart ached too.

The rusalki were able to communicate with other Wild Women once they located where to project themselves. They only needed to learn where I was to make a connection with me and speak into my mind, to visit me. If I could tell them where we were being held, they could all move forward with plans to attack this complex and free the last of the Wild Women imprisoned by Hunters.

If they were all still alive.

Just as quickly as my hope soared, it crashed and burned...a lot like our attack on the Maine complex. I kept that depressing bit of news to myself. Goddess, I hoped they'd all made it out of that complex okay.

"I've tried to escape this place before. It ended badly," Rose said grimly. "But I was on my own in that attempt. This time there are three of us. Better odds, I'd say." Her lips lifted into a hopeful grin. Her brown eyes also seemed to grin. "I suspect you're being kept a secret, even from other Hunters. The Brotherhood knows there's human women here, and the top tiers of leaders know about your mom and me, but you've been kept a secret. I will spread word of your arrival."

"Huldra eight-two-zero-one-three," a man boomed from right outside the door to the brick monastery.

I tried to ignore him.

"Oh, honey," Rose said, shaking her head. "They'll get what they want in the end anyhow. If you don't go to him, he'll make your walk back to your room very painful. Believe me, I know from experience."

I let out a huff and wished I could hug her goodbye. "I'll get us out of here," I assured her.

Her tired smile revealed her unspoken response. She highly doubted it.

* * *

I lay on the lumpy bed and gazed out the window. A half-eaten tray of toast and chicken noodle soup sat on the nightstand. I'd tried to gulp down the food, I'd tried to sleep, but knowing my mother slept under the same roof as me kept my body buzzing. It was a strange thing, but I missed my huldra. She had to have had a connection with my mother, even if I didn't remember it. I wanted to feel her reaction to the news, feel her jittery excitement and eagerness to break down the door and track our mother down.

Did my huldra have a separate and deeper connection to my mother's huldra? I'd never asked my sisters if mothers and daughters experienced such a thing; I'd never thought to.

I wondered this as I watched clouds move through the dark sky, barely lit by the bit of moon they hid from view.

For years I'd believed my mother to be dead, until my hunt for Shawna revealed the truth behind the missing Wild Women and my own mother's abduction. After that, I worried I'd never get the chance to see her again, worried she'd died in captivity. And when I was told she was still alive, another worry lived in my heart, the worry that she'd go the way of all huldra in their fifties, that she would die young. Each passing day was one less I'd get to spend with her.

A muffled knock created a soft sound on my door. I sat up in a hurry and sucked in a quick breath at the stinging in my side. I wished one of my aunts were here to care for the wound.

A dark-skinned man peeked his head in. "Faline?" he whispered, barely audibly.

My muscles tightened with fear and the need to defend myself when he crept into the room without my invitation. He wore the black uniform of a Hunter. His dagger glinted in its holster along his hip from the small amount of light coming through the window.

I had no weapon. I had no huldra abilities. And I was wounded and weak. I could not protect myself. But hell if I'd let him take me without a fight.

He quietly closed the door behind him and stood with his back against it. It looked as though he were waiting for his eyes to adjust to the darkness. Thanks to my lack of huldra abilities, I'd had some recent experience in that necessity.

He spoke again with quiet formality. "Faline Frey of the Washington huldra coterie, are you awake?"

Hunters don't know our names, and even if they found our names out through a little digging, they'd never call us by them. To them we were numbers, not worthy of names.

I paused my thoughts of using anything and everything in this room to bash over his head and into his stomach, including the cross hanging on the wall made of wooden daggers. Why they thought that'd be a safe item to place in a detainment room, I had no idea.

I tried to smell his emotions, but with my non-existent abilities, nothing registered.

"Marcus sent me," he whispered, his voice nearly as low as a growl.

"Yes?" I answered, squinting to get a better look at him.

It could be a trap, but what else did I have to lose?

"Is he okay?" I asked, to gauge whether this Hunter was friend or foe by his response.

He took a step and his boot hit the leg of my bed. "He was shot, but the xana was able to use water manipulation to get the bullet out and the succubi healed him. Same with the incubi leader and your sister. They are all well and healed."

I breathed a sigh of relief.

I highly doubted anyone other than a person who knew Marcus would have that sort of information, those details. But to be sure, I pressed further. "Why did Marcus send you?"

He suppressed a laugh and it came out as a type of scoff. "He'd said you wouldn't trust me 'til you tested me and asked a personal question only Marcus and you could know."

I nodded and realized he probably couldn't see me. Just like I barely saw his chest rise and fall to know he'd stifled a laugh.

"Since I can't possibly remember all the answers to anything you'd ask, he told me to tell you about a time that only he, you, and a rusalka would know. A recent instance in which powerful erotic energy was used to physically transport you?" His statement sounded more like a question and I didn't blame him. A rusalka using a huldra's orgasm as energy to teleport her to a forest? That sounded like something out of a sci-fi novel, not my actual life.

Goddess, I wished I could see the Hunter's expression.

"Okay," I said as a signal that he'd passed that part. "You know who I am, but I don't know who you are."

"I'd rather not say," he whispered, shifting in place. "They don't know I'm a rogue."

"A what?" I asked, trying to remember where I'd heard that term recently before.

"A rogue. That's what we call ourselves, Hunters doing what we can on our way out of the brotherhood. Some are already out."

I wanted to ask more about Marcus and Shawna, but I'd been needing a saving grace to get out of this place and I figured I may have found one. I had to learn more about the current Hunter situation. Marcus would have expected me to dig, anyhow.

"So then he was right," I said more to myself than the man in my room. "Are there a lot of rogues?"

"Our numbers are growing every day." He paused. "Rod is helping me and a few others get out. He told Marcus about me, that he had a guy in the North Carolina complex, and Marcus had me ask about you, to see if you were brought here."

"And someone here told you?" I asked.

"Nah, only the leading officers know about you; the leader of the revolution, they're calling you. They're keeping your stay with us top secret. The harpy made sure I found out. Told a guy who told a guy."

Thank Goddess for Rose.

"Are they coming for me?" I asked and then clarified. "Marcus and the rest of them?" I made sure to not mention any other Wilds. Obviously, he knew about some of them, but I didn't want to give anything away either.

"I'll send a message to Rod to let Marcus know I've confirmed that you're here." He turned on his heel to leave. Before he opened the door, he said, "I'll try to let you know what he says. If I can get back here."

He silently opened the door to reveal a dimly lit hallway.

"Wait," I whispered harshly, only to grab his attention.

He paused.

"Where is the other huldra? I know she's here," I said.

"Are you of the same coterie?" he asked, clearly uneducated in the existence of American huldra. We only had one coterie to speak of.

I didn't know how to answer in a way that wasn't too revealing.

He took my omission as an answer unto itself.

"Ah, yeah. Okay. I'll let her know you're here." He left my room and secured the door behind him.

My mother. A nervous excitement rolled through me. Would she be proud of my efforts? Would she be disappointed that I'd gotten caught and put the whole Wild revolution at a blatant disadvantage? Or a complete halt altogether.

Since learning she lived, I'd imagined meeting her for the first time, as an adult, by rescuing her. Here I lay in a room that might as well be a prison cell, praying a rogue Hunter would honor his word and send a message to my mother. Not quite the image I'd created in my head.

I hadn't thought to ask the rogue Hunter how he got the key to my room. But some questions were better left for later. And plus, the moment Marcus found out I was here, the rusalki would know. I rested my head on the single pillow in the room and went back to staring out the window.

It was only a matter of time before I'd be receiving a visitor, one in animal skins who spoke in parables and had a propensity to use orgasmic energy.

SIXTEEN

THE NEXT MORNING, the boot steps of the Hunters woke me before the keys jingled against the door and two men dressed in black walked in my room. Clarisse squeezed past the two pillars of strength and rigidity, carrying the red shawl.

"Good morning," she chirped, as though I were a guest and she had come to fetch me for tea or a leisurely stroll through the gardens.

I'd made it a point to be standing, waiting by my bed before any of them entered the room. I only looked at Clarisse with daggers for eyes.

"Well," she huffed, "if you don't want to make the most of your stay here."

Whatever that meant. Not that I put much stock in the ramblings of a deeply confused human.

By the time we made our way to the nearly empty courtyard, the harpy's mother, Rose, was already in her cage using a talon to pick at the pink feathers along her right wing. She'd been turned away when I stepped foot onto the barren dirt, but quickly twisted in a sharp movement to eye the newcomers in silence. She studied me as though we'd not just had a conversation the day before.

I played along, hoping she meant to act like we were long lost enemies rather than comrades, hoping she hadn't forgotten about me due to whatever the Hunters had done to her and any types of pharmaceuticals they'd pumped into her. I moseyed toward the single tree in the courtyard, pretending to have no set goal for my time outside and no idea how to spend the minutes or more.

The Hunters and Clarisse watched for less than five minutes before deeming us harmless and leaving us alone. I wasn't so naive to think there weren't cameras recording every square inch of the courtyard, but it wasn't like I had better options for the taking.

I rushed to Rose's cage, but not close enough for her to reach out and swipe at me with a talon. I had to make sure she remembered me.

"One came to me last night," I said, to see how coherent she was and how much she knew.

"A rogue?" she whispered under her breath, turning her face away from the building and toward the chain link fence.

True to harpy form: whip smart.

I nodded and followed suit, speaking away from the building. "He's going to get word to my mother that I'm here."

"Did he mention a plan to escape?" she asked, getting straight to the point. Also a harpy quality.

"No," I said. "He wasn't very forthcoming with any details."

"Oh," she said somewhat sadly. "I was hoping he'd have a tip or two on getting that thing off you." She motioned to my shawl of doom. "You can't escape with that thing hanging around your shoulders."

The back door opened with a loud bang, as though someone had shoved the thing open hard enough for it to smack the outer wall. Rose and I swung around to see what all the commotion was about. I jumped away from the cage. One Hunter escorted a woman out. She wore a red shawl like mine that seemed to weigh heavily on her back, causing her shoulders to slouch. Her red hair hung long and scraggly, with a thin braid on each side to keep strands out of her face I figured. The Hunter whispered something into the woman's ear and backed into the building, quietly shutting the door.

The woman's face lifted. Her gaze bore into mine.

My throat tightened. My breath stopped. Tears filled my eyes. I began to shake and fought against weak knees to stay standing. "Mother," I whispered.

"Meet her at the tree," the harpy commanded. "On the back side, facing the fence. There's a sliver of a blind spot for the cameras, so they won't be able to read your lips."

I gave an absent nod and walked to the tree without recognizing the ground beneath my bare feet or basically anything else around me, only the one other huldra in the courtyard.

The woman, my mother, held my gaze as she neared the tree, her steps strong and deliberate despite her hunched shoulders. I remembered those eyes, only now crow's feet played at the edges. I remembered those lips, only now they were thin and chapped. A tear escaped my eye and I swallowed to keep more from revealing my emotions in view of the cameras.

I found myself behind the tree, my hand pressed against the bark for support, staring into my mother's eyes. With a gasp she wrapped her arms around my shoulders and pulled me to her chest, as though I were still her little girl, the little girl she'd been stolen away from. I leaned down, happy to be held, unaware of how much I needed to be held in such a way by my mother until my face pressed to her shoulder and my tears dampened the fabric of her red shawl.

My head spun, so I pulled away from her bloodstone shawl. The fabric so close to my face was too much to handle. My mother placed her palms on each of my cheeks.

"You are the most beautiful thing I've ever seen in all my life," she whispered through sobs. "I always knew I'd get to see you again. I always knew."

"But I was captured," I heard myself whine, as only a child would say to her mother, presenting her most vulnerable side full of insecurities.

"Yes," she said, releasing my cheeks to push hair from my face and hold my hands. "So that we can escape together."

"I got word to the others," I remembered to tell her. I cleared my throat and stood straight, still holding my mother's hands. "I'm awaiting their response. Probably by way of a rusalka visit."

"So you were successful then?" she asked, her expression beaming. "In uniting the American Wild Women?"

I nodded. "For the most part, yes." I wasn't sure how she'd take the whole truth, but pleasant or not, she deserved to know it. "We've also attracted the attention of snake Wilds and a few others. As well as males."

"Which males?" she asked, her dark reddish-brown eyebrows raised.

"Incubi and ex-Hunters," I said, studying her expression before I told her the bigger revelation.

She only smiled. "Yes, the Hunters are losing their ranks these days. The young men of this generation are not like those of earlier generations. There's a difference in the way they see the world."

I'd meant to ease the topic, but I blurted, "I'm with an ex-Hunter...romantically."

My mother inhaled.

"We liked each other before we knew what the other person was," I added. "And then he helped us take down the Washington Hunter complex, and he saved Shawna when my huldra was too erratic to do it."

"So you've released your huldra then?" she asked. Her eyes dropped to my waist area.

I nodded and turned, lifting my shirt to reveal the deep russet bark on my lower back.

My mother gasped. "It's gorgeous, truly gorgeous."

The harpy coughed and my mother eyed her cage for a quick second. "We don't have much time left," she uttered. "Does your thigh ache?"

I rubbed the area of my thigh where my tattooed identification number lived. "Yeah. How'd you know?"

"They've tattooed you with bloodstone. It's a relatively new procedure they've started doing; they ground it into a powder to make ink with. It's why you feel weak even when they take the shawl off." Her eyes bored into mine with all the seriousness in the world. "You'll need to carve it out before you try to escape. Find something to do it with, something sharp. I'll do the same. But only shortly before. They can't have enough time to realize it's gone."

The harpy coughed twice, clearly signaling us to finish up.

"How will I know when to do it?" I asked. "Will they let you out with me again?"

She pursed her lips, holding tightly to whatever she wanted to say. She shook her head. "This was a payment for a favor owed to me. They'll be back any second to get me." She pressed her hand to the tree. "The harpy will relay our messages to one another."

The sound of the door from the building to the courtyard opening cut through my thoughts. I didn't want to tell her goodbye, didn't want to let her go.

She peeked around the tree. "They're here." She kissed my cheek and held her face only inches from mine. "According to the Hunters, they're winning. They are creating a warrior race, mixing our two kinds. They may think they've hit the jackpot with you. They plan to collect your DNA to create offspring with."

"You think?" I said. "They've been doing this for decades and haven't been successful yet."

Her expression darkened. "They have been. They've created a male in Europe. Spain, I believe."

"When?" I whispered.

She squeezed my hand one last time before releasing it and turning to walk toward the Hunter waiting anxiously for her at the door.

"Between twenty and thirty years ago," she answered. "The product of a powerful Wild Woman leader and a commanding Hunter. I've heard complaints about the last warrior they created; he may be dead. I believe you are the powerful Wild Woman they're looking to repeat the experiment with. The leader who's released her inner Wild."

She walked away, not turning back to look at me as I leaned against the tree and held back tears. If they were planning on using me to create their warrior species, what were they waiting for?

I clung to the maple tree and watched my mother walk into the building. I peered at the harpy. She paused from her preening to glance at me. These two older Wilds knew things I didn't. Perhaps they also knew what was in store for me at the hands of my Hunter captors.

SEVENTEEN

MY PHONE VIBRATED in my pocket. The Wild Women lingering around the fridge didn't even look my way when I left the kitchen and walked out to the front yard. The grounds looked more like a park than someone's yard, with tall hedge-type trees blocking the view of the road and absorbing the sounds of car engines along with it. I waited until the front door closed and was at least ten feet behind me before digging the phone out of my pocket. These Wild Women had super hearing and I didn't need them listening in on my conversation. Since Faline's capture, her coterie reached a tension level I'd never seen before, which didn't bode well for my Hunter side.

"Marcus?" the Hunter on the other end of the line whispered, his voice echoing enough to make me think he called from a bathroom.

"Who is this?" I asked the person on the other end of the line, just to be sure. The number was one I recognized, a rogue Hunter from the North Carolina complex who'd been talking to Rod. Rod had given me the guy's number and instructed me to wait for his call of confirmation.

"You were right. She understood the code question," the man said, his voice low and deep.

I'd never spoken to him personally before. We'd gone through Rod.

But if his size matched his voice, Faline was in good hands, because size mattered when it came to Hunters.

"So then it's confirmed. She's at your complex," I stated. I exhaled and closed my eyes. Fuck.

While I'd left the beliefs of Hunters behind, especially those involving a woman's place in the world and in a relationship, my DNA couldn't help but hold an unbreakable claim on the woman I loved. According to the most basic instincts pulsing within me, Faline Frey was my partner, my female, and the one life I was compelled to protect at all costs. Nearly everything in me demanded that I hunt down and torture each and every being involved with her absence.

Couple the huldra's anxiety levels with my need to hunt my enemies, and each second was a match waiting to be lit in a room full of gasoline.

"She is," he started. "We were able to connect her to her mother this morning. She'll have to take it from there."

My eyes flung open. "Her mother's there?"

"Yes, and a harpy."

"Well, shit." I paced to the line of tree hedges, thinking. I rubbed at a bruise on my forearm, courtesy of Aleksander. The incubi leader and I couldn't be in the same room since Faline had been taken. We'd tried once and almost killed each other. While I couldn't rely on that guy, I also couldn't deny I needed backup. "Rod tells me you've got your own army."

"I'd hardly call it an army, but our ranks are growing," the Hunter responded. I hadn't asked his name and I didn't plan on it either. Not until we met in person. He needed to feel safe in helping my Faline. The safer he felt, the more likely he was to keep an eye out for her and report back to me.

"Are your men willing to fight with the Wild Women when the time comes?" I asked. I made it to the trees and back to the brick porch a third time. If my hard-working logical side waned just a little, I'd run through those trees and wouldn't stop until I broke down whichever door Faline was trapped behind.

"Fight alongside them?" the man asked, skepticism dripping from his words. "Rod never mentioned that."

"Alongside them, for them, whichever is necessary," I clarified. If Rod hadn't mentioned that fact, what had he said? "What exactly did Rod say?"

"That the leader of the Wild Women revolution may have been taken to my complex and he needed confirmation on her whereabouts." The man paused. "I tried to call him before you, and he didn't answer. He never not answers."

"I don't know," I said, not wanting to spend time on the topic of Rod when the topic of Faline was all I could think about. "He hasn't contacted me since he said he'd talk to you."

The man at the other end cleared his throat. "Listen. I have nothing against the Wild Women, but I can't speak for all the men. Yeah, some think what's happened to them is a shame, but others are only joining our rogue ranks after seeing what their leaders are doing to the human women. It's wrong. I don't care what religion the human women are. It's wrong."

I scratched my head and stifled a guttural noise akin to a growl. It took a few seconds before I could speak again without reaming this man through the phone. I pushed the words out through clenched teeth. "Fine." I took another breath, forcing myself to continue. "Then you'll not fight against the Wild Women at least? If they show up at your complex?"

Now the man took a while to answer. Finally he said, "I'll have to take a vote. I can't know for sure."

I pulled the phone away from my face, to hang up on the asshole, but his next words stopped me.

"We'll focus on helping the human women and you can focus on helping the Wild Women."

I hated his lack of commitment to the Wild Women, but it was important to Faline that the human trafficking victims be rescued and the ones in charge be taken down. My cop side saw the importance too. But the cop in me took a back seat to my need for a certain huldra who'd turned my world upside down in the best possible way. My focus was to get Faline back. Everything else came second. If the rogue Hunters agreed to deal with the human women, that was one less thing on my plate to make sure got done.

"Okay," I said as I shook my head. "Fair enough." I started to head up the paved rock path leading through the large front yard to the porch. "Is this a good number to call back with updates?"

"It is," he said. "Have a blessed day."

The line went dead before I could respond. A blessed day, my ass.

* * *

"Marcus?"

My bedroom door flung open before Aleksander burst through like a bat out of hell...or an incubus out of hell.

"What the fuck?" I yelled, jumping from the bed and backing against the furthest wall from the incubus. Since Faline's capture, my patience with the incubi leader waned with each second. His behavior shifted from controlled leader to half-mad, love-sick energy manipulator. It wasn't pretty or pleasant, and it pissed me off.

"Marcus! There you are!" he shouted, his eyes wide and crazed.

I almost called for Mason to come control his leader, but the boy was staying with the succubi in a separate house, and anyways, we had no prison cell to keep the irrational incubus in.

"Dude, get out," I seethed, clenching my fists. I closed my eyes and tried to count to ten, taking a deep breath with each number. Marie had shown me how to do it the night Faline had been taken, the night I'd almost forced my dagger through Aleksander's gut.

Aleksander backed into the hallway, but still spoke to me. "Rod is on his way. He just texted to say he's coming."

I ran my hand through my hair. "Why did he notify you and not me?"

Aleksander seemed to think clearly for half a second. He stilled and met my eyes. In a mischievous tone he answered, "It is not my news to tell."

EIGHTEEN

"GOOD EVENING, FALINE," John, the leader of the previous Washington State Hunter complex said as he walked into my room escorted by two Hunters.

I'd spent the afternoon running my fingers over my numbered tattoo, only noticing the fresh traces of red when I studied it hard enough in the natural light of the window. I'd been so preoccupied with my dagger wound that I hadn't noticed the faint new lines on my thigh.

The Hunter on John's right carried what looked like an old-fashioned leather doctor's supply bag. He placed the bag on the empty dresser and unzipped it from the top. He wore his light brown hair high and tight, like most of the other Hunters I'd seen. I watched him carefully as John continued drabbling on as though I were a guest in his home and not a prisoner.

"Any headaches since you woke this morning? Any nausea or upset stomach?" John asked.

His question surprised me enough to make him my new focus. I tilted my head.

He behaved as though the last month of fighting had never happened. As though I were attending a check-in and he was still pretending to the be the nice guy we huldra could go to for whatever reason.

"Oh," he gave a short laugh. "The medication we gave you should have worn off by now. If it hasn't, we need to know. So, any headaches or nausea to report?"

Out of reflex to his question, I shook my head, and then immediately scolded myself for giving him any information at all. How I felt was none of his damn business. Clearly, he didn't care if he was going to hole me up in a tiny room against my will.

"Perfect," he said with a gleam in his eyes.

He turned and nodded to the Hunter with the medical bag. The Hunter pulled a syringe from the bag and I crab-crawled on my bed backwards to the headboard. My slowly healing stab wound in my abs made itself known in a nasty way.

"Now, now," John said, his friendly voice returning but with an edge to it. "Don't make this harder on yourself. Don't make me call Clarisse in with the shawl I know you love so much."

"What's that for?" I said, motioning with my chin to the syringe.

John put his hands out like he was leveling with me. "How about this? If I tell you what we're doing, you'll sit still and be a good girl. How about that?"

I considered my lack of options. I either got poked with Hunters holding me down and a bloodstone shawl draped across my body, or I got poked without Hunters holding me down and a bloodstone shawl draped across my body, along with an explanation.

I relaxed my body and un-plastered myself from the headboard.

"Good, good," John said, interpreting my body language correctly.

He waved away the Hunter with the syringe and sat beside me on the bed. I wanted to shove him off but controlled my urge. "You have been our target from the very beginning of all this," he started. "At least this round. You see, we're trying to help your kind, trying to unite our two species into a master species, but you all fight us at every turn."

"Stealing us away against our will, holding us in captivity, and forcing us to create a race that you'll brainwash into conquering us is an odd way to unite our two kinds," I critiqued.

John's smile dropped. "There's something about mixing the DNA of leaders that has proven successful."

"Huldra have no leader," I corrected. "I thought you were a specialist of my kind."

John gave a harsh laugh. "No, you don't have a leader, that much is true. This is why we had to create a leader, why we had to force one of you into that role."

I couldn't help but let my expression give away my whirling thoughts. It made so much sense. The Hunters triggered the release of my inner huldra because they knew it'd put me in an impossible position: either be found out and jailed at the next monthly check-in, or stand up and fight back. If I stood up and fought back, I'd be the leader of a revolution, a revolution Marcus had told me our first night in the motel room the Hunters believed had been prophesized hundreds of years ago.

I thought back to Marcus's words that night.

"The old monks," he'd said, *"who went rogue from the church to raise and train the first Hunters, told a story that a Wild Woman would rise up from her station and challenge the Hunters. If they were weak and allowed her to win, they'd cause the demise of not only Hunters, but of all civilization. If they gave her a deserved bloody death, they'd squelch future uprisings and secure their future as masters over all."*

They were forcing the prophesy to play out, forcing a Wild Woman to challenge them and at the same time, become the ultimate leader of the American Wilds and therefore a secure mother for their master race.

"If your focus was me, why did you take other Wild Women?" I asked.

"Simple," he answered with a shrug. "To weaken the ranks and test out our newest methods before using them on you."

My stomach turned and I swallowed the lump in my throat.

Another, more disturbing realization settled in. I studied my enemy as he sat on the same bed as me, his grey hair cut high and tight like a true military man. "You're building a master race to take back control of Wild Women from all over the world."

John's lips curved into an evil smile. "Your time with our traitor has increased your wisdom. We Hunters have that effect on females of all species, I suspect."

I refrained from punching the asshat in his sour face. I wished I could grow branches through his lungs and watch him choke on his own blood. Soon. Very soon.

John nodded to the Hunter waiting at the dresser, the syringe still in hand. He accepted the signal and walked toward the bed where I sat.

"So," John went on. "Now that I completed my end of the deal, explained to you how well you've managed to fit into our plan to rule over each and every one of your kind for the foreseeable future, it's your turn to allow us to take a sample of your blood."

I sat still while the Hunter hastily shoved the needled into my left arm and drew enough blood to fill the vial. He walked my blood back to where he had left the bag and placed it in a small insulated box, then zipped the bag up and waited beside the door.

John stood and opened the door, allowing the two Hunters to go through before himself. Standing outside the open door, he turned to me. "Once the test results reveal that the medications have been cleared from your system, we'll be back to begin the process of invitro fertilization. The male's specimen is ready and waiting." He winked like he'd just let me in on a secret. "We've learned the uselessness of trying to impregnate a medicated huldra, thanks to your sister."

I couldn't hold myself back any longer. I lunged from the bed. He slammed the door shut right before I reached my hand out to wrap my fingers around his neck and choke the life out of him.

NINETEEN

AFTER A TENSE DRIVE, locked in a vehicle with my current least favorite incubus, I stepped from the blue truck Aleksander had rented with a fake ID and surveyed the woods around me. According to the ex-Hunters we'd scheduled to meet, about a half a mile into the forest we should find a clearing where they'd be waiting.

Aleksander's stillness caught my attention from the corner of my eye and I turned to watch him. He stood from the truck's bucket seat, eyes closed, hands out. His lids fluttered open and I gave him a questioning look. The incubus read energy, not minds. My time with him had taught me the power of energy, that energy couldn't lie in the same way a mind or mouth could lie. The body held onto truths, new and old, whereas the mind had the ability to bury those things it didn't find useful.

"Yes," Aleksander said on an exhale. "They're out there, waiting."

"And?" I urged him to continue. Knowing they'd held up to part of their bargain was helpful, but that other part of the bargain was what concerned me. Where they here as allies or enemies?

"They mean well," Aleksander commented as he began walking forward, lifting his loafers high enough from the ground to keep them semi-clean. I'd warned him to wear boots, but the old incubus refused to "sully himself." His words, not mine. "Rod is among them, as is another incubus."

I narrowed my eyes and started walking to catch up to him. "What do you mean another incubus? Is this something you agreed to ahead of time? I thought they had to pass everything by you."

Aleksander shot me a side-glance before looking forward again. "Yes, they passed it by me already."

Goddamn this incubus. I'd been able to handle him with Faline nearby. His affections for her grated on my nerves, but I respected him as a fellow supernatural and I knew he disliked the idea of his mate bond connecting to a huldra almost as much as I hated his affections for her. I'd be kidding myself if I said joining his brotherhood wasn't more than a little tempting, just to get him to back off her. But without Faline to keep the energy-manipulator in check, the guy behaved like a lovesick teenager—one whose personal logic had a hard time connecting with reality.

I exhaled long and loud to release just a portion of my irritation before speaking to him. "And why is this thing they've already passed by you something you've failed to tell me?"

Earlier the Hunter had texted Aleksander rather than me and now he was passing information by the incubi leader as though Rod needed Aleksander's permission? My girlfriend was being detained by my own kind, which was why I gathered the rogues together to meet with me —to incorporate them in the Wild Women's plan. When my own brothers, my own rogues, answered to the incubus and kept me out of the loop, it made me want to impale things...or beings...with my new-to-me dagger.

"I would have told you, but out of respect for Rod's wishes, I have chosen to refrain," Aleksander answered, skirting around a muddy patch by choosing a path of dead pine needles. So he chose now to behave dignified and use his brain.

I sloshed through the mud, splattering wet earth onto my pants legs.

I grumbled and grit my teeth.

One positive thing about all of this was Aleksander had stopped hanging around the house so much without Faline's presence calling him to be near. He'd taken to staying at a nearby motel, the one the harpies occupied, said it enabled him to rest better. I moved around a fern, not to keep from getting dirty, but to keep from crushing the bright green living thing. When I got Faline back...and I *would* get her back...we'd need to come up with some way of dealing with Aleksander. Neither she nor I accepted Aleksander's claim to her as his mate, and after this little stunt, I didn't know if I could spend another hour with this man hanging around once she returned.

Thoughts of our reunion was what kept me going. Not the actual retrieval of my huldra woman, but the hours and days afterwards. Holding her in my arms, caressing her hair, taking in her sweet scent, kissing her lips, her shoulders, and beyond. More of me than my lips and arms yearned for Faline. I slowed my gait to readjust my pants and my thoughts.

If everything went as planned, we'd be Hunter establishment-free very shortly and while I knew we couldn't go back to life as usual, I had hope in the new life we would create for ourselves.

"They are past this line of trees," Aleksander said, pausing to wait for me.

I gave a nod and walked by him, intent on approaching my brothers first.

The clearing lay before me, a circle of field grass, wet and muddy from the autumn weather. Evergreens surrounded us, tall and mighty, while other types of trees stood barren, asleep for the coming months.

Seven men stood before me, two holding hands, and the others spread out, standing at attention. None wore the black cargos and shirts of the brotherhood. A few had begun to grow facial hair, their chins and upper lips scruffy with early signs of beards and mustaches. All but one wore daggers at their waists. I imagined they'd been given those daggers when they'd reached their teen years. Before that, as little boys, Hunters carry around wooden daggers to practice with and get used to.

"Thank you for coming," I said, spreading my hands wide and making sure to create a visual connection with each man in attendance. "You've made the right decision, done the right thing." I motioned to Aleksander. "Now, if you'll just give Aleksander here a few moments to assess the loyalty among you, once he's done we can begin."

Aleksander nodded his head and went to work absorbing the energy of each individual man, a decision we'd discussed on the way over as an extra precaution. I needed to make sure these men were true rogues before I offered them any intel on the Wild Women or our strategies.

"They're clear," he muttered with a quick glace toward me. "And we are the only ones within earshot."

I thanked him and addressed the men, loud and clear. "I had wanted to jump right in on battle strategy and the sharing of helpful information." My words held a little more irritability than I'd wanted to show. "But I'm told one of you has an announcement to make and that I'm apparently the last to know."

"Yes." Rod stood taller and released the hand of the man beside him, a blond incubus. His perfectly slicked hair had grown longer, more tussled since we fought together in Oregon. Hints of silver shone through the black on his temples. "I do have an announcement to make. I wanted to tell you, Marcus, but the truth had to flow through the proper channels before it reached you."

I held back my retort.

"And as such," Rod continued, "I am glad to finally share the news. You are not looking at six rogue Hunters and one incubus, as you may have thought. You are looking at six rogue Hunters and two incubi."

I sighed. "You were changed, then."

"I was," Rod answered, proudly. "The process is much less involved for gay men than it is for straight men."

The incubus beside him chuckled and the two shared a look. They clutched hands again. "Edward here is my mate, and I am his. Our bond has been sealed and I am now in the incubi brotherhood under Aleksander."

Aleksander pressed his palms together in a prayer pose and gave a nod, smiling. "And we are most happy to have you."

For the life of me I couldn't figure out why Rod felt he needed to keep such a thing from me. Did he assume I'd be upset?

"Congratulations," I said with sincerity. "Will there be a wedding when this is all over? A reason to celebrate?"

Rod looked to Edward and the two smiled.

"Incubi don't usually marry," Edward said, his voice happy and in good spirits—a feeling I missed right along with Faline.

"We also don't usually participate in the wars of others," Rod joked.

"True, true," Edward agreed. "But let's not take up any more of the group's time with our talk of romantic endeavors." The incubus gave me a nod and I returned one to him.

"All right," I started. "One other incubus, Mason, will be joining us in the fight, besides the three you see here today. Outside of that, it'll be us and the Wild Women joining forces. I recently spoke with another rogue Hunter, one who hasn't left the complex life yet, and he wasn't so sure his comrades would be willing to do this. Before I continue, I need to see a show of hands. Who all here is willing to fight alongside Wild Women?"

Every hand went up. I didn't think my expression changed or my body language, but Rod answered my unasked question. "The rogues have factions, as I'm sure you know," he said to me. "This faction doesn't have much to do with the larger group of rogues."

"Why?" I asked.

"Because we're all gay," another Hunter answered. "The other rogues would probably dislike fighting beside us almost as much as they dislike the idea of fighting beside the Wild Women."

I rubbed the back of my neck. I'd only re-joined the Hunters for a short while before Faline and the other American Wild Women overtook the Washington complex. Before that, it'd been years since I'd stepped foot in a complex, years since I'd surrounded myself with the Hunter ways and beliefs. Within every large group lived divisions, but to divide over such a thing as personal preference made no sense. It only weakened a group, which was probably the opposite of the intentions of those determining the divide.

The Hunter establishment clung to the popular term "sanctity of marriage," but those few of us on the inside, who thought for ourselves, knew their exclusion of homosexual rights within the brotherhood had nothing to do with sanctity and everything to do with their thoughts on women and the roles of women. To them, women were lesser than men and each romantic and sexual relationship needed to have the controller and the controlee. The idea of a same-sex relationship upset this ideal balance of theirs. Plus, in their finite thinking of gender roles, they couldn't wrap their heads around why on earth a male would want to lower himself to a female's status by taking the controlee position of a coupledom.

I withheld my grumblings of how fucked up it all was and shook my head to show my thoughts on the subject before moving on. "Okay, so then each and every one of you is comfortable with fighting alongside Wild Women?"

They nodded.

"Have you had much experience around them?" I asked. "Outside of check-ins?"

They shook their heads.

"All right," I said. "Well, for starters, they will release their inner Wild Women in your presence, and your inner Hunter will feel it. As in, your muscles will grow rapidly, causing soreness. And you'll feel like you've just been given a steroid shot full of testosterone." I caught their eyes. "You'll have the inescapable urge to either fight or fuck with no particular preference. I suggest you fight and then fuck."

A few men laughed and I quickly pushed all thoughts of a naked Faline from my mind. "If you go into it knowing these will be your triggers, you'll be better able to channel them effectively. Except for you, Rod. You don't have to worry about that anymore," I said jokingly to decrease any fear of the unknown I may have planted in the men.

"As long as I still get to fuck after I fight," Rod joked back.

The other men laughed louder, certainly on board with Rod's plan.

"Now that we have that taken care of," I said more seriously. "Let's talk tactics."

When their laughter died down, I continued. "We have multiple Wild Women groups here from other countries, as well as our own. They are gearing up to attack the North Carolina Hunter complex tomorrow morning." The men exchanged glances. I raised my hands. "I know that's short notice, and I apologize. But the sooner the better. Not only do they have three Wild Women against their will, but every day we wait more innocent human women are taken and prepared to be sold and deported like livestock. None of this is acceptable."

I nodded to a few of the rogues' waists. "I see you all brought your daggers. I know each of you has been extensively trained in hand-to-hand combat with the types of Wild Women from your region. Today I'll quickly give you an overview of how these and the other Wild Women will fight, so you may better fight alongside them. And a reminder that tomorrow morning you won't be fighting folkloric women. You'll be fighting your brothers...men who are as thoroughly trained as yourself."

I pulled my dagger from its sheath and raised it in front of my chest, at the ready.

The rogue Hunters, including Rod, did the same.

I advanced on the group. "Then let's begin."

TWENTY

MY ARM ACHED where the Hunter had plunged the needle and stolen my blood. I lay on my right side, away from the window, to keep it from aching. I stared at the empty wall, cursing its existence. I wanted to see my mother again, hoped the rogue Hunter would enter my room tonight with more information, and wished I were lying with Marcus in my bed at home in my tree house, alone, and safe. I tried to cling to hope, but my reserves were about as full as the wall I stared at.

"You mourn an experience you are not having."

I knew the voice well. I took a breath and slowly turned to my left side, toward the window. My arm pulsated with the movement, so I used my right arm to heave myself up to sitting.

"Drosera," I said on an exhale. "They took my blood. They're preparing to remove my eggs and inseminate them with Hunter sperm. So don't tell me I'm not having an experience that I most clearly am having."

The rusalka didn't even blink. "They have not yet taken your eggs. They have not yet created offspring with them. The experience has not happened."

She had a point, but I heaved out a sigh anyway. "My mother is here and so is the harpy flock's mother."

Drosera gave one quick nod. It appeared as though she'd run a few fingers through her hair since I saw her last, in the hotel after her forest had burned down. She'd changed too, into a less bloody animal skin skirt and no top. She brought with her the scent of dirt and pine needles.

One thought led to another, sisters and mothers in captivity, and I remembered to ask the rusalka about her own sisters. "Did your sisters make it out okay? Are they all right after the whole Maine complex shitshow?"

"Oleander and Aconitum are well, thank you," she answered. "Their connection to Mokosh has been reestablished and they have been working on healing themselves."

"How did they take the news about Azalea?" I wondered aloud.

Drosera closed her eyes for a moment before opening them and responding. "Telling them was to experience the loss anew."

My heart ached for them all. What awful news to come home to.

"Your Wild sisters hurt for you," I added, not as consolation, but as affirmation.

"We know," she said. "It is appreciated."

She stood in silence and I watched as though we both contemplated what this path to freedom had taken from us. I wondered what else it aimed to steal.

"So," I started, to rescue us both from unhelpful thoughts, "is there a plan to get us all out, my mother, the harpy Rose, and me? Sooner rather than later?"

"Yes," she answered. "Tomorrow morning, during your courtyard time."

I sat up a little taller with a new sense of energy. Hope did strange things to a person.

"Wait," I said, only now realizing what her words meant. "You've been here before? While I was here?" How else would she know I spent my mornings in the courtyard?

"Azalea," she answered, which was enough for me. Her sister in spirit, lost by Clarisse's hand to save my sister.

Which brought up another memory. I'd warned Clarisse that the rusalki would avenge their sister, and I never went back on my word. "Clarisse is here," I said.

"Yes," Drosera answered with a smile and eyes full of malicious plans. "Azalea has been watching the Hunter woman as well, waiting for when her usefulness to our sisters, to you, has worn out."

Oh, how I wished I could be there to witness their deadly birch scissors—one snip of the hair to cut a life short—and Clarisse's terrified pleading for her own life.

"We cannot guarantee your desire will be met, but we will try," Drosera said.

So the rusalki were still reading minds. Good. I wondered if having to bring up old wounds, telling their newly rescued sisters about Azalea, had stolen some of the energy needed to not only transport themselves, but read minds as well. Although, the incubi and succubi could have helped too.

Come to think of it, I did feel a bit of tingling deep beneath my skull. I'd initially passed it off as the bud of a headache caused by the damn blood stone tattoo. It'd been a couple weeks or so since a rusalka had spoken into my mind. With all that'd happened in that time—my visit to the rusalki's underwater funeral home, my visit to the incubi's Portland underground lair, my visit to the Airbnb and then the Oregon Hunter complex and the city of Atlanta and the Maine Hunters' complex, and now here—it felt like an eternity. But I'd forgotten about my telepathic conversation with Drosera the night I met the alae in the burning Maine forest.

When this was all over with...if this ever ended, I wanted to take a break from visiting anywhere and anyone. Traveling no longer held the same wide-eyed wonderment it once did.

"Ha." I laughed and Drosera's eyes twinkled with knowing at what I was laughing at.

Before I was attacked at the Westin in Bellevue, before Shawna was taken and I went on my multi-state hunt to find her, I wasn't allowed to leave Washington State, by order of the Washington State Hunter organization. Before I'd released my inner huldra and basically killed my ability to ever pass a Hunter check-in again, I'd never left the state. I'd accepted the rule, but secretly wondered what it'd be like to cross borders from one state to another, from one country to another. If we took down the last Hunter complex, we'd have complete freedom to travel. But because of all the traveling I'd have done to get to that point, I'd likely never want to travel again.

Life is full of the kind of irony that makes you shake your head and want to give life itself the finger.

"They will come soon, so I must go," Drosera said, eyeing the bedroom door. "Be brave in the knowledge that this will soon come to an end."

I thought to ask her exactly what she meant, what was going to happen between now and tomorrow morning that I needed extra bravery for. But I worried her answer would have the opposite effect of bravery.

"Can you see the future?" I asked. I had asked this question before, and the answer they gave was less clear than a dirty snow globe. Now more than ever, I needed to know the end results—if all of this was actually for something rather than a slow and painful descent into death.

If the answer was yes, and the future for American Wild Women looked dim, for all Wild Women, would I have wished I'd never started this thing in the first place? Knowing the future, would I have preferred a caged life over a free death?

Drosera cocked her head and studied me, the sense of tingles rummaging through my brain clearly explaining her focus.

"Do you understand your own answer?" she asked.

As I lay in captivity in the second oldest Hunter complex in America, my inner self felt accomplished, fulfilled, like I'd lived a life of purpose and meaning. A life that touched others. Whether or not my path in life would soon end, it was a path I was proud of and glad I'd stepped onto. Yes, I would have chosen a death of freedom over a life in which I lived by the lies of an oppressor. Connecting with my inner huldra, helping other Wilds to connect with their inner Wild Women, was worth anything the Hunters threw at me as punishment.

"I do understand," I said, even though Drosera's soft smile told me she already knew my answer.

"My sisters and I, Azalea included, will come to your aid

tomorrow," Drosera said as she faded from existence. Her last statement, she spoke into my mind. *Until then, be well.*

The tingling sensation of a rusalka sorting through my mind filled my body with a state of euphoria, to the point of feeling as though I floated above the bed.

"Freyja," I whispered, the name of my Goddess, a sweet tingle on my lips.

Four sets of Hunter boots tromped down the hall and grew louder as they neared my door. The cadence halted at once and the lock rustled before the door knob turned.

"Freyja," I said again, stronger, louder. "Strengthen me for what they're about to do."

TWENTY-ONE

SHAWNA, Olivia, and I waited at the half-way point in the dark bootlegger tunnel under the harpies' home we currently stayed in. I held a steel flashlight, on its lowest setting. I turned the stream of light away from the huldra, who could see well enough in the dark and preferred that I not shine the thing in their eyes, temporarily blinding them.

"They're coming," Shawna whispered, just loud enough for me to hear.

I pulled the beam of light from the tunnel wall to the center of the ground in the distance, the place our guests were to come from.

While Aleksander and I had been meeting with the small group of rogue Hunters in the woods, Shawna and Olivia had made their way through the secret hutch door, into the basement of the house, and further into the tunnel, in search of a mermaid. They'd found two who'd been on their way to the harpies' home. Despite what the Hunter teachers taught me growing up, and even my more in-depth trainings as a man, Wild Women seemed to have an unseen connection, one that I doubted even some of them realized.

From the outside looking in, I noticed the more they worked together as a team, the more they seemed able to move forward when the other moved back, to anticipate the needs of another Wild Woman outside their group. This morning's chance meeting between the two huldra and the mermaids only served as proof of my theory.

Rock curved around us, leaving a semi-flat floor for the flashlight beam to bounce off of, hitting pebbles and dirt. No one had gone through the trouble of smoothing the walls or rounding the ceiling. Jagged edges of sharp stone still held the lined marks of rock cutters. This tunnel had a specific function and ease of use or safety were not priorities. I considered removing my boots to widen the gap between the top of my head and the protruding rock edges, but two mermaids rounded the bend in the tunnel before I bent to untie my laces.

The mermaids, holding hands, walked into the beam of my flashlight, their feet bare and jeans dirty. I raised the light to point just beside the one on the right, to view them without shining the thing in their eyes. They were of similar height and build. One had red hair and the other was a brunette. Both wore serious expressions as they clasped Olivia and Shawna's hands in greeting.

"We came as soon as we found out about Faline," the red-head said, concern lacing her tone.

Shawna thanked her and turned to address me. "I'd like to formally introduce you to a couple friends Faline made during her travels to the mermaids' island. Marcus, this is Sarah." Shawna motioned to the red-head. "And her partner, Elaine." She motioned to the brunette.

I remembered Elaine, but not Sarah. I looked between Elaine and Olivia and wondered what a succubus or incubus would feel in this moment, between the two Wild Women who, when they first met, began a physical altercation in the huldra's common house kitchen. Understandably, Elaine hadn't taken the news of Gabrielle's death sitting down. She'd wanted to pull out of the whole mission and go home.

"We're wife and wife now," Elaine said with a smile in her eyes as she looked to Sarah.

"Congratulations," Olivia offered. "That's actually really positive news in such a negative time."

"Thank you," the two mermaids responded. "With everything

going on, we just felt we needed to declare who we were and our love and devotion for one another, who and what we're fighting for."

Either my officer mind or my Hunter mind kicked in, making me ask, "Was this through the traditional government system? Because Hunters keep a close eye on government documents submitted by females in areas where Wild Women reside." I added my intention behind the question after I realized my query had the components of a douchy remark. "I don't want you two separated so soon after celebrating such a commitment."

God, I had a way with words. Not really.

Sarah spoke up, assertive, but not offended, as far as I could tell. "We don't respect or adhere to human systems of government. We decided to pledge ourselves in a more traditional way for our kind, officiated by the leader of a council that governs beings much like us, but who aren't Wilds."

There were no non-Wild Women supernatural females in America, as far as I knew. I wasn't going to ask, though, having already reached my douchy comment quota for this meeting. Knowing me, the question would come out as a know-it-all statement or an accusation, neither of which would do me any good in earning their trust.

Apparently Shawna and I were on the same wavelength because she asked, "Wait, others here in the states?"

The two mermaids shared a look.

"Yes, our two kinds broke the connection many years ago due to differences of opinion about the humans," Sarah answered. "When our shoal fragmented, Elaine, our daughter, and I sought them out."

Elaine nearly interrupted her wife. "Yes, but we prefer not to share much more about them." She gently touched Sarah's arm. "If they want to be known about, they'll make it happen."

Sarah nodded her agreement. "So," she said to Shawna, Olivia, and me. "What's the plan to get Faline back? I know there's got to be a plan."

"She's done so much for the Wild Women," Elaine agreed.

Shawna tensed and lifted her chin.

I held back the urge to press a hand to her back in show of support and safety. Faline's partner sister had been through nothing short of trauma at the hands of my brothers in a building, on a property, where I was raised and played as a kid. Entering that cabin where my father used to sit with a cigar and tell me the stories of his father and his father's father, and seeing an innocent woman drugged, held against her will...it turned my stomach and solidified any disdain I held for the brotherhood. I took it as my duty to support Shawna in any way needed. Now, though, what she needed was to be given space to flex her strength and power.

"Tomorrow morning," she answered the mermaids. "Are your sisters going to take part as well? We haven't told them the strategy, that there is one, but they knew we were planning on taking down the North Carolina complex before Faline was taken. That's still what's going to happen, but with an added rescue. Last they told us, when they called they were deciding how it all worked with their current arrangements."

"And I bet they didn't share what their current arrangements happened to be? I'm sorry they're so secretive," Sarah interjected. "It's an old habit."

"One that's kept our kind safe, for the most part," Elaine added. "Until recently."

"It's okay," Olivia said. "Trust is earned over time, not something that should always be freely given. It makes sense, seeing we've only known each other for a few weeks."

"They are planning on helping," Sarah continued. "Those that are here, at least. They're actually searching the area around the complex as we speak, looking for water access."

"Great," I said. "According to the rusalki, Faline will be spending roughly a half hour outside in the morning, in their courtyard. They give her outside time daily."

Elaine shot me a look. "The rusalki."

I'd thought to keep their coven unmentioned to the mermaids, after what Faline said transpired in her kitchen between Olivia and Elaine over the news that the rusalki killed the mermaid's sister, Gabrielle. But the mermaids who'd shown up to help at the rusalki's forest didn't seem to have any issues. And we didn't have time to skirt around uncomfortable topics and prance around to avoid stepping on toes. Not when it came to rescuing Faline, to having her safe in my arms.

"Yes," I answered and then continued on with the subject at hand, the topic that transcended bad blood between Wild Women groups. "Their fallen sister, Azalea, has been keeping an eye on Faline and the others at the complex, gathering information. We only get one shot to enact the final blow against the complex; it needs to be as destructive as possible."

Which was why I suffered myself enough to work with the rogue Hunters alongside Aleksander, training the men how to fight with Wild Women and not against them. With Hunter DNA coursing through their veins, it was no easy task. The alae offered to join us tonight in the woods, to give the rogue Hunters a taste of tapping into their Hunter strength and fighting techniques with Wild Women present, but not as their foes.

"Despite any issues we may or may not have with the rusalki, we have a much larger bone to pick with the Hunters," Sarah nearly growled. "They've driven us from our island home, fragmented and dispersed our shoal, manipulated those within our ranks to do their bidding for fear of their sisters' deaths, and now they've taken Faline, the one Wild Woman raised by the Hunters' lies to break from their cage of fear and reach out to unite us all. We will be there tomorrow."

Elaine added, "We look forward to killing anyone wearing that black uniform."

I made a mental note to remind the rogue Hunters to dress differently than their brothers.

"Here's the number to the house where we're staying." Shawna handed Sarah a folded piece of paper. "We'd leave the barrier between the home's basement and this tunnel open, but we can't be sure who else knows of this entrance."

"Thank you," the mermaids said. The women exchanged smiles and nods and each turned to head back to where they came from.

I re-centered the flashlight on the dark path ahead of me, walking silently beside Shawna and Olivia. Inside I buzzed with impatience to see Faline again and raged at the thought of what darkness she was currently encountering at the hands of my ex-brotherhood.

TWENTY-TWO

"GOOD NEWS," John announced as he burst through the door of the tiny bedroom they'd been imprisoning me in.

I turned to meet whoever entered my room face-to-face. From the dresser I glared at the leader of the Washington Hunter complex.

"Your blood came back clean. The drugs are all out of your system." The man motioned his head toward the door where Clarisse strolled through carrying the red shawl.

I wondered if Azalea saw this, watched how willingly the woman did the men's bidding, oppressed another woman to stay in the men's good graces. Still, I said nothing.

Freyja, keep me strong. I absently reached up to stroke the Freyja charm on my necklace, but found nothing there. The Hunters had removed it when I'd been brought here. I could only imagine why, with their poor excuses of an explanation about it being demonic or of the occult or some bullshit that basically meant any deity without a penis was an evil creation meant to lead humans and supernaturals astray.

Clarisse seemed more confident with John around. Without hesitation, she shook the shawl to unfold and threw it over my back to drape across my shoulders. "This looks good on her. Don't you agree, father?" Clarisse asked, taking a step back to get a better view of her handiwork.

John was her father? Was this biological or more like a spiritual leader sort of father?

John paused a moment, as though her speaking threw him off. He quickly composed himself. "Submission always looks good on females," he agreed. "It increases the feminine qualities, softens them, makes them more appealing."

I tried to un-hunch my shoulders, push against the weight of the bloodstone fabric and fragments woven in the shawl. The weight gave ever-so-slightly, but it wasn't enough.

John, in a cheerier mood than usual, exhaled and called in two Hunters who'd been waiting outside the open door. "Let's get this started!"

The two Hunters moved to each side of me and began escorting me from the room, with the expectation that I join them. Glad they hadn't yet put hands on me, I did as expected, walking between them down the hall after John.

Clarisse walked ten feet behind our row.

Keep me strong, Freyja.

They led me down a wide set of carpeted stairs to the first level. No light streamed from the stained glass windows situated near the vaulted ceiling. We made our way along the reddish-brown tiled flooring of the large and open entry of the monastery-turned-complex, past a lone water fountain standing in the center of the circular entry, and toward a set of elevator doors.

"What was that?" Clarisse asked from behind the group.

No one paid her any attention. Not until she screeched and ran to the Hunter on my right, clinging to his arm. Eyes wide and hands shaking, Clarisse begged the Hunter, "Did you hear her? Did you hear?"

John paused his whistling and turned right before pressing a button on the elevator panel. "What is it now, woman?" he said, his jovial attitude gone.

Clarisse froze. She grabbed her head, squeezing her skull, and fell to the tile. "She's in my head! Get her out! Get her out!"

Neither of the Hunters moved from my side, but John ran to the writhing woman on the ground. "Who's in your head? The huldra?" He shot me a glare before returning his focus to the brown-haired woman screeching and clawing at her head, ruining her bun.

"No, don't make me tell them, please, don't make me," she screamed.

Clarisse's body froze in an eerie stillness.

The hairs on the back of my neck rose and my instincts told me to back up, get away from whatever transpired on the entry way floor. I stood in place between the hulking Hunters.

John pulled his dagger from the sheath at his waist and knelt beside Clarisse.

Her body writhed again, only enough to curl into the fetal position and freeze. "I tried to escape you, father. I tried to become one of them," she muttered under her breath, her words quick and slurred. "One of them!" she yelled.

John flung his arm back and positioned his dagger right above her boney back, at an angle to penetrate her heart from behind. "How is this possible?" he demanded. "Have you sold your soul?"

"I killed a Wild Woman because they refused to make me one of them," she whimpered, her lips barely moving.

The two Hunters at my sides fidgeted, staying in position, but straining their necks to search for the unseen cause of Clarisse's struggling.

John stood slowly, his focus on the young woman at his feet. She muttered a string of words incoherently. I glanced around the room, in search of a rusalka.

Azalea? I thought.

Clarisse's body shot up and hovered, her feet dangling inches from the ground. Her chin rested on her chest and her eyes fluttered behind her closed lids. John ran in a circle around her, shoving his dagger into the air, within inches from her loose clothes and skin.

"In her weakness, she's sold her soul to them," he gasped, jabbing his dagger at nothing but air. "She's possessed!"

A handful of her brown hair, loose from her bun, raised straight up from her head. She jolted her head up to stare, her eyes filled with insane fear, into my eyes. Her mouth opened, a silent scream on her lips. The sound her lungs produced rushed out past her tongue in an ear-splitting octave that left the Hunters and me covering our ears against the pain.

The chunk of hair standing straight up looked as though it held her in the air. With unseen scissors, made of birch I guessed, the chunk of hair separated from Clarisse at the scalp. In an instant the woman dropped to the tile floor in a sprawling heap.

John rushed to kneel beside her. He checked her pulse. "She's dead," he said quietly at first, contemplatively. "She's dead!"

He jolted up and rushed me, his dagger still at the ready in his right hand. He shoved a Hunter out of his way and wrapped his left hand around my upper bicep. "Any mercy I would have shown is gone now," he seethed.

He yanked me toward the elevator and slammed his finger onto the open button again. When the doors opened, he jerked me into the elevator and hit the basement button with the palm of his hand.

The two Hunters hurried to join us before the doors shut.

Downward movement threw my stance off, and John tugged my arm painfully to keep me in position. I looked to my fingers, willing vines to ease from their confines. But nothing came to my aid, not with the bloodstone shawl draped around my shoulders and fastened at my neck like a choker.

The elevator hit the bottom floor and the doors sprang open to reveal a surgical-looking underground with white, empty walls, white tiled flooring, and steel doors. John wrenched me into the hallway and pulled me to match his quick pace. A woman's sobs echoed from behind one of the steel doors and my eyes filled with tears. This was where they kept the women they were selling, the human trafficking victims. It had to be.

"Let's get this over with," John commanded as he stomped down the hall, his Hunters moving quickly to keep up with us. "As soon as the seed takes we can be done with this abomination. The sooner I can dispose of it, the better."

TWENTY-THREE

DOUBT ISN'T a regular piece of baggage I carry around. That's not to say I don't have baggage. I own my fair share, just like the rest of the world, aspects of myself brought on by upbringing and mistakes—pieces of my own thinking that I've fought against and tried to stay on top of. For example, maintaining a certain degree of closeness with women took an embarrassing amount of effort on my part. Growing up with no sisters and no mother, in a culture that flowed with the pride of a brotherhood, created a sense of wonder and fear when it came to the opposite sex.

During the awkward teen years, I watched those in my brotherhood who'd grown up with sisters and mothers, saw their familiarity with females in the way they'd converse with their female cousins and the Hunters' wives during holiday celebrations and birthday gatherings. As we aged, though, nearing our own Hunter careers, their comfort with females mattered less and less, as we were expected to estrange ourselves from our sisters and mothers and female cousins, and draw closer to our brothers, our father, and our leaders.

When I'd first left the brotherhood, I felt like a lone wolf, unsure how to operate within other packs, but unwilling to return to his own.

I had been truly alone. My father had continued contact, though it grew strained and shallow—our discussion topics relegated to politics, work, and weather. Now here I was, trying to figure out how to interact with women on a casual basis again. Funny how life is cyclical like that.

By the light of a moon barely visible above the blanket of trees circling us, I surveyed the small group of rogue Hunters before me in the forest clearing. These men were not alone and would never be alone, even after leaving the brotherhood. For that, I envied them, because they would always have a part of their foundation, their brotherhood, beside them. When I left the brotherhood I had no one.

Still, my rarely seen bag of doubt weighed on me as I considered the reality of our situation. Did these men have what it would take to fight and kill the very brothers they grew up with? The men who'd covered for them during their early years of Hunter training when they'd dropped their dagger or failed to study the night before an important exam on Hunter history?

I thought back to my first time fighting my brothers, to the day when I had to walk past a line of them on their knees in front of Wild Women I'd never met, as they, one-by-one, breathed their last breath. Just remembering their faces, the confusion and pain, made my stomach knot and my throat tighten.

"Remember why you're fighting," I started, bellowing out to the men in the clearing, with the exact sentence I used to keep me fighting forward. "These are your brothers you'll be killing. The Wild Women you've been conditioned to hate will be taking down the men who used to be your allies, with their energy manipulation, their speed, their talons, and their song."

I didn't know why, but I left the huldra out of my speech. Maybe out of a sense to protect the coterie who held my highest loyalty, or maybe out of my desire to forget the scenes playing through my head.

"I cannot express this enough—it will be the hardest thing you've done." I paused to let that sink in. "Trust me, deciding to leave the brotherhood is nothing compared to standing by while a Wild Woman chokes the life from a childhood playmate." I watched their faces and gave that a beat to sink in.

"In these moments you'll need to have your reason for fighting solidified. So, I ask again, why are you fighting? What and who are you fighting for? Figure it out before tomorrow morning, and ingrain it in your skull. If you think it's hard, keeping this a secret, that you'll be rushing their complex tomorrow, just know that this secret is nothing compared to what you're about to do. Trust me, you will need to repeat your reason for leaving, for fighting back, over and over from the moment you step foot on the complex property as an invader, to the moment you wash your brothers' blood from your skin tomorrow night, to the wee hours of the next morning, when you are tossing and turning, unable to unsee what you wish you could."

I thought back to the whispered conversations shared in the middle of the night between Faline and me, over her sleeping sister, Shawna.

At first, I'd fought for morality reasons. I'd fought for what I believed the Hunters had done to my mother—the miniscule trail of breadcrumbs left that painted a picture of deceit, manipulation, and murder. But after those nights, filled with inner turmoil and Faline's comfort, her acceptance and listening ear, I began fighting for more than morality, more than ethical beliefs and the inkling that my mother had been at the receiving end of the Hunters' control. And it made all the difference.

I began fighting for Faline. For a future with the woman I loved, an existence not governed by the Hunters and tradition, but by us.

"I fight for love," I continued. "And I suggest you do the same. Fight for the love you deserve, a love of your choosing, a love free of shame and gossip and secrecy."

The men grew somber in contemplation. I'd hit a nerve. Good.

"You may have those things now. I don't know. But what I do know is that if the Hunter establishment, as a governing force, isn't taken down, you may not have that again." I took a breath and gave them a moment to sit with that thought. I paced in front of them, down the line of seven men. "You know as well as I do what they're capable of. And if we do not fight for love, if we do not fight for freedom, we may very easily lose both."

A woman's melodious voice came from behind me. "Freedom for

loved ones is the very thing the Wild Women began fighting for when they rose up, if I'm not mistaken."

I swung around to peer in the direction of the voice, in the direction the men suddenly shifted their gazes to.

A tall, tan woman, with sweeping black and silver hair, who looked to be in her fifties, stood at the edge of the tree line.

When she had all of our attention, she spoke again, her Spanish accent saturating each word. "It began as the desire to free loved ones and it has morphed into a thing of absolute beauty—the desire to free themselves."

"Are you alae?" I asked, though her accent had already answered that question.

"No." She looked toward the woods, behind her. "Though they are only minutes away."

"But you are a Wild Woman?" I clarified. "Here to help us practice for tomorrow?"

She studied my face before leaving the tree line and making her way toward me. Her dark green cloak shifted as she moved, revealing a long white dress underneath. As this unknown Wild Woman approached, I expected to feel my Hunter react, but I only met with acceptance at her close proximity.

"I am not here to help them," she said, without so much as looking in the direction of the rogue Hunters. "I have come to help you, Marcus Garcia, son of Paul Garcia."

Her features intrigued me—her forehead, somewhat wide like my own, the shape and set of her nose and how her eyebrows—thick and dark—matched her face perfectly. She felt, she looked... familiar.

I gave a slightly uncomfortable laugh. "Well, it seems you know a bit about me and yet I know nothing about you. Are you a friend of Faline Frey?"

The woman studied my face, squinting her eyes as she stared into mine. "I've never met the huldra," she said. "No, as I stated, I only came on your behalf." She tilted her head as though she were reading an inscription across my face that she couldn't quite figure out.

Her expression shifted in a breath, from deep in thought to jovial.

"Ah," she said as she turned in place to peer at the direction in which she'd come from. "They have arrived, our alae friends."

The group of fire-wielding Wild Women entered the circular clearing and stopped short when they rested eyes on the cloaked woman less than an arm's length in front of me. The alae leader, Ailani, bowed first. Her sisters soon followed.

"Madam," she said, coming up from her bow. "We are honored with your presence."

"The honor is all mine," she said graciously, giving a small bow to Ailani.

"Did the pregnant harpy and her bad choice in mate bring you to this land as well?" Ailani asked, her sisters following close behind in a huddle. A few trained their gazes on the rogue Hunters and held fire in their palms as what I could only image was a warning.

"No," the woman answered. "Talk of this man has brought me here. My sister, Conchita, believes there to be a strong resemblance between him and me. I had to come see for myself."

"Who is this man to you?" Ailani said. "Surely, you do not wish to create another daughter with him."

Something about her statement brushed me the wrong way.

The woman gave a short laugh. She turned to me. Her smile fell from her brown eyes and a sense of depth, of wanting, replaced it. "There has been talk from the Wild Women who've recently traveled to aid in this cause," she started, her cracking voice barely noticeable, "that my son lives."

"Your son?" Ailani asked in shock.

"Your son?" I repeated.

"You were born in Spain to a mother you no longer have?" the woman asked.

I nodded absently before finding the words to answer. "I was, and then brought to the States by my father."

"I gave birth to a son, in Spain, with a man I loved, who I'd believed loved me in return. I was sadly mistaken shortly after passing my second trimester, when he revealed his affiliation with the Hunters. It had all been a ruse, our love a sham, perpetrated by a Hunter seeking to gain rank and notoriety through bringing the first Hunter/Wild

Woman hybrid into this world." She reached to touch my cheek and I flinched back. "The moment my son was born, I knew he was lost to me, that Paul Garcia had succeeded. For Wild Women are unable to birth males with the weak Y chromosome sperm of human men."

Now, more than ever, I relied on my legs to keep me upright, because what this woman said just about bowled me over. Could it be true? My eyes retraced the woman's face, the familiarity of it. But how could I have remembered her face as just a baby? Or was the familiarity from looking at myself in the mirror all these years? The wide forehead. The thick brows. The tan skin.

"I cannot know, though," she went on, as though she were partly talking to me and partly to Ailani, but mostly speaking to herself. "I have not seen my son since he was only a little one. He would be a man now, having lost all of his childish features."

The cloaked woman exhaled and nodded, looking me straight in the eyes. She held out her hand to shake mine. "Hello, my name is Avera and I am a xana, Wild Women of pure water, our hearts flowing with pure love. We were created by the Goddess Danu, and the only way for me to test whether or not you are of my blood is to test the purity of your heart. I must sing for you."

The fire wielders gasped.

"Okay," I said, stealing a glace to see what the other women gasped at. "Is that a bad thing, you singing?"

She sighed. "The song of a xana can only be heard by a pure heart, otherwise it has the power to drive the listener mad, or worse."

"Oh," I said. Well, that changed things. "I guess it depends how you define pure as to whether or not I'll pass the test."

I'd waited years to meet my mother, to look into her face and realize the other half of myself. To, on top of it, know I wasn't full Hunter, that I belonged to another family, would fill me with more gratitude than I had the power to express. But Faline needed me to be battle ready by tomorrow morning. And if somehow I wasn't found pure, by some undefined and possibly outdated concept, I could lose my mind and my fighting capabilities along with it.

She asked my birthdate and the exact town I was born in. I told her, and she responded with a nod. "I believe you to be my son," she finally said after some contemplation. "And if you are my son, I would very much like to fight for you, help you to finish strong, as the opportunity to do such things for you over the years has been stolen from me."

I swallowed hard. Could she really be my mother? I ached to allow her to sing to me, but... "I cannot lose my mind," I said. "Faline needs me. I need Faline."

She gave a comforting smile. "A xana can feel a pure heart, one that pulses along the same vibration as her own. I feel this from you."

"Then why do you need to sing to prove it?" I asked. My desire for confirmation gnawed at me too, but considering the risk I had to ask.

"Because I have never wanted anything more in my life than this to be true," she said, her words full of strength and softness.

I took a deep breath. If Faline were here she'd already have agreed to the xana woman. Having grown up without her own mother, she'd understand my heart's desire and she'd insist I take the test for nothing if not confirmation. She'd tell me between the succubi, incubi, and rusalki, we'd be able to reverse any mental or emotional confusion failing the song's test could bring. My resourceful lover, watching out for me even when she wasn't here.

"Then I'll hear you sing," I said. "But promise me first, if I fail, you will take me to the huldra coterie and ask them to bring the others to help heal me. If they fail, you will fight in my place."

"Very well then," Avera agreed.

"And perform the test in a place that doesn't put others at risk, so not out here," I added, glancing back to see the worried expressions on the rogue's faces.

She grunted, probably just as frustrated to wait as I was. "Then where?"

"Come back with me to the house I'm staying in, when I'm done here. There's a basement, hidden, under the house. I think that'll be a safe enough spot."

For the first time, she noticed the men behind me. "They fight for you?" she asked.

"No, more like with me," I answered. "And I've promised them an in-depth lesson in fighting alongside Wild Women that I need to get started with." These men had pledged to help us, to stand up against the establishment that excluded their romantic lifestyles. I owed it to them to show them how. "If you don't mind, I'll need you to wait 'til we're done."

"Then I will help the alae in their training endeavors tonight." The xana winked. "I do not sit by and wait for any man. Not even my son."

TWENTY-FOUR

"OKAY, IT SHOULD BE SAFE NOW," I told the cloaked woman before me. I couldn't figure out whether I should call her mom or Avera. So, I called her nothing. I'd decide after she sang, if I had my wits about me enough to still talk.

The look on Shawna's face when I'd brought the woman through the front door and into the living room where the huldra coterie sat with a map of the area strewn across a coffee table, was priceless. I made a mental note to let Faline know her sister was incredibly loyal, if she had any doubts.

Introducing my new guest calmed Shawna's icy glares enough for us to make our way to the hidden door behind the empty hutch without Shawna feeling the need to follow us. I'd warned the coterie that with their sensitive hearing they may want to leave the house for a few minutes, but Olivia assured me she'd done some research on the house and the basement had been insulated to be sound proof. It kept the sounds of alcohol production from visitors or nosy officials.

Avera and I stood alone in the dank, cold basement. The flames of two candles danced along the brick walls, casting shadows across the floor and offering not much in the way of light or warmth. The woman opened her mouth to begin singing and I threw a hand up to stop her.

"What should I expect to experience?" I asked. "In either scenario." Guilt tugged at me. I had important duties that needed to be done tonight.

Each time I wondered why the hell I had to do this now, rather than wait until Faline was safely in my arms again, I swore I heard her voice chastising me for my thoughts. And plus, Avera offered to help us if I proved to be her son. We could use all the help we could get.

"It is different for everyone," she answered, her accent and voice playing along the words as though she told a story. "But, for me, when a xana sings, I am filled with an overwhelming sense of love. The kind that brims over and splatters with giddiness."

"And if I'm not your son?"

She considered me a moment.

"Others—not only our xana children—can hear our songs and be filled with peace. This is not why I suggested the trial," she started. "Others, of pure heart, pass the test fine. Hunters do not. If you are full Hunter and not xana, your ears will bleed; my voice will split your head with a migraine, and the voices my song places in your mind will draw you to madness."

I shifted in place, eager to be done with this and yet not wanting to start.

"You offered to give this test in front of Hunters," I reminded, irritated that I'd nearly put their lives in jeopardy. "Why, if you knew what it'd do to them?"

She tossed back her black and silver hair from her shoulder. "I do not care for the lives of Hunters."

I chewed on that a second, letting the first wave of offense wash over me. The men in the clearing were Hunters who had left the brotherhood—same as me. If she didn't care for them or how she could have hurt their lives, even if she was my mother, that meant she didn't care for half of me. Because whether she or I or Faline liked it, I still had Hunter blood running through my veins.

But, then again, I could only imagine the hell my father had put her through. I guessed she had more of a hate for his kind, his way of thinking and being, than my actual Hunter blood.

"I have questions," I said, thinking of her and my father. Questions

I'd held on to, never speaking out loud, for as long as I could remember.

"I will give you answers once we are done," she responded.

I shook my head. "No. If I fail, I won't be able to comprehend them." The angry little boy in me bubbled to the surface.

"If you fail," she said slowly, "I won't give you any answers. I will leave and you will never see me again."

Before the little boy in me had time to feel hurt and open that scabbed wound of abandonment, the woman tilted her head back, closed her eyes, and sang.

The most beautiful melody exited her throat, as though it completely bypassed her lips and came from somewhere deep and dark and magical. Her lips began to move, to form words I didn't understand in a language I'd never heard. Glowing symbols danced from her mouth and floated toward my ears.

They struck my eardrums with a vibrating sensation, before entering my mind. I closed my eyes and heard myself groan as my shoulders slumped and I leaned against a cold brick wall. I'd never heard anything so beautiful. I leaned my head to the side, nearly touching my chin to my shoulder, and relished in the warmth flowing through my body. Tingles rolled up and down, from my feet to my skull and back down again. I had to remember to breath and in that moment, it felt as though I breathed in pure acceptance and the feeling of truly being known.

The song abruptly stopped and sounds of dripping and the creaking floor boards above jolted me out of the trance. I straightened my shoulders and blinked.

The woman huffed and turned on her heel to climb the basement steps back to the main level of the house.

I followed behind. "Wait, why'd you stop?"

She didn't turn to respond. "You are not my son."

"I felt it, though. I felt the love and the vibration," I explained.

She reached the top of the stairs and shoved the door open. "You lie. You are only repeating back to me what I told you you'd feel."

This woman had come to me, not the other way around. I had

enough to do and worry about before she showed up, claiming to be my mother. And now she acted like I'd put her out?

"You know what?" I said, moving quickly to get in front of her and open the door to the walkway for her to get out of our way. We had shit to do. "That's fine. You can make up whatever excuse you want for hating me because of my Hunter blood. I'm not the one who decided to get involved with a Hunter; I'm only the result of it."

She scoffed and shook her head, her eyes narrow and seething. "I made up nothing. The blood dripping from your ears tells me everything I need to know." She swept the hood on her cloak up over her head and hurried away from the house and away from me.

I looked to the shoulder I'd rested my head on in the basement when the woman's song had me so relaxed I wanted to curl into a ball and fall asleep. A smattering of blood stained my shirt. I turned and closed the door, standing in the entry.

Shawna stood beside me, her concerned expression asked wordless questions.

"It didn't go well," I grumbled.

"Because of your lineage?" she asked.

"Who the fuck knows," I growled. I shouldn't have gotten my hopes up. My mother had kept hidden for a reason. She didn't want to be found. I needed to be okay with that and move on. There was a woman, Faline, who loved me, who accepted me, whose touch made me feel those things the woman's song gave me and more.

This was for the better. My focus needed to be on Faline and getting her out safely.

I started to walk past Shawna, toward the room Faline and I had shared, when she reached a hand out to stop me. Softly, she said, "Why is blood draining from your ears?"

I reached up to touch both of my ears and viewed fresh blood on my fingers.

"Because," I answered sarcastically, "it turns out I'm a Hunter."

TWENTY-FIVE

JOHN WALKED BRISKLY into an operating room as the two Hunters held me by my biceps and basically dragged me into the room after him. A circular light lit an operating table directly beneath it like the sun itself. I squinted at the harsh light.

"Go behind there," a grumpy John demanded, pointing to a panel of white curtains creating a makeshift wall. "Get undressed and put the gown on. It's back there on a stool."

The two Hunters released their hold of me. I peered at my shawl. "But what about—"

He cut me off and rushed toward me, raising his arm to threaten a beating if I didn't obey. "Just go behind the damn curtain," he said between tight lips and a clenched jaw.

I shuffled, already feeling weak and fatigued from the bloodstone shawl, past the curtains. Two women met me. Neither smiled, which shouldn't have bothered me, but it did. I missed seeing smiling women. I missed my sisters and aunts and the other Wild Women. I stopped in front of the two women and unbuttoned my jeans, pushing them down to my ankles and stepping out of them. One woman quickly grabbed them up and folded them neatly to set on the stool, replacing the paper gown she'd pulled from the surface. I couldn't remove my shirt with the shawl still tied around my neck.

"My shawl," I muttered.

"First your panties," the woman holding the gown said. She wore a sour face and an ankle-length jean skirt.

I was a Wild Woman. Nakedness felt more comfortable to me than clothing. Yet in this moment, removing my panties felt like baring a piece of my soul to soul-eaters. I could only imagine what these women believed about me, how they found disgust in my existence. To bare myself completely to their harsh scrutiny turned my stomach. We stared at each other for a couple breaths before John ordered the women to move things along and fear flashed through their eyes. They were grown adults who had chosen to remain in this situation, living in this culture. But they also probably didn't know anything better existed, anything just as holy. I wiggled my cotton panties down my legs and handed them to the woman holding the paper gown.

She gave a curt nod and the other woman went to work unlocking and unfastening the bloodstone shawl. As she struggled to unlatch the thing without actually touching my evil skin, I considered my options. I could make a run for it once the heavy thing no longer held me down, but the bloodstone tattoo still kept me from using my huldra abilities. And how far would I get without my vines and branches?

I could still try to at least make it outside. I'd noticed surgical instruments on a metal stand beside the operating table. If I turned and ran, stabbed the Hunters on my way out of the OR and made my way upstairs, there was a possibility I'd get off the grounds alive. I hadn't seen many other people lurking around the main floor when we'd passed through.

But if I left, I'd have to leave without my mother and the harpies' mother. And if I wasn't successful, it would jeopardize my rescuers' plan to attack tomorrow morning.

The distinct heaviness of reality sunk in. I'd have to do this. I'd have to allow them to essentially torture me, steel my eggs, my daughters, to save my mother and other mothers.

The woman in a black ankle-length skirt who wore her long hair in a braid removed the shawl from my shoulders and carefully folded it, placing it on my jeans and panties. I breathed deeper, thankful for the lifted weight, the absence of the shawl. I pulled my shirt over my head and handed it off when both women gasped. I looked down to see what they saw. Were they shocked I didn't wear a bra?

And then I noticed it. I peered up at their faces, the disdain. One even curled her lip up at the sight. The sight of my bark, how it creeped from my lower back onto my sides. I felt the sudden urge to cover myself, to wrap my arms around my side and back away. The mermaids, Elaine and Sarah, popped into my mind, their expressions of awe drowning out these women's expressions of disgust.

I had nothing to be ashamed of and everything to be proud of. These women's ignorance would not determine my worthiness. I stood taller and turned on the ball of my foot to walk, stark naked, out from behind the curtain and right toward the operating table. They could find revulsion in the Wild form all they wanted; I wore my skin like the priceless heirloom it was.

John stood glaring at my act of insolence while the other Hunters shielded their eyes and turned away. I couldn't help but giggle. The two women quickly caught up to me and went to work dressing me in the paper robe like a child.

"Go ahead," John scoffed. "Laugh it up now. Soon you'll be begging for mercy."

I stiffened and swallowed. Once I was dressed, a Hunter moved to force me onto the table. I swatted his hands away and stared John in the eyes as I climbed onto the table myself, lay down, and closed my eyes.

Freyja, please keep me strong.

TWENTY-SIX

"RELAX YOUR MUSCLES. This will only hurt a little," the man in the white medical jacket assured me as he held a needle above my abdomen. I recognized him as the same man who'd taken my blood earlier.

He'd entered the room after I'd lain on the table to spite John, refusing to show how my wounded abs still ached with the controlled movement. He'd prepared my lower stomach area by cleansing it with yellow liquid and then placing blue paper cloths around the patch below my belly-button so that only a square of my skin showed. The women had covered my legs with a thin sheet before exiting the room.

The operating room looked much like the hall—stark white and clean. Except, it held a tray of sharp objects and against the far wall stood a metal cabinet.

I shivered with a chill that had nothing to do with temperature.

The man, whom I assumed was a doctor, plunged the large needle into my skin and deeper into my abdomen. Stinging and intense pressure ripped through my stomach. I screeched and flailed my arms to push him away, to escape. Freaking liar—it hurt way more than a little.

Two Hunters ran to each of my arms and held them at my sides.

Trapped. I was trapped and despite these men, I was alone. I closed my eyes against the pain. Warm, wet tears trickled dwindled down my cheeks. *Concentrate on the tears,* I begged myself. *Concentrate on how they feel along my skin.*

My breathing stilled for two seconds before the doctor shifted the needle while still inside me and I screamed again, clawing my nails into the table I lay upon.

"Almost done," the doctor said to the Hunters holding me down, reassuring them rather than me.

I stared at the ceiling to keep from watching the pain he inflicted on my body. The needle moved again, and I ground my teeth and squished my eyes shut to keep from crying out.

These Hunters, every one in this room, would pay for this.

The doctor walked out of my peripheral vision and I looked down. He was done. I exhaled and moved to rub my stomach, but the Hunters still held my arms in place.

"It'll be a few days before we know if these ova inseminate or not," the doctor said, messing with glass bottles in the cabinet. He bent to place a bottle and the needle he'd used into an insulated box on the ground I hadn't noticed before. "Until we know, keep doing what you've been doing. No pharmaceuticals or supplements of any kind, daily sunlight outside, and refrain from intense physical harm. At least until the ova take with the sperm."

He lifted the box and his white coat opened just enough for me to notice the dagger in its sheath, hanging from his belt.

"Are you the one who drugs the women too?" I let slip. "Before you sell them off to the highest bidders?"

The doctor rolled his eyes like I'd been nothing more than an annoying fly buzzing in his vicinity. "What are you going to do with it once the ova produce an embryo or two?" he asked John, the "it" being me.

John put his hands on his hips like they were discussing cars. "Oh, I don't know. Sell it? Use it for target practice? He hasn't decided."

He? John must have been referring to their leader, the elusive Hunter in charge of all American Hunters.

"Well," the doctor said, his shoulder pressed against the door to open it, "let me know. We could make top dollar selling its parts to a few fringe scientists I know."

John gave him a nod and the man in the white coat left the room, having just stolen my eggs as though he were doing nothing more than plucking fresh eggs from a hen house. I hoped he would be around tomorrow.

The two women entered the OR again and hurried to the space behind the curtain.

"Like we'd let humans know the existence of Wild Women," John scoffed under his breath. He motioned to me with a wave of his hand. "Get up and get your clothes back on."

They were done with me. They'd forced me down here, commanded that I strip my clothes from my body, that I lie on this cold table and allow them to pluck my future daughters from my womb, and now they were done with me.

I vowed to Freyja to make it my personal responsibility to see that each person in this OR burned in this building.

I eased from the table, not fast enough for John by the way he urged me to hurry. My stomach muscles burned as I twisted my torso to climb down. My breath hitched as I shuffled slowly toward the white curtain, toward the women and my clothing. My dagger wound smarted with the addition of the large needle prodding around my belly.

The women dressed me without touching my skin and without making a sound. After fastening the shawl, they presented me to the Hunters who stood on each of my two sides to escort our group from the OR. The bright circular light above the table shone down on the rolling tray and glinted off the scalpel sitting beside gloves and a glass bottle of solution.

I needed that scalpel.

My abs burned with each step, my uterus cramped, but I had no choice. I needed that weapon. A foot away from the tray, I took a step in front of the two Hunters, held my stomach, and heaved over, howling in pain. The commotion bought me a second to swipe the scalpel on my way upright. The Hunters rushed to my sides.

"Stop messing around and get moving," John demanded harshly.

The Hunters grabbed my elbows before I could slip the thing into my pocket. I held tight to the sharp metal object, its tip poking my inner wrist.

I almost wished the men would have dragged me back through the building and up the stairs the way they'd dragged me to the OR, with how badly I cramped each time I used my core muscles. But no such luck. They dropped me off at my room as though we'd just gone for a leisurely walk and I hadn't had a huge needle plunged into my abdomen. Call me cruel, but I dreamed of watching someone shove a needle into their testicles and then see how quickly they walked after that. Or hell, even their stomachs. But unless a magical revenge fairy showed up tonight, I highly doubted they'd get to experience what they'd put me through. I took comfort in knowing their ends would be much worse than a needle to the groin.

Alone in my locked cell of a room, I sat on my bed and considered my next move. I didn't want to do it, but what choice did I have? I unbuttoned my jeans and slowly pushed them down my legs, taking care in how much I used my core muscles for balance. I hoped to Freyja my abs didn't ache this badly tomorrow morning when the Wilds came calling for a fight. What I prepared to do would compromise me even more, affect my ability to use my right leg. If I didn't do it, though, I was as good as dead, unable to access my huldra. Goddess, I missed my huldra.

She'd become a real part of me, not some aspect of myself I hid away in shame. Anger and a sense of vindication rose through me. My lower back ached, my bark missing a key component of its existence. The tips of my fingers, my palms, the soles of my feet, tingled with want.

The Hunters had silenced my huldra, they'd tried to remove my power—called it evil and unsafe. I yearned to feel her pulsing through me, to grow vines from my fingers, branches from my palms, and roots from the soles of my feet.

I wanted my huldra back. I wanted all of me back.

I grabbed for the scalpel sitting beside me on the bed and carefully inserted it into my thigh, just deep enough to trace around the hastily tattooed new tiny red crosses at the edges of my identification number.

Blood met the blade and still I cut. I ignored the pain and let raw anger push my hand to press on, to go deeper, to cut their handiwork out from my skin. And when the red crosses were nothing more than bits of bloody skin on the wooden floor beside the foot of my bed, something in me demanded more.

My huldra.

She was waking up.

And she was pissed.

Tomorrow, I would fight for my freedom and for the freedom of those I cared about. I wanted nothing belonging to the Hunters on my body, nothing symbolizing the years of oppression my kind had lived under by their hands. The identification numbers they'd tattooed into my thigh after I'd had my first menstrual cycle covered a larger portion than their newest red crosses. And while I'd tattooed tree branches over their numbers a while ago, in an act of rebellion, that was no longer enough.

I sucked in a breath and pressed the shiny, sharp metal to the top edge of where the first number started, and drew it down, past the other numbers, to create a box of blood. My heart beat sped, along with my anxious need to get them off of me. Vines slowly protruded from the tips of my fingers, and the scalpel lost its shine, the metal covered in slick, warm blood, but I kept cutting. As the last piece of my numbered flesh fell away and left the fatty flesh beneath, I dropped the scalpel and closed my eyes.

My huldra thrummed inside me, the sight of my own blood amping up her killer desires, her need for revenge. Goddess, I loved her.

"Thank you, Freyja," I whispered, waving my hands in front of me while vines grew from my fingers and wound their way up my wrists.

"I see you're feeling more yourself," Drosera said before her body came fully into view, as though she stepped out of some unseen existence and into the seen. She stood beside the window, wearing the same animal skin skirt she'd been wearing last time she visited. Her messy hair hung in knots, part of it pulled back with plant roots and twigs.

"They took my eggs," I uttered, returning my focus to my hands, woozy with the intense pain and loss of blood, but mostly mesmerized by my vines.

"Yes, and we shall burn them down along with this building," she responded. When that didn't garner my attention, she added, "You have more eggs."

I peered up at her. "Do I though?" I asked. "I don't know how many of mine they took, but huldra only have one daughter each. What if they stole my ability to have my own daughter, Drosera?" Although, they'd taken my mother after she'd had me and kept her for twenty years, so apparently she had more than one egg. But how many more?

I hadn't realized how much that idea upset me until the rusalka walked closer and placed a hand on my shoulder. "You are experiencing a reality that is not yet yours, again," she warned. "Think on what is to come, not what has yet to be seen."

Her words did nothing to calm my racing mind. We couldn't know the average amount of eggs Wild Women, and huldra in particular, carried; there'd never been scientific studies. The scientific community didn't even know we existed, outside of Hunter medical professionals and I figured their goal had more to do with how to create a hybrid warrior and less to do with the Wild Women make-up.

Unless.

"Do you think the Hunters know how many eggs we have?" I asked the rusalka. "The ones who've done studies on our reproductive systems enough to piece together how to create hybrids?"

Drosera's sneer shocked me. Very rarely had I seen a rusalka show much of any outward emotion. "They have dissected Wild Women, yes. But studies done on living beings in captivity are always skewed. The body changes in captivity; it reverts to survival mode."

"So there's no real way to find out if I can have a daughter," I said, looking back to my vines, the way they created bracelets along my arm. The wooziness edged away with Drosera's touch.

"I cannot reveal too much; it is not our way. But do not fear. A daughter will come." She rubbed my shoulder and I peered up from my vines. "We need to discuss tomorrow. The harpy ancestors have rejected our invitation to take down the descendants of their oppressors."

"I had no idea having dead Wilds take up arms was even an option," I remarked.

"They would have been a great asset, but they have declined, and we will continue on," she said, as though she simply briefed me on a fact and moved on to the next. She looked to my naked and blood-smeared thigh. "Are you able to fight?"

TWENTY-SEVEN

"Yes, I will," I answered Drosera's question, meeting her eyes. My huldra stirred in excitement. "I will definitely be able to fight tomorrow." Even if I had to limp my way to each Hunter and get close enough to shove branches through his heart and vines around his neck, I'd do it.

"Good," she said, removing her hand from my shoulder. She focusing on the blood stone shawl the women had left folded neatly on the dresser. Drosera ran her dirty fingers across the thing. "The harpy will break this from your body as a signal to begin. We will be waiting in the tree line outside the fencing, hidden from the cameras."

"How?" I asked. "She's stuck in a cage when she's out there."

"She will call you over, tear this horrid thing from you, and you'll in turn use your abilities to release her." Drosera turned and eyed my blank room. "The rogue Hunter has agreed to bring your mother out."

I sighed with relief. "That was my next question."

Drosera smiled. "I know."

Two emotional expressions from a rusalka in one discussion. Must have been a record.

Her smile dropped. "There is something else we must discuss this night."

"Okay?" I shifted on the bed to rest my back against the headboard and stretch my legs out in front of me.

"Your coterie and Marcus have been reading through the files in your briefcase," she started.

I knew the one she referred to. After taking down the Washington Hunter complex, I'd started gathering information on the human trafficking cases I thought were connected to the Hunters, Clarisse, and Samuel Woodry—the last bail jumper I'd had the joy of hunting down and taking in before everything went to shit. That briefcase had gone everywhere with me, up until the day I was captured, thankfully. If the Hunter leaders learned how much I knew about their human trafficking operation they'd forego the whole hybrid thing and kill me execution style.

Drosera continued, "They have been adding more to the files and piecing together a case to present to the local police force investigators as well as local and major news stations."

I stilled. "Marcus is going to out the whole Hunter establishment?"

"He is," she said. "Along with himself."

I sat up straighter and hissed as a hot shot of pain ripped through my ab muscles. "But he's done nothing wrong, why out himself?"

"He says either he reveals himself or another arrested Hunter will reveal him. Also, it will increase his believability."

"But they'll know he's supernatural and run tests on him," I argued. Every supernatural lived with the hidden, but very real, fear of finding themselves under the knife and microscope of an eager human scientist searching for answers. It had been one way the Hunters were able to control us—their rules were to safeguard us from that exact reality...or so they said.

"We do not know what the humans will do, but he is willing to place himself at risk to save many," she stated with no inflection of any kind.

"Did you try to talk him out of it?" I asked.

She tilted her head in confusion. "A person's decision is their own."

Not when that person is the one I'd chosen to spend my future with, the one able to break through my carefully constructed walls and reach my heart to hold it tenderly to his own. That person's decision was not his own.

But I doubted Drosera would understand, so I pressed on. "What kind of evidence is Marcus collecting? Other than his own word and the existence of this complex?" Sure, he could have the officials all over the North Carolina Hunters, but what about the others? If they didn't go after every American Hunter, the Hunters in higher government offices, and in the police force, would make everything Marcus said and found go away. It was one reason Wild Women of the country never went to the police—they knew it'd do more harm to themselves than good. I hoped Marcus wasn't making the same mistake.

"Heather wore a camera to the coven circle meeting she attended," Drosera said. "The video shows an undercover Hunter's woman lying about leaving the sexist confines of religion and embracing the Wiccan ways of female freedom."

"Uh, that's not evidence, Drosera."

"Marcus said the same. The footage of the woman offering to host the next circle, only for the most devout of witches, at her property, is the damning evidence."

"True," I responded in thought. "It shows the missing link, the connection between the online chat group and the circles, how they lure the women in, and how they pick them." Their evidence would also link Samuel Woodry, seeing as the barista he'd hit on in front of me, who'd also filed a police report of harassment by him, fit the Hunters' criteria for their trafficking victims. Maybe with this new evidence they'd be able to get Samuel to talk, to share everything he knew about them.

"I know where the victims are being held," I added.

The woman's cries from the other side of the door in the underground hallway John and the two Hunters had escorted me through tonight gave me chills just thinking about, just imagining the young woman's terror and possible future.

"That's the best evidence. The women themselves can point fingers at the Hunters. I'm sure there's captured women from each state where there's a complex who can indict their local Hunter groups. Although," I said, remembering who exactly we dealt with and how many times they'd escaped legal scrutiny and gone under the radar, "we'll need all the information we can get to tie everything together and prove it without a reasonable doubt."

Minutes of silence hung in the room and I waited to hear Drosera's words in my mind, or the massaging fingers within my skull. "Clarisse would have given solid evidence if we'd promised to change her," I said. The woman had taken the rap for a group she didn't even want to be a part of. I could only imagine what she'd do to gain access, or what she believed would be the ability to gain access, to our Wild Women kind.

Drosera's lip raised to a smirk. A first, from what I'd seen. "Clarisse is gone from here."

"Did you enjoy her death?" I asked without blame or shame. We'd promised Clarisse she'd get what was coming to her when she least expected it. The rusalki followed through with that promise.

Drosera's smirk morphed into the biggest smile I'd seen on her. "We accomplished what had to be done."

"Yeah you did," I joked. "But seriously, I only saw the thing from a near-human perspective." I'd had the blood shawl draped over me, and even if I hadn't, I doubted my huldra would have sensed the rusalki near if they hadn't wanted to show themselves. "Who all was there? Who held the scissors? And why now, before the attack?"

"We were all present," she answered, a smile still pulling at her lips in a way that proved the sweetness of revenge. "Even our missing sisters who have recently rejoined our coven. To take care of old business, before taking care of new business, is our way. Clarisse was old business—a promise to be upheld." She paused. "Azalea held the scissors, as was her right."

"Ha!" I said, during a moment of feeling like maybe the world was a place of fairness, maybe those who'd done wrong *did* end up paying in the end. Clarisse had helped in the trafficking of countless human women, not to mention her role in my sister's imprisonment and her murdering of Azalea. "I knew it!"

Drosera's smile dropped and she peered toward the door. "I must leave."

"Wait," I said, partly because I wanted more information and partly because I didn't want to be left alone. "I need to make sure the human women get out alive tomorrow, and I don't know how to do that while I'm fighting. Can you tell that rogue Hunter to come to me tonight?"

"The rogues' first priority is the human women, not the Wild Women," Drosera reminded me. "Many do not care how our kind have been treated, only the human women."

"But does it really matter if our end goal is met?" I asked. "I just want to make sure they're on board to help the humans tomorrow."

Drosera took a step closer to me. "They cannot know when we plan to attack, not the rogues who still live among their Hunter brothers. They may change their minds and alert their brotherhood. It is too risky."

I considered the parameters I had to work within. "Okay, I won't let him know. But I'd still like to talk to him tonight."

"I guarantee nothing," Drosera said, her image fading from existence until she was nothing more than a silhouette of light and then nothing at all.

Drosera guaranteed nothing, but she came through all the same. Thankfully, by the time the rogue Hunter who'd told me Marcus was well and fine unlocked my door and crept into my room, I'd cleaned up all the blood and already climbed under the covers. If the rusalki didn't fully trust these rogue Hunters, I wouldn't either, which meant he didn't need to see my mutilated thigh, my lack of identification number and bloodstone addition. He didn't need to know I now operated on full huldra capacity. And there was no way my raw, wounded thigh was ready to be covered by tight jeans. Even the sheets' slight movements across my open skin caused my breath to hitch and my sore abs to tighten. Why couldn't one of my abilities be to heal immediately?

The large, dark Hunter shut the bedroom door behind him with a muffled clink. "Rod said you needed to talk to me," he stated without inflection of any kind.

This time, my dark room posed no hindrance in my seeing the man, the way he stood rigid and his blank facial expression. This time I could smell the rotten scent of his indignation for me and see how much he really didn't want to be here—in my room or this Hunter complex. Was he even from North Carolina or had my band of Wild sisters displaced him from his home complex and brought him to this one? His voice lacked a southern accent.

So many questions whirled around my mind, but only a small percentage were safe to ask, and even then, I'd have to carefully choose my words.

"Thanks for coming," I started, despite his obvious irritation by my presence. "I wanted to see if you knew much about the human women being held here."

He shifted his weight from one leg to the other and stuck his hands into his pockets. "I do."

"Is that why you were brought here?" I asked, hoping to reach a soft spot of his and use it to get information.

"It's one reason," he answered.

Ugh, this guy wasn't giving me much to go on. He held onto his information like his life depended on it, which it kind of did.

"Is their safety a priority of yours?" I said.

"Yes."

"Okay, good." I slouched more in my bed, trying to use body language to draw the Hunter out of his tightly confined protective shell. My huldra couldn't help but think of ways to lure him in. "And you know where they're at, to get them out when the time arises? Are there others who feel the same way you do?"

"Why? Is there something coming I should know about and be prepared for?" he asked.

I kept from shaking my finger at him and letting him know he didn't get to ignore my questions to ask his own. This would be a give and take or nothing at all. Seriously. You could take the Hunter out of the complex, but you couldn't take the entitlement out of the Hunter.

Wait. No, that wasn't right. We *were* still in the complex and Marcus had never displayed such a sense of entitlement.

I brushed aside the needless rabbit trails from my thoughts. Clearly, my mind needed a good rest.

"No, I'm not aware of anything coming you should know about. But you didn't answer my questions," I reminded.

He grumbled. "Of course there's others who feel the same way I do. And yes, we know where they're being held. It's no secret."

I thought to ask how the operation worked, who was in charge of the human trafficking part and when were the latest group of women supposed to be shipped out. Had they already found buyers? But I figured none of that mattered because they'd be free and telling the police everything tomorrow anyhow. At least I hoped. And plus, I doubted this Hunter would tell me anyway.

"Okay, thank you," I said, laying down in the bed, signaling we were done.

He seemed more than happy to leave. But before he touched the doorknob, he turned and whispered. "If you're planning anything for any time soon, I'd highly advise against it." When I didn't respond— even though everything in me wanted to—he went on. "They aren't only using the human women to sell off to the highest bidder. And if you think you'll succeed in taking on the beings in this complex, you're wrong. You have no idea who and what they've got on their side. No idea."

The Hunter left my room and locked my door behind him.

The sleep I'd planned to get to heal my mind and my thigh...it now seemed like nothing more than a ship tossed upon thrashing waves of worry and doubt. What had he meant? Which other beings, other than Hunters, humans, and Wild Women did they have locked up in this complex? I thought of the etchings on the cabin door where Shawna had been held at the Washington Hunter complex. Marcus had told me the door displayed an array of supernatural beings, many of which I'd never known existed.

I'd since met incubi, who'd been the love children of a succubus and a vampire long ago. Which led me to my next question, if incubi and vampires were real, what other folkloric monsters roamed the world? And which ones were in cahoots with the Hunters?

TWENTY-EIGHT

THE HARPIES' large historical bootlegger house felt cramped with the number of Wild Women filling the spaces. Groups convened in the living room, the kitchen, the front room, and the dining area. They shared information and tactics and stories. Neither of the xana showed up, Conchita or Avera. I assumed they were already on a plane headed home to Spain, seeing as I wasn't the long-lost child of Avera and therefore our battle against the Hunters failed to grab their attention.

I stood from the couch to stretch my legs. "I'll be right back," I told Shawna, who sat on the couch in the living room, listening to Drosera re-explain her latest conversation with Faline to their coterie. Shawna's little white dog slept on her lap and only looked up when Shawna moved enough to give me a nod.

I appreciated Drosera filling us in, but I couldn't listen in a second time. I didn't need the reminder of my inability to get to Faline right at this moment. I'd have to see her in the morning as I fought my way into the complex and she fought her way out. And on top of it all, knowing she'd cut up her thigh and they'd stuck a needle in her abdomen, I worried for her safety and strength. Would she be able to fight at the capacity necessary to get out alive?

But what bothered me the most, made me want to head down to

the complex right now and bust through the doors, my dagger swinging, was what Drosera and her sisters felt in the complex when they'd visited to take Clarisse's life. She'd said she hadn't told Faline because they couldn't be sure why they'd felt it. Something had been different, a new presence—one they'd never experienced before—in the complex entry earlier today, and its energy still lingered. An energy they believed wasn't human, Hunter, or incubus and was incredibly male and aggressive. She'd mentioned it to the coterie and me, hoping I'd know what they may have felt. And I wished I had, but an aggressive non-human male with the energy similar to water and the scent of seaweed rang no recollection bells for me. It just pissed me off that I couldn't get Faline tonight, that I had to wait for tomorrow, knowing other males roamed the halls outside her door.

Renee burst into the house, revealing the dark night outside. She slammed the door against the cold wind and slumped her bag and purse on the entry table. "Eonza has given birth to her baby girl," she announced, her cheeks flushed and hair frizzy.

The house erupted in excitement as Wild Women made their way to Renee, squeezing through openings connecting rooms like bottlenecks, full of questions about the size and appearance of the new harpy baby.

Renee regaled them with details. "Or, I mean the egg. It was my first harpy birth, so I'm used to saying baby. The egg was much smaller than a newborn huldra baby, and came out a soft green, gorgeous." She paused in thought. "I suppose that's how they name their daughters, based on the color of their egg at birth, because they'd mentioned different stones of a similar color and tried those names on their tongues." She laughed. The other Wild Women hung on her every word. "I didn't hide my shock very well. They said once her egg cracks and she comes out, her feathers will be soft and fluffy and the color of her egg's shell. Then her feathers will fall out and smooth skin will replace them all." She sighed and made her way to the kitchen, finding a chair to rest her body. "So strangely amazing."

A nagin woman gave Renee a glass of water. "When will Eonza be back to normal?"

Renee drank deeply before answering. "She'll need to rest in the nest they've created. She and her sisters will take turns keeping the egg warm until the baby girl is strong enough to crack through the shell."

"Will none of them fight with us tomorrow?" the nagin, Anwen, asked.

Renee sighed and leaned back in the wooden chair. "Their mother, Rose, is still at the complex. Eonza will stay behind with the egg while the others join the fight. Rose certainly has a gift to come home to."

She finished her water. "And did you know Clarisse is dead? The Hunter's woman? I heard it on the news while Eonza was in labor. The police found her body in the woods, from an anonymous tip. They're still deeming her the leader of the human trafficking ring, so they're theorizing the parent of a missing girl found and killed her, or maybe a deal went south with some foreign buyers."

"The rusalki killed her," I said. "But I'd bet my motorcycle the Hunters used her death to their advantage to make the cops think the whole human trafficking thing is over, ended with her." I decided to add what I'd discussed earlier with her coterie and the rusalki while she'd been helping a laboring harpy. "I'm going to call the local police department, as well as the FBI and a few local and national television stations after we get to the complex. That way if there's any Hunters among any one of those groups, they won't have time to be notified of our plan. I'll call, give them the location of the complex and some key information about the human trafficking, and hopefully by the time we've leveled the place, the truth will be out about these missing women."

"The news people can't show up when we are there," an echidna said, her tone assertive and wary at the same time.

"None of us can be seen," Anwen, a nagin, agreed.

"I know," I assured them. "I plan on staying behind."

Drosera and her sisters didn't seem shocked, but the huldra coterie shook their heads. Yeah, I hadn't mentioned that part in our earlier discussion. Shawna's eyes fill with tears. She stood beside the kitchen table and held her dog tighter.

I hadn't meant to let them know my plan, to stay after and make sure my brethren paid for their transgressions, to out the elusive leader in charge of all the American Hunters, and make sure he was brought to justice. But the random sharing moment helped to solidify my decision. Sometimes, speaking the words of the heart rather than the mind helped more than it hurt.

"I have to," I told Shawna.

"What about Faline?" she asked. "She won't agree to it."

"She knows," Drosera answered. The rusalki must have read my thoughts last time we'd talked about this. I wondered how Faline reacted when they told her.

Shawna shook her head. "There's got to be another way."

"I can't think of one," I said honestly. "If we want to know the Hunters are outed for good, stricken from their high places in government and law enforcement, unable to hurt you all ever again, I have to be the one to do it."

I'd made the decision last night in the clearing, before I spoke to the rogue Hunters about their dedication to the cause, told them how they'd be tested and possibly change their minds when push came to shove, how they'd have to live with themselves long after they had washed their brothers' blood from their hands. I'd said those things because I knew the heartache. I'd let my father go that day in Oregon, when I shouldn't have. And Faline, my lover and friend and hopefully life partner, was a Wild Woman. If any ex-Hunter had enough inspiration to stand against his own father, it was me. And in a moment of weakness, I had fallen. I couldn't ask another brother to stand strong, to not give in, when law enforcement came calling and wanted the names of his loved ones to indict. I had failed once. I would not fail again.

TWENTY-NINE

THE MOMENT the heavy footfalls of boots reverberated along the stairs that led to the hallway outside my bedroom door, I started the process of getting out of bed. Sleep had been impossible, so I'd spent the night stretching my muscles, trying not to let my abs and thigh stiffen from inactivity due to soreness. Before the sun came up, I'd used a piece of torn bed sheet to wrap my thigh and keep it from leaking through, then pulled on my jeans.

Did my mother and Rose already remove their tattoos? Did they even have them? The Hunters hadn't given Shawna one. Maybe they reserved that honor for the leaders of revolutions. That particular honor didn't feel too wonderful as I hobbled around the bed, tidying it up enough to keep the Hunters or their women from noticing the missing strips of sheet and blood stains.

I quickly double-checked my hands to make sure I'd cleaned my blood from beneath my fingers well enough to keep from bringing suspicion upon myself.

I blamed my lack of sleep on night-before-battle jitters, but I couldn't deny the other part of the equation—the return of my huldra abilities. As though someone had turned the volume up, noises I'd always just been used to became blaring irritants. What had once been simply white noise—floor boards creaking, wind in the trees, birds calling out warnings—had taken on a whole new threat while I lay in bed, wishing my leg would stop pulsating and morning would hurry up and come.

But now morning was here and so were the Hunters.

I had no choice but to go with them to the courtyard and meet my fate.

A woman entered my room first, one of the women who'd met me behind the white curtain yesterday before my procedure. She wore a different colored jean skirt today, a darker one, with a black top. In a twisted sort of way, I wondered if she unconsciously knew she'd be getting her own blood on her clothes today. Her eyes bounced around my room to find my shawl. She unfolded it and, without touching me, placed it over my shoulders to clasp around my neck. She was a master at not making eye contact, clearly someone who had years of eye aversion practice under her belt.

The bloodstone shawl weighed heavily across my shoulders, and I slumped lower without trying. I hated the thing, a piece of clothing that carried its own secret identity as a cage woven within its threads.

Two Hunters stood outside my door, which was cracked open, while the woman worked. She cleared her throat once she finished preparing me, and on cue the men entered to retrieve me. The woman scurried out and away, and my more merciful self hoped she had an appointment to get to or some reason to leave this property in the next twenty minutes or so.

For as secret as the rogue Hunter said my being here was, they sure did use a lot of Hunters to transport me. Since arriving here, I hadn't seen one Hunter more than a couple times, other than the rogue guy and John. I breathed deeply and caught faint traces of a very non-Hunter scent. Damn, if it weren't for the bloodstone shawl I'd probably be able to get a better idea of the odd smell. These particular Hunters had been near the sea recently, or had eaten sushi, because I picked up faint traces of salt water and seaweed.

The mermaids. I glanced up and down the hallway. Were there mermaids here, working with the Hunters, betraying us on a whole new level? They were probably talking to John, in his stupid temporary office, giving away all of our secrets and plans.

"Where's John?" I asked, although the Hunter leader rarely escorted me to the courtyard. Still, the moment shit went sideways I hoped he'd be nearby for me to plunge my branches into. And if it came down to fighting my mermaid foes, I was game.

One Hunter stared forward as if I hadn't made a peep. The other gave me the death glare and shook his head.

All right, then.

I concentrated on pretending my thigh didn't burn each time the scabs pulled to reach the next step as we headed down the stairs. To keep them from noticing the real reason behind my stiffness, I accentuated the soreness of my abdomen, grabbing it whenever I accidently moved wrong or sucked in a breath to keep from cussing.

The Hunters didn't seem to care either way, and didn't slow down for me either. Heartless bastards.

With little care for my physical state, the Hunter on my right opened the door to the

courtyard and shoved me out of it. It slammed behind me with finality. I nearly fell onto the dirty cobblestone, but righted myself just in time, which my abdomen did not like at all.

"You okay?" Rose whispered.

I glanced at the harpy in her cage. Her brownish-blonde hair sat bone-straight atop her shoulders.

"They took my eggs," I said, nonchalantly, as I hobbled over to her.

Her green eyes softened in a way I'd never seen on a harpy. "I'm sorry. I know how much that hurts...and it's more than physical pain."

"It is," I agreed. But I couldn't think on that right now; it would get me down in a way I couldn't afford at the moment.

"And then *I* took my tattoo," I added in a whisper, cautious of any cameras or listening devices.

Rose gave one nod, returning to her distant, harpy self. "That will help."

I neared her cage and leaned in. "Did they give you a bloodstone tattoo, too?"

She shook her head.

"Then why do you stay in that cage? Why don't you bust out of there and fly away?"

She sighed. "They have cameras. I tried once, when I first arrived. They came out before I could untangle myself from the cage wires I'd ripped." She pointed her nose to the top left portion of the cage where a quick repair job was made obvious by the contrast of new silver wire against the slightly rusty-looking chain link wiring of the rest of the cage. "After that, they broke my wings and ensured that they didn't heal correctly. I cannot fly. And they began using the bloodstone shackles. I believe their use of bloodstone ink in tattoos is relatively new."

It occurred to me that since the bloodstone worked on Rose, she had yet to reach menopause. I wondered if they still took her eggs, but my curiosity wasn't worth bringing up a possibly painful subject for her, not after finding out about her wings. "I'm sorry they broke your wings," I said, truly sorry for her. I couldn't imagine losing the ability to jump through trees. I'd only been forced to go a couple days without my huldra and I thought I'd lose my mind.

"We each pay our price," she uttered.

Unfortunately, I knew exactly what she meant. Whether we kept our heads down in obedience, like the Hunters' women had when undressing and dressing me, or whether we rebelled, we each carried scars forged by the Hunters. Some lived with deeper scars, burned into their minds. Others could point them out along their skin. Oppression is like a box of bricks placed on the backs of the oppressed as they're forced to continue on with their lives despite the box cutting into their flesh, breaking their backs, and making them believe they're weak for not being able to match pace to those who aren't carrying a box of bricks.

"Drosera didn't tell me when—"

"Shh!" Rose commanded and shot a glance at the camera perched at the edge of the roof, pointed down at her cage.

Goddess, could I have felt any stupider? Yesterday my mother had insisted we talk behind the one tree in the courtyard because we were being watched and our lips were probably being read, if they didn't already have another device catching the sounds of the yard. Nerves and pain skewed my ability to think straight.

Rose faced away from the camera and whispered under her breath, "You will know when."

I strode away from her cage, to keep from looking too suspicious, and sat with my back to the maple tree living in the middle of the courtyard, out of view of the camera, facing the forest beyond the fence. I ran my fingers along the dark ridges of its bark and wished I could reach my roots into the ground and connect, ask the tree what it had been like having to live among Hunters who had no appreciation for nature, who saw nature as a thing to dominate and subdue. I discretely removed my boots. The soles of my feet ached to press into the moist dirt, to communicate with the earth. I tried, too, but only received a headache for my troubles. Damn bloodstone shawl.

An odd echo, one that didn't sound like it naturally came from the woods, resonated from deep from within the forest. I squinted to see if any Wilds waited past the tree line and hoped to spot my coterie and Marcus. I saw nothing outside the ordinary.

The door to the building swung open with a creak and I peeked around the trunk of the tree. My mother, a bloodstone shawl wrapped around her shoulders, ambled into the courtyard and paused to take it all in.

I hated not knowing the details of today's attack. I liked to have exit strategies in place, layers of what-ifs at my disposal, ready to switch plans up at any time. I couldn't be sure why Drosera chose not to fill me in, but I hoped it was to keep the strategy safe and not because there was no definite plan. No, that didn't make sense. My tired mind played tricks on me, gave me a defeatist attitude. I couldn't let it.

I stood and met my mother halfway between the building and the tree. Rose watched us like a hawk, her unblinking eyes taking everything in. My mother gave me a half-smile and walked right past me, toward Rose. I followed, thoroughly confused. My huldra shook with anticipation; she too hated not knowing our next move.

"Faline," my mother said when we reached the cage. Rose looked away and watched the monastery door. "You are the one, you've always been the one."

I opened my mouth to respond, to ask for clarification, but my mother's raised eyebrows and sharp eyes told me to stay quiet. All these years away from her and I still knew *that* look.

"I'd tried to tell you through my stories to you, in a way that would keep you from being a target. I'd first connected with an ancestor when I was pregnant with you. Your father was a forest ranger, and we'd take long hikes through the Washington woods. We'd fallen in love quickly, and I'd told him of my huldra ancestry." Her smile reached her eyes as they softened. "He'd been studying the secrets of trees, their root systems and how they communicated. It's why he visited our state. He was ahead of his time." She brushed her tender memories away with a wave of her hand. "It had been his idea for me to try to connect with the tree roots, to learn more about them. And I was fairly successful, but the day I found an ancestor, I'll never forget. She felt you within me and gave me a promise: If I agreed to pass our truths along to you, she would reveal them to me. It was risky and would endanger my life, but I could break the cycle of oppression by raising my daughter to stand in her truth, to embrace her power. It's why the Hunters chose to take me over my sisters, why they'd tried to take you over your sisters. Somehow they'd figured it out and they sought the strength we carried in our knowing."

I looked down at my clenched fists and relaxed my shaking hands. The mermaids had told me a tree woman would save the American Wild Women. Even the Hunters had a prophesy of a Wild who would rise up against them. "Why me, though?" I whispered. "What's different about me?"

My mother released a breath of laughter. She held my shaking hands in her still ones. "You were not born in chains the way the others were, yet you believed you had been. Because of this, your mind was able to break free from the Hunters' brainwashing, and yet you still had the oppressive experiences to fuel your fire."

She released my hands and wrapped her arms around my shoulders. "I love you," she whispered into my ear before shoving my back into the harpy's cage. "Now burn bright, my daughter, burn!"

A sharp talon reached through a square in the chain link cage and ripped at the neckline of my blood stone shawl, tearing skin from my neck in the process. The shawl fell to my feet and I kicked it away from us both. Suddenly the full capacity of my huldra abilities careened into me.

Vines grew from my fingertips and branches pierced outward, through the flesh of my palms.

An ear-piercing alarm blared from the Hunters' complex.

Shouts and screams from the forest rang through the trees.

Rose tore my mother's shawl from her shoulders and she sprang onto the top of Rose's cage, pulling back the wiring at the weak spot where new wire had been spiraled in to the old.

An army of Wild Women ran, flew, and slithered from the forest, toward the courtyard. Hunters burst through the door behind me in droves, their daggers drawn, and muscles twitching and growing. I stood between the two groups, unsure which to head for.

I spun on the ball of my foot toward the Hunters. With a blood curdling warrior cry, and my hands out in front of me, branches at the ready, I ran toward my enemies.

THIRTY

Two harpies, Lapis and Azul, arrived first, landing near their mother's cage and pulling her out from the top. Lapis left with Rose, clinging to her mother as she soared toward the woods. Azul grabbed my mother and flew them both toward the building, gaining speed on me. The two Wilds dropped from the sky. We attacked at the same time, three Wilds amidst a blur of black cargos and swiping daggers.

With my mother and Rose free from their confines, I shouted to Lapis and Azul, "I'm going in to get the women!"

My mother's greenish yellow vines shot from her fingers. She flicked her wrists so quickly, I barely saw her hands clearly. She choked out two Hunters who'd made it their mission to block me from the wooden door.

The fencing behind us crashed to the ground as Wilds and what had to be ex-Hunters and incubi tromped the chain link fencing and barbed wire into the moist dirt. A ball of fire flew over my head and landed to the right of the door seconds before I'd reached to open it. I turned to see where it came from. There were still innocent lives inside; we couldn't burn the place down yet! The group of alae we'd met in the rusalki's woods ran toward the building, each holding handfuls of fire and taking turns throwing their flames at the Hunters and the building. I looked up and noticed a portion of the roof in flames.

"Faline!" His voice rang out over the others, over the shouting and cursing and screaming. I searched the crowd for Marcus, turning away from the building and toward the battlegrounds that had been a quiet unkempt courtyard moments before.

"Marcus?" I yelled, zig-zagging through the fighting and the killing. "Marcus?"

"Faline!"

"I'm here, Marcus! I'm here!" I scanned the crowd in search of my ex-Hunter like my life depended on it.

He broke free from a pocket of men who looked to be Hunters, but without the black uniforms. Marcus ran for me, shoving his enemies out of his way. He caught me up in his arms and lifted me from the ground, wrapping his hands around my back and squeezing. "Thank God," he said on a whispered prayer. "Thank God."

With my feet off the ground, my lips reached his face and I planted a long-awaited kiss on his mouth. My vine-covered fingers wove through his dark hair. I pulled away and kissed his cheeks, his forehead, his lips again. His nearness lessened the ache in my abs and thigh.

Another ball of flames hit the building.

"I know where the women are. We have to get them before the house burns down," I pleaded.

He gave a nod and ran, with me still in his arms, toward the monastery. I didn't push off of him, and the other Hunters didn't seem to think it was worth stopping a Hunter, out of uniform, carrying a Wild Woman back into the complex. He flung open the door and ran through the first level hallway, past the stairs leading to my upstairs bedroom cell.

"Let me down," I finally shrieked with a laugh. "It'll be faster."

He gently dropped me and I grabbed his hand. "This way!"

We ran through the entry, across the tiled floor, and to the elevator. I slammed my hand onto the basement level button beside the elevator, but nothing happened.

"Lockdown," Marcus said. "Elevators won't work."

Clinging to my hand, he pulled me—neither of us wanted to let go of the other—to a door twenty feet away from the elevator on the left side, toward another hallway out of the entry. He swung the door open and led me through to a set of stairs leading both down and up. We descended the steps, two at a time.

"Is the basement level locked?" he asked past his panting.

"I don't know," I responded, a little fear-stricken. What if we'd done all of this and couldn't get the women out safely? Parts of this building were already on fire. Soon all of it would be, and I highly doubted Hunters would rush back into a flaming building to save women they believed were going to burn in hell anyway.

We reached the bottom level and Marcus tried the push handle on the white metal door. We breathed a sigh of relief when it opened without a problem.

"This way!" I led him through the white basement hall, sterile and uninviting, along the path I'd taken only the night before.

We turned a corner to stare into the eyes of a huge Hunter guarding the corridor, who I hadn't seen last time I was here.

Doors hiding trapped women lined the walls and my stomach tightened.

"Hello?" the shaking voice of a woman called. "Is there anybody out there?"

Another voice cried from the door on the opposite side. "Please, help us. We've been taken. Help us."

The Hunter stood in the middle of the hall and widened his legs as though challenging us. Marcus and I shared a quick glance before running, full speed, at the Hunter. The male in all black brandished his dagger, but didn't move from his place. Marcus got to him before me and barreled into him, shoving him farther back down the hall, away from the doors where the women's shouts came from.

I tried to turn the knob on both doors; neither would work. "The doors are locked," I told the women now frantically trying to turn the knobs from the inside.

I looked to Marcus who took a fist to the face before returning a punch to the Hunter's gut and then a swift heel to the Hunter's shin.

The Hunter tripped backwards and Marcus took that opportunity to brandish his own dagger and finish the job.

"Move," Marcus told me, wiping his blade on the dead Hunter's shirt before standing. I backed up. He repeated himself, louder, to the women in the room. He positioned his right forearm out in front of him as a barrier. "One, two, three!" On three he ran and shoved his weight into the metal door. The thing popped off its hinges and fell to the cement ground with a loud clang.

I ran in to assist the women and he turned to knock down the other door.

"Are there any more of you here, other than these two rooms?" I asked the women, peering around the cell to take in their living conditions of squalor. A bucket wedged into a corner for waste, and sleeping pads and blankets covered the hard floor. I fought from shielding my nose to block the intense stench.

"I don't know," a young woman said. She clung to the black sweater wrapped tightly around her. "We came for a special moon ritual, and when the girl invited us in, a bunch of men grabbed us and threw us down here, said witches shouldn't be suffered to live, so they were doing us a favor by not burning us at the stake."

A new anger raged in my gut and sped my pulse. "No," I seethed. "You won't be the ones burning today."

I ran out to the hallway where Marcus escorted women from the other cell. "They don't know if there's anymore down here," I told him.

"These women don't either. They just came for a ritual," he said.

We went to work, checked the rest of the doors lining the hallway, the locked ones without windows. Only one other held women. Those females looked to have been here the longest, their clothes torn and dirty, their waste bucket full to brimming. I couldn't enter the space without gagging.

"Follow me!" I instructed the group. Marcus hung back to protect them from behind. I led them through the hall and toward the stairs. One limped and I grabbed her, throwing my arm under her side and hoisting her up enough to walk with me.

We made it up the stairs to the main level of the huge house and I held the stairwell door open for the women to pass through. "Down the hall, to the front door," I repeated to every new group of women that passed.

Marcus held the door for me and we walked through together, behind the women quietly trying to escape the house of hell.

Without the bloodstone tattoo or shawl to inhibit my huldra abilities, the scent of seaweed and saltwater hung much heavier in the house, especially the entryway. I almost asked the human women if they smelled it too.

"Here," Marcus told them as he opened the great front double doors and stuck his head out to look around. "It's clear. For now." He pulled his head back in and addressed the women. "I'll open this door again and I want you all to run. Those of you who can, help those who can't. Run straight down the driveway. You'll see an iron gate. Either open it or climb over it, but keep going until you're met by cops. They're on their way."

I hadn't thought of the gate, but as long as the women weren't in the house, they'd be safe. The Hunters had supernatural women to deal with; I doubted they'd go chasing after twenty or so human women.

"Ready?" he asked, his hand on the doorknob.

The women nodded.

A woman nearest me, the one in the black sweater, touched my arm. "Thank you so much," she said, her gaze bouncing from me to the door, to her freedom.

"You're very welcome," I said. "Tell the police everything. Don't leave out anything, even if they try to convince you some of these things never happened."

"I will," she assured me.

Marcus flung the door open and urged the women, "Go now! Run!"

In a mad dash, the women left the house, through the paved circular driveway and past the perfectly trimmed hedges. A fire ball hit one of the hedges and the women passing it jumped and ran faster, down the driveway, escaping through a wall of smoke.

Marcus shut the door and grabbed my hand. "Let's get back to the action."

We made it halfway through the large, circular entry area, past the water fountain and toward the hallway leading to the back of the house, when Marcus's father appeared at the end of another hallway that fed into the entry. He leaned against the corner wall with his hands in his pockets. "Well, don't you two make a cute couple."

His black pinstripe suit looked expensive and personally crafted for his height and broad shoulders. A silver dagger emblem attached to a black ribbon hung from his neck in lieu of a tie. "You do realize you just let a human run to her death. She's carrying a hybrid warrior in her belly, one that'll surely kill her on its way out."

So the rogue Hunter hadn't been misinformed. They *were* impregnating the human women with Wild Women/Hunter hybrid embryos. I made a mental note to make sure we found the impregnated human women when this was all over and help them. Renee, ever the nurse, would be happy to assist in whatever they chose to do with their pregnancies.

"What are you doing here?" Marcus growled. He placed me behind him.

"Now, that's no way to talk to your father, son. I raised you to be more respectful than that."

My heart thrummed in my chest. We needed to join the others, get out of the building before the fire outside burned through to become a fire inside. But we couldn't leave Marcus's father alive in the process. And my poor ex-Hunter had a track record when it came to confronting his father in a fight to the death.

Marcus pulled his dagger from its sheath. "You raised me to take orders without question, to hate beings who only want to exist in peace, hell, to hate everyone who's not us." He shook his head. "Apparently, the way you raised me didn't take."

"Apparently not," his father said, pushing off from the corner wall to stroll toward Marcus and me. "What's all this going on out there?" He waved a hand toward the back of the building. "A rescue mission for your revolution leader?"

"Something like that," Marcus answered, his voice low and his dagger hand at the ready.

His father laughed mockingly. "Do what you will. We've already got her eggs; we were going to dispose of her soon anyhow."

Marcus's muscles tensed as though he were going to rush his father, drive his dagger into the man's gut and slide it up as far as it would go. But the front door flung open and froze him in place. A tall, regal woman with long silver and black hair peeking from one side of the hooded portion of her cloak, marched from the door to stand in between the two men.

Marcus's father's face softened for less than a second before his brow furrowed again. "Avera."

Her lip curled and her eyes shot daggers. "Paul Garcia," she said in a Spanish accent, her tone making it sound as though each syllable left a disgusting taste in her mouth. "I should have known. Where my son is, his father will also be."

THIRTY-ONE

"AND HERE YOU ARE, AVERA," Paul, Marcus's father said. He ran a hand through his thick silver hair. "To remind me how our son, my son, is a half-breed." He shook his head, eyeing his son. "Ironic isn't it? My heroic efforts at bedding a Wild Woman to create you is what gained me my high station, as commander of all American Hunters. When I saw you with this huldra, in Oregon, I had hoped you would follow in my footsteps. I knew you'd figured out the gist of our taking the Wild Women and, I don't know, maybe it was foolish hope, but I'd thought that if the huldra proved to be with child, your child, you'd turn from your rebellious ways and take your place at the helm with me." He shook his head in disappointment. "But when we tested her blood, and the pregnancy test came out negative, I did what had to be done, went ahead with our original plan." Paul looked over Marcus's shoulder to me. "Don't worry, when they inseminate your eggs with my sperm, I'll make sure our son is raised under a harsher hand."

Marcus rushed his father like an angry bull seeing red.

I saw red too, but for a different reason. My huldra pushed her way to the surface, ready to take over. I'd been told they'd realized the combining of genes, Wild and Hunter, only worked with a Hunter leader, and that it'd worked in the past. It seemed Marcus had been the product of the first time they'd been successful. His father was the leader of American Hunters. His mother...was a Wild Woman.

I hitched a breath, not able to fill my lungs with enough oxygen to keep the dizziness of shock away. Suddenly, it all made sense, Marcus's ability to be around me and other Wilds without losing his control, his deep desire to protect the Wilds and our ways.

Paul swung at Marcus, but Marcus ducked to the side just in time to force Paul to stumble forward and lose his balance. Marcus swiveled and planted an uppercut into the kidney area of his father's back.

My huldra thrummed with the need to join in, to defend my man. But my rational self knew Marcus needed this, needed to stand his ground and break ties with his brotherhood in this real and physical way, especially after what he'd done in Oregon. Avera only watched the two men fight, and my huldra hated her for it, for her lack of any kind of empathy for her own damn son.

Paul jumped, unsteady from the blow to his back. He fell forward, but quickly righted himself within a couple steps. He turned to face Marcus and brandished his dagger. He ran toward Marcus, aiming his dagger for his son's throat. Hurt flashed across Marcus's face and my heart ached for him as he jumped up and back. Paul's dagger failed to hit its target, but he made quick work of righting his miscalculation. The Hunter leader spun in a circle, crouched low, and shoved his dagger up into Marcus's gut. Marcus stumbled backwards, clutching his bleeding stomach.

I moved to rush Paul, my branches out and ready to push into him like a pin cushion.

Avera intercepted me, blocking my path. "The honor is not yours," she commanded.

I paused, only inches from the xana, and watched my man. Marcus was strong, but everyone needed to tap out sometimes.

"I didn't want to have to do this," Paul said, walking toward his son as Marcus tried to get back into battle position with a wound that had to have cut deep. Blood pooled along his shirt and dripped to the tile floor, creating a puddle. "But I knew there was a chance it'd come to this. And when you left the brotherhood, left your chance at moving up the ladder, I figured it was only a matter of time. Even when you rejoined, I didn't foresee that lasting very long. You've got too much of your mother in you."

I tried to get around Avera, unwilling to allow her screwed sense of honor to govern my need to help Marcus. But she grabbed my elbows and whispered into my ear, "This fight began before you were born. Back down huldra. Paul's death does not belong to you."

I shook my head, but didn't move.

Marcus laughed. "You created me for a purpose." He exhaled and composed himself again to talk through the pain. "And you'll kill me because I no longer fulfill that purpose. Don't pretend I was anything more than a science experiment to you."

"A failed science experiment," Paul stated, rushing forward to offer Marcus the final blow.

"Enough!" the cloaked woman bellowed, stomping a foot to the floor in a way that seemed to shake the house and crack the square tile beneath her foot. She raised her hands in front of her and water from the decorative fountain in the entry flew through the air, in a ball, to unroll like a curtain between the two men, blocking them from reaching one another.

She marched toward the two Hunters, her raised hands keeping the water in place.

"You, Paul, forced me into a disadvantageous relationship, under false pretenses, to use me. You took my son, stole him from me, and ordered your goons to end my life." She stopped at the edge of the water curtain, the liquid swirling and shifting within itself. "And now you seek to kill my son." Her voice lowered and the water vibrated in place. She glared at Paul. "If you end my son, I will end you."

Paul chuckled. "I'd like to see you try—wouldn't be the first Wild Woman I've taken out, and you won't be the last."

Paul thrust his hand and dagger through the water to stab Marcus's throat. Marcus dodged and reached back. Only, when Marcus pressed his arm into the water, the liquid melded around his skin like a protective glove, breaking formation around the dagger's blade and hilt. Paul tried to push his son away, but the water absorbed the movement. Marcus aimed his dagger down and thrust it into his father's solar plexus. Paul coughed and stumbled back, clutching his abdomen. His legs gave out and his tailbone hit the floor with a thud.

Marcus pulled his hand back to his body, out of the water, and began to walk around the water curtain to finish the job.

"Please," his mother, Avera, said, "allow me the honor?" Her eyes searched her son's, as though she knew having to take his own father's life, no matter how badly it needed to be done, would scar him forever.

Marcus gave her a nod.

With a swoop of her hands, the water rushed together and formed a waterfall, landing on Paul's chest.

Terror filled the Hunter leader's eyes. "No, no, no!" he shouted, as a thick stream of water inched its way up his chest, toward his mouth and nose.

"Your heart is impure," Avera declared. The water halted, swirling in place, and she opened her mouth to sing.

The melody sounded like the voice of an angel. I fought to stay alert, to keep my eyes open, because I wanted nothing more than to follow that melody into a place of inner peace, to close my eyes and absorb her song into my being.

It had an entirely different effect on Paul Garcia. Blood dripped onto the floor from his ears. He squirmed and clenched his jaw and hands, and when he could take no more, he shouted out, begging her to stop.

She only raised her voice and the strength of her song.

Paul thrashed along the tile, unable to get up due to the water holding him down and his ripped gut. "Please," he cried, "please stop! I can see them. I can see them coming for me!"

She paused her singing. "Paul Garcia," she bellowed, "you have been found impure. I sentence you to die."

The water on his chest gushed into his nose and mouth, drowning him in the middle of the entry of the North Carolina Hunters' complex. Within seconds, Marcus's father, the leader of all American Hunters, died.

Marcus clutched his own stomach and fell to the ground.

I ran to him and held his head in my lap, brushing hair from his forehead. "Marcus," I fretted, "hold on. Just hold on long enough for us to find a succubus. She'll heal you."

"I'll heal him," Avera announced. She knelt beside Marcus and closed her eyes. Her breathing slowed. She raised her hands from her lap and held them above him, palms down. Water streamed from Paul, across the floor, up her body to her hands, and down to Marcus. As the liquid streamed along her hands, it cleared, the blood and other impurities fading out of existence before the water touched him.

It pooled on Marcus's abdomen, where his father had stabbed him, and a portion of the water disappeared into his wound. The rest of it stretched along his exposed skin, leaving openings for his nose, mouth, and eyes. It spread up his forehead, and over his head, his hair, his temples. Some of it dripped onto me and my jeans greedily absorbed it.

"What are you?" I whispered in awe. "What is he?"

She spoke softly as she worked. "He is the first male xana to be born. I am xana."

"Are xana like the mermaids and the rusalki?" I asked, her connection to water unmistakable.

"We are not. We cannot breathe water, yet we are of water." She inhaled deeply and exhaled slowly, as though a battle wasn't being fought outside the building we sat in, as though our last stand for freedom wasn't currently being made. "The water tells me you too are wounded."

Before I had the chance to confirm her statement, a handful of water splashed onto the right thigh of my jeans, and made its way through the sheet strip I'd used as a bandage to my cut-up skin where my identification tattoo used to live. My thigh tingled and warmed. The pain I'd been fighting lessened and comfort eased into its place.

Marcus opened his eyes and blinked, reaching down to check his stomach. He gazed at me and a goofy grin lifted the corners of his lips. "What happened?"

I smiled down at him. "You scared me there. I thought we were going to lose you. Your mother saved you."

His gaze shifted to the woman kneeling beside us, pulling the water from us to herself to gather and hold it in a swelling ball. His grin dropped. "You said I wasn't your son."

"I lied," she stated. She collected the remaining water and splayed her fingers wide, causing the ball to unwind into a line that she directed back to the fountain with a wave of her hands.

"Why?" he asked as he sat up.

I moved back to give him space. He stood and reached to me, pulling me up to stand. He wrapped his arms around me and kissed the top of my head.

"I know," I said, sensing his mixed emotions of battling his father. I would be his sounding-board later, when we were alone and he felt safe enough to let it all out. For now, I just hugged him back.

Avera stood and smoothed her cloak. She pushed the hood back to fully expose her face and exuded even more regality than I thought possible. "Your ears bled," she said. "I knew you weren't full Hunter, or your reaction would be more like your father's, writhing on the floor. But you have enough Hunter in you to cause your ears to bleed. Too much for my comfort."

Marcus absently touched his right ear. He studied the bit of fresh blood on his finger. "Then why are you here?"

She sighed. "Because you are still my son and I could not risk losing you again."

I expected to have to release him so he could hug his mother, but they only stared at one another.

"I have questions," he told her. "A lot of them."

"I imagine you do," she responded.

Was nobody going to share a happy reunion hug? I'd never heard of a xana, but seeing as I'd spent enough time with the rusalki and the harpies, I couldn't be too shocked that a type of Wild Woman acted so nonchalant about a major life event.

I pulled away from Marcus. He was half Wild Woman, half xana. I couldn't wrap my mind fully around that fact, only the ways it made sense.

"There's a war going on outside," I reminded them.

Marcus stiffened. "Shit, I've been standing here."

"No, you've been fighting and almost dying and then healing," I corrected. "But yeah, we need to get out there."

"They've already made it into the building," Avera said, turning toward the hallway that lead to the courtyard. "There's a shift in the air."

I poked Marcus's arm. "You're gonna need to figure out if you can do that too, because that's really cool."

"Tomorrow," he joked. "I'll get to it tomorrow."

We held hands, jogging through the entry, past the fountain, and into the long hallway. Screams caught my attention and my huldra rose. "One of those is a huldra scream," I exclaimed.

"The fire is in the house," Avera warned as we ran toward the screams.

My heart thrummed. My sisters, my aunts...my mother.

A door in the hall flung open and we skidded to a halt. John stood in the center of the hall, blocking us from passing. Marcus pulled his dagger from its sheath and moved toward the Washington Hunter, his old boss.

John smiled a slimy, disgusting grin. "My friends have arrived. And they don't like you approaching me like that."

Four handsome, rugged-looking men walked from the office, each of them filling the space with the scent of seaweed and saltwater. The mermaids weren't helping the North Carolina Hunters. These men had caused the mermaid-type scent lingering around the monastery hallways and entry. Who the hell were they?

As though John had read my mind, he spoke. "These here are kelpies. Ever heard of them?"

Of course none of us gave him the satisfaction of an answer. I needed to get past him, get to my coterie. I didn't give a shit who these men were, business associates of his or something. Well, the human women they'd probably come to buy were gone. They needed to leave before they fell by the hands of a Wild Woman.

"Kelpies," John said with a gleam in his eyes, "are supernatural males. Their power?" He laughed, thoroughly enjoying himself. "Is killing women."

THIRTY-TWO

WHY I HADN'T REALIZED it as soon as he said what they were, I don't know. It must have been the trauma of being in captivity. "Hold on," I said, interrupting John's twisted moment of pride over his "friends." "You're selling human women to these, these...kelpies...for them to kill?"

I hadn't thought highly of John since his response to Shawna's disappearance, but this was a new low for him.

His boastful smile dropped. He looked confused for a moment. "No, of course not. They're here to kill you and your kind."

Smoke rolled along the first-floor ceiling like the slow creep of a menacing fog. The old monastery was on fire. I could smell it, and now I could see signs of it. How much worse were the conditions outside the complex building?

My coterie was fighting for their lives and freedoms and every fiber of my being needed to join them, to fight alongside them, in what I hoped would be our last battle. Time to process this news of yet another male supernatural species would have to come later. I gave a quick glance to each of the four kelpies. None displayed any type of obvious weapon. Two stood on each side of John, their hands in their pockets like they were just here to kick back and have a few beers, not kill an entire species of females. But if I'd learned anything in these last weeks, it was that looks could be deceiving.

"No they're not," I responded to John, before I shoved my hand to his pec, right over his heart, and grew the sharpest, most rigid branches I could muster from my palm.

His look of shock didn't last long before he pulled backwards, knocking two kelpies out of the way to take refuge along a wall. He moved slow enough that I followed him, still attached to his heart as it beat faster and faster under the pressure of my branches wrapped around and squeezing it.

Words filled my mind, statements I'd wanted to blast him with since he'd shown his true colors outside the Washington Hunter complex the day I went to him, asking for help. How he'd betrayed us. How we'd trusted him and he'd thrown that loyalty away as though it meant nothing, as though our existence meant nothing. But in this moment, I didn't care enough about him to say one word. He didn't deserve to know my thoughts and feelings. He hadn't earned the right to know my mind. So I kept quiet and stared at him, waiting to see the light in his eyes extinguish for the good of all.

Whether Clarisse had been his biological daughter or just his pawn, he'd soon meet her wherever her soul had gone to.

I noticed, out of the corner of my eye, a kelpie move toward me. Marcus stepped between us, his back to mine as I kept watch on John, now sagging against the wall, a line of blood smeared on it where his back had been. Huh, guess a few of my branches went all the way through.

"I'm not going to do anything," the kelpie said to Marcus, his voice deep and smooth. "We're not here to kill the Wild Women."

Avera only watched the exchange quietly.

"Then what are you here for?" Marcus asked, his own voice demanding and mistrusting.

Another kelpie answered, "We were sent here to help her." He pointed to me. "But from the looks of it, she's got things handled."

John's eyes widened as he glared at the kelpie, then his heart beat one last time against my branches. His head fell to the side of his lifeless body. I retracted my branches and let his form slump down the wall to the floor. I'd thought maybe I'd feel a sense of satisfaction after killing the man who'd controlled my adult existence, who'd made sure I didn't join the police force and who watched as his peons tattooed an identification number on my teenage thigh. But I felt nothing. I wanted to be done...with all of this. And I wanted to find my coterie.

I sighed and turned to view the kelpie straight on. "You were sent to help me?"

"Yeah," he said with a nod.

"By whom?" I asked. "The incubi leader?"

He shook his blond head. "We don't know any incubi. No, the sirens sent us."

"Faline!" Shawna yelled from upstairs. "Faline!"

"We'll pick this back up later," I told the kelpie before racing to my sister.

"I'm coming, Shawna!" I ran down the hall, back toward the entry, to the wide set of stairs leading to the second floor. I made it halfway up the stairs when a portion of the roof caved in and landed in front of me, blocking the stairs in flames.

"Shit!" I ran back down the stairs and through the hallway past Marcus, Avera, and the four kelpies, toward the door to the courtyard where the back set of stairs led up. "The house is on fire!" I yelled to them as I passed. "Get out!"

They ran after me, and all but Marcus left the building out the back. Marcus followed me upstairs, shouting for Shawna. Smoked filled the upstairs hallway. I pulled my shirt collar up over my nose and mouth and called for my partner sister.

"Faline!" she shouted amidst coughs that had her doubled over. "There you are! I went looking for you and found your scent strongest up here. Then the roof caved in."

I grabbed her hand. "You found me. Let's go!"

She stood in front of my room, her eyes filled with tears, probably due to the smoke, but her raised eyebrows told me her heart broke for me too. "Did they do the same to you that they did to me?" she asked.

I stopped trying to pull her away long enough to relieve her worries. "No, they didn't. And Shawna, I killed John. He's dead. We don't have to worry about him ever again."

Marcus touched her arm. "My father is gone too," he said solemnly.

"You killed my captors?" she asked both of us.

"We did," I said, sparing Marcus from having to relive the hurt he no doubt felt. "Can we go now?"

"Thank you," she offered before clutching Marcus's hand and pulling us both with her toward the back of the building.

We burst through the thick, wooden door to the courtyard, gasping for clean air. I blinked to clear my vision from the burning smoke and froze as I took in the war scene in front of me. The kelpies fought nearest to the door and probably hit the battle the moment they exited the building. I couldn't differentiate their supernatural abilities by their fighting styles, but strength had to be a component of their talents.

Avera fought farther away, using her hands to pull out water from the Hunter she attacked by placing her hands on his skin and easing them away, taking a stream of blood with her.

The alae pummeled their foes with handfuls of fire, sending men screaming and running in agony. The shé, covered in snake scales, strummed their instruments as though they were playing in a concert while the chaotic audience burned around them. Hunters within earshot stilled, swaying to their music, until the echidnas picked them off, slithering over and using their long snake tails to squeeze the men to death. The nagin worked beside most of the succubi, standing in a large circle with their backs to one another, harnessing each other's energy to push out toward the Hunters closing in with daggers drawn. Daggers dropped to the dirt and the Hunters soon followed, twisting in excruciating pain.

"Are those the rogue Hunters?" I asked Marcus, eyeing the small group of men who stood as tall and broad-shouldered as a Hunter, but wore colors other than black. They fought alongside Aleksander, who I noticed had been staring at me, analyzing my health, probably, as he scanned from my bare feet to the top of my head. He gave a nod and returned to fighting.

My coterie worked with a handful of fish-scale-covered mermaids I hadn't seen since the first time we took out a Hunter complex. My aunts and sisters shielded their skin with bark, their vines twisting like tiny snakes from their fingertips. Marie kept Celeste close—the two fought beside one another between our coterie and Marie's succubi galere.

I looked for my mother. She stood bent over, catching her breath, behind her partner sister, Abigale, who protected her.

The Hunters hadn't anticipated such a quick retaliation from the Wild Women. If they had, there would have been bloodstone hanging on the walls, and the Hunters would be covered in it. As it was, only a few had the foresight to throw a few pieces on them. Two had draped my mother's and my red shawls over their shoulders and tied the connecting portion around their necks to hold them on. Those two seemed to be fairing the best, the added bloodstone automatically weakening any Wild of menstruating age within arm's reach to challenge them.

Shawna, Marcus, and I ran to join my coterie beside the maple tree, when I caught the faint sound of sirens. I tightened my vines around a random Hunter's neck and paused as he fell to the ground, his dagger half through my vines before his body expired. The other Wilds, those with the ability to hear from long distances, paused and looked toward the driveway and the front of the house, out of our vision.

Celeste and Marie were among those who paused for a half second. Their Hunter foe, who wore a bloodstone shawl, used his opportunity and lunged forward just quick enough to catch Celeste off guard. She noticed too late, pushing her branches out and missing his chest as he crouched low and slid his dagger into her inner thigh.

"Celeste!" I screamed. Before I had a chance to run to her, Marie squared her monstrous gaze at her lover's offender. He froze, clearly under her energy manipulation, for only one breath before a chunk of cobblestone flew through the air and hit Marie in the head, knocking her to the ground and forcing her to lose her power over Celeste's attacker.

In the blink of an eye, Heather stepped from her circle of succubi and shoved her hands in the direction of the Hunter as he dragged his blade deeper into my sister's thigh. I rushed to her, to knock the Hunter off her, but the nearness of his shawl weakened my attempts. His blade neared my sister's femoral artery and she screeched. Marcus ran up behind me and used the hilt of his dagger to hit the Hunter over the head. The Hunter wasted no time by turning to see who his attackers were. He moved to finish the job, when Marcus fell to the ground and clutched his chest.

Heather walked closer, her arms still raised. My head pulsated with a sudden headache and my legs began to wobble beneath me. The closer she came, the stronger my symptoms became. To get past the Hunter's bloodstone shawl, Heather pulled energy from me and Marcus—another Hunter whose energy only strengthened with bloodstone. I felt it in my bones, an ache of fatigue. Apparently, Marcus felt it in his chest. The Hunter trying to kill my sister froze, mid-strike. Heather moved two more steps toward us and the Hunter fought his muscles, his whole body shaking, as his right hand opened and dropped his dagger.

The Hunter slurred out something indistinguishable before falling to the earth and pulling himself into a fetal position.

"You will not touch my leader's reason for living," Heather breathed out, her hands nearing the Hunter's heart to give the final heart-stopping blow. If she needed me and Marcus's energy for that, she could have it.

She bent down to crush her palms into the Hunter's chest, when another Hunter cloaked in bloodstone rushed up behind her. I tried to open my mouth, to yell a warning, but I hadn't the energy to push words from my lips.

In an instant a Hunter's blade plunged into her back. Red patches spread quickly through the front of her green cotton shirt. She didn't cough or cry out. Her gaze caught mine as her eyes registered shock, pain, and what looked like sadness. She fell forward, her face in the dirt.

The moment she no longer used my energy, I jumped up, as did Marcus.

The twisted roar of love lost rumbled through the courtyard. Mason. If incubi developed mate bonds, and their mate died...

Marcus snatched up the dropped dagger and pulled his own from its sheath. With a dagger in each hand, he crouched to finish off the Hunter on the ground, spun in a circle, to pop up and surprise the standing Hunter with a blade to the throat, finishing both enemies in under thirty seconds.

Mason found the body of his mate, Heather, on the ground and careened to a halt. He kneeled down and picked her up, cradling her in his arms. He shouted his breaking heart to the heavens and the earth, his emotions of torment pulsing out to those of us closest to him.

Celeste stroked Marie's forehead, crying over the succubi leader, begging her to be okay.

Marie sat up with a sudden jolt to see Mason wailing over Heather. Shock and hurt twisted her face as she fought back tears. "Take her to the woods," she commanded the incubus softly. "Take her away from here."

Mason turned from us to run over the broken fencing and into the forest, holding his dead love close to his heart.

"Go!" Marie yelled to her sisters, probably sensing the incoming humans. Like a hoard of battered warrior women, the succubi galere followed Mason, crying out for their fallen sister.

Aleksander hung back, watching. He and Marcus shared a tense second of staring, before Aleksander shook his head and followed his cousins.

Wilds were dying and human law enforcement were too close for comfort. We had to finish this once and for all.

"Avera!" I yelled. "Can you end this?"

The Wild Women, the kelpies, and the incubi needed to leave before the police arrived. I figured some of the cop cars would stop to help the human women who had to be down the road by now. But others would pass on by to get to the scene of the fire, where Marcus had tipped them off they'd find the key players of the whole human trafficking ring.

"Retreat!" I yelled to all those fighting for our cause. "Retreat!"

Before Avera began her song and lulled me to a relaxed state I couldn't afford, I called for the leader of the alae. "Ailani!"

She jogged over to me, flames licking her fingers as she moved through the crowds, her palms out in warning. She pushed her long black hair from her face, her tresses impervious to the fire.

"How are you with technology?" I asked.

"Proficient. Why?" she responded with a smile that made me think this fire warrior enjoyed battle. "Is this the part Marcus mentioned?"

"I need someone who's immune to fire to go into the house and gather as much information from a particular office computer as possible." I peered at the house, flames covered the roof and corners. "It could collapse any minute, and take all the proof we need with it."

She nodded. "Yeah, but you want me to grab a whole motherboard?"

Marcus pulled a lanyard from beneath his shirt and over his head. "Here." He placed the lanyard with the attached thumb drive in Ailani's hand. "It's in the office I showed you on the building's layout schematic we got from the rogue Hunter," he reminded.

She snickered. "Who uses thumb drives anymore?"

"It was a last-minute purchase," Marcus said defensively amidst the chaos of a stampede of women running for their lives, a spitting house fire, and Hunters yelling for help.

The alae leader placed the lanyard over her neck and skipped into the burning building as the sirens grew louder and closer.

Avera belted out her song. Another, woman, who looked similar, stood beside her and began singing along. As though a choir of heavenly angles blessed us with their presence, the chaos-filled courtyard slowed and then stilled to listen to the entrancing melody. The last of the Wild Women who hadn't left yet began slowly swaying with the music, their eyes closing and smiles lifting their lips, yet the Hunters screamed and fell to the ground, covering their bleeding ears.

I looked to Aleksander who watched me from the forest's tree line. He swayed, with eyes open. He caught me watching him and winked. I jumped my gaze to the kelpies, who covered their bleeding ears, but still stood with eyes closed. The rogue Hunters faired about as well as their Hunter brothers, and I hoped a succubus or a xana would be able to reverse whatever damage had been done out of necessity.

When the wailing car sirens were loud enough to be in the driveway, the two xana—I assumed the woman singing beside Avera was also xana—quieted long enough to instruct their allies to run, get away. Like a stampede, those of our allies left made for the forest, trampling the already felled chain link fence that had held in my mother and I earlier in the day. Wilds even helped the few ex-Hunters unable to get up on their own.

Marcus and I hung back, watching the others run, fly, and slither away. My coterie didn't budge.

"Let's go," my mother said, grabbing ahold of both my hands and tugging. "It's over. We can go home, be together again, daughter."

Goddess, it broke my heart to tell my mother the next part of my plan. "I can't," I said. "Not every Hunter is here to be taken in and seen for what they really are. There's Hunters in high places in our government that need to be outed, or else nothing will change. And Marcus and I are going to be the ones to do it. To out them. It has to be done."

Tears filled my mother's eyes, and Abigale wrapped an arm around her shoulder.

"Be proud of the leader your daughter has become," Abigale told her sister. "She is capable and willing. She is strong, Naomi."

My mother released my hand to wipe a tear from her face. "Please come home to me. There's so much I need to make up for." She gave my hand a squeeze and let go. With one last look, she turned and ran toward the woods with the rest of my coterie.

Please, Freyja, let me see my mother again.

THIRTY-THREE

THREE FIRETRUCKS BLARED TOWARD THE HUNTERS' building, following more than five police cars. I couldn't see how many from the courtyard, but from the sound of it, Marcus's call before storming the building had been effective. Unlike the other Hunter locations in the United States, the monastery building encompassed the whole complex, except for a couple smaller outlying mobiles acting as extra bunk houses for the recent influx of Hunters.

The Wild Women, rogue Hunters, incubi, and kelpies escaped into the woods outlying the complex property, leaving Marcus and I alone, among dead Hunter bodies, holding hands and waiting for the next step of our journey.

The Wilds had removed all Wild bodies: one echidna, one mermaid, and two succubi who'd lost their lives in the fight. If the Hunters had been prepared for our takeover, our death toll would have been much higher. Thank Freyja for the strategic planning of my coterie and the others.

Still, my heart beat wildly as Marcus and I waited for our fate to be determined. Growing up, a Wild's biggest fear was to be caught by humans and forced to undergo painful tests, possibly to the point of death. From childhood, our mothers and aunts spoke of the real threat. After coming of age and being forced to attend Hunter check-ins, the fear grew exponentially, as the Hunters taught us, in great detail, what would happen to us if we were ever found out to be non-human. They'd taught us we needed them to protect us from the humans, to keep us from being outed or exposing ourselves.

And here Marcus and I stood, knowing full well that one of my biggest and most instilled fears had a huge chance at becoming my reality by the end of the day. Would they torture me, cut me open, experiment on me?

If it meant freedom for my sisters and mother and aunts, and Wild friends, and all their daughters and their daughter's daughters, then being detained would be worth it.

"If they ask," I thought to tell Marcus as the sound of boots running in our direction grew louder, "I'm the only one of my kind."

"If there's only one Wild Woman, it makes no sense for Hunters to have complexes," he responded.

"The humans don't need to know why the Hunters think they were created, what they believe their life purpose to be," I said. "We don't even need to out Hunters as a supernatural community. All the humans need to know is that the Hunters used their secret organization and its high-reaching members to traffic human women."

Marcus nodded. "Most people like having a group to rise up against and a good reason to do it. They probably won't question much beyond that."

"No, I don't think they will."

"They'll separate us," he said, as though he were going through the next steps in his mind. "We need to have the same story, about where you came from and how we met."

The middle, pointed, portion of the huge building's roof collapsed in on itself, spreading flames in a hurry, and billowing smoke in every direction.

A pit formed in my stomach. Since I set out on this journey, I never imaged Marcus and I would go down with the Hunters. And yet, here we stood.

"We can be honest with how we met. That'll help us to appear trustworthy, since I'm sure they have footage and will quickly gather paperwork on the times I brought skips into your Everett police station," I said. "And as far as where I came from, we can tell them I'm part of their organization, that they've been doing experiments on women. This will further incriminate them."

Marcus release my hand and turned to me. He cupped my face in his large hands and gazed into my eyes. "No, I won't say that."

"Why?" I implored. "You don't want to dig a deeper hole for the Hunters?"

His brow creased. "I refuse to bury you in that hole. I'm going to tell them that you contacted me, as a bounty hunter who stumbled across evidence to a huge case involving members from higher up in the police department, when you captured Samuel Woodry. I went snooping for proof before I brought it to their attention."

"Then don't tell them you're a Hunter," I pleaded. "Tell them you infiltrated their ranks or something."

Marcus's eyes darkened. "I can't, Faline. When they bring in living Hunters for questioning, it's bound to come out." His gaze softened, probably due to the pleading in my own eyes. "I won't offer that information off the bat. I'll wait."

That was all I could ask of him. "All right."

Huge streams of water sprayed over the top of the building from the front. The firefighters had begun their work. Police ran around both sides of the house, trampling the broken fence. One look at the bodies and they drew weapons and pointed them at us. "Get down!" they shouted. "Get down, and put your hands above your heads!"

In the middle of the courtyard, beside the maple tree, and in the midst of bloodied bodies, Marcus and I slowly lowered to the ground, on our knees. We placed our hands behind our heads, and waited. Police zig-zagged through dead bodies and burning debris toward us. Four of them cuffed us before jerking us to standing.

"You one of the women from the road?" an officer asked before escorting me toward the car where the other officer had Marcus standing beside it, patting him down. "One of the kidnapped?"

"No, I'm a bounty hunter," I answered. "The man you arrested beside me is a police officer with the Everett, Washington police department. We were following leads to a case that started in Seattle, Washington. We are not criminals."

The officer grunted. "Really? You sure you weren't in the middle of killing your captors when we got here?"

I shook my head.

"Then why were there dead bodies all around you and blood on your hands?"

Ailani jetted from the burning building, out the back door and through the courtyard. I stared as she ran past us, past the many police officers, without being noticed. She slowed enough to offer me a wink and a thumbs up.

"You have the right to remain silent," the lean, male cop said as he pushed me away from the tree and to the right side of the house, walking me toward the squad cars in the large, round driveway at the front of the building. As he finished listing my rights, I heard the larger male cop saying the same to Marcus, directly in front of us.

I snuck a look to Ailani out of the corner of my eye. She appeared as a flame, flickering along the ground, jumping from one spot to the next. I almost laughed to myself. So that's how she got past the cops without being noticed. Marcus hadn't even seen her.

"Do you see her?" I whispered to Marcus who stood beside me.

"Who?" he asked, looking around.

A cop opened the back door to a squad car, and they escorted me into the backseat, lowering my head and shutting the door. I watched as another set of cops escorted Marcus into a separate car. Blue and red lights spun atop vehicles. Sirens blared. Water spilled and wet the ground. Smoke and steam filled the air, the heat cooking the bodies, leaving a stench of burning flesh in my nose. The two cops crawled into the front seats and clicked their seatbelts. We roared down the driveway, hurtling to the station.

As a bounty hunter, I knew what would come next. I literally had the blood of others on my hands. I knew they'd silently drive me to the local police station, process me, and throw me in a private room for questioning. I gazed out the window at the trees seemingly speeding by, replaying every possible scenario through my mind.

Shit. They weren't taking me in as a witness. They'd cuffed me, read me my rights. They'd arrested me. When they processed me, I'd be stripped and looked over by female cops. They'd see my back, my bark. The pit in my stomach grew and I ground my teeth to keep the bile in my stomach from coming up.

It was only a matter of time before they realized I wasn't human.

The officer in the front passenger seat, the one who'd led me to the car, turned to me. "What case where you referring to back there?"

"A country-wide human trafficking case," I said, trying to sound professional and confident, but unable to keep the pleading from my voice. "Their base was moved from the Seattle area when their cover, a woman named Clarisse Callixtus was captured. She was eventually released on bail and then went missing. I'd followed her to this complex here in North Carolina. Marcus met me here."

He tilted his head as though he were in thought, but I could tell by his lack of expression that he doubted my words. "Why weren't we notified that there was an investigation happening in our backyard?"

I thought to look him and his partner over for hidden dagger necklaces, or revealing tattoos, or some sign they were Hunters. But their sizes alone kept me from believing I was dealing with the enemy.

"Because," I said, nearly stuttering. So much depended on whether or not they believed me. If they processed me as a suspect, it'd be over. My bark patch had grown too pronounced to miss. "The building we just left, was the operation hub of the human trafficking ring. It's also the compound to a private group of individuals who've infiltrated the government and law enforcement. We had to procure solid evidence before telling anyone. If information leaked before we had the evidence, it would have all fallen apart and more women would have been abducted."

"Look it up," the driver told his partner.

The front passenger turned away from me and began punching keys on the laptop attached to the car's dashboard. He sucked in a breath. "Shit."

"My name is Faline Frey," I added as an afterthought. "Check the records. A month ago, I brought in a skip named Samuel Woodry, a serial rapist. He'd been bailed out by the leaders of the human trafficking ring because he'd agreed to work for them, procure their victims. I believe it's because their organization had grown so much that they were gaining interest from law enforcement and needed someone not linked to their secret association in any way to do their frontline work."

"She checks out so far," the passenger cop said, scrolling through uploaded documents.

"How'd you find out about this?" the driver asked me.

"Something Samuel said when I captured him," I responded. "I dug deeper. And got a tip from Clarisse Callixtus." Mentioning Clarisse was a gamble, but I couldn't afford to walk into that police station as a suspect, and I had to think we were nearly there.

Our car turned a corner with a small park on one side and old brick buildings lining the streets on the other. A two-story beige brick police station took up a corner, a clock tower positioned at the top. I had to pull out everything I could before we parked along the road at the side of the station.

"Marcus Garcia, the officer your co-workers just arrested, took leave from the force to go undercover in the Washington complex, where this was supposed to have started, where Clarisse was hiding out after she skipped bail. He'd tried to bring her in when he found out she was staying there, but angry buyers, from another country, I'm assuming, attacked the complex and burned it to the ground."

We pulled into the parking lot.

"Please, look it up. He went to the Oregon complex next, it was right outside of Portland. But he was too late, they'd already caught on that they were being watched and they burned the evidence and moved the women to the building in North Carolina."

"So then why is their current building on fire?" the driver asked before he pulled the parking break lever into position. He unbuckled his seat belt and turned to look at me. "Do they have pyro enemies following them around the country? That makes no sense."

Please, Freyja, please, help me.

"The women, your coworkers found women at the end of the

driveway, women who'd been kept in the basement of that monastery building," I said, pulling out everything I had.

He nodded.

"Marcus and I rescued the women. We were caught by a couple members and fought the men off. A few candles were knocked over in the process. The women will attest to us rescuing them and fighting the men." I doubted the women saw a fight, but I hoped they'd at least heard it as they fled the front yard.

"And what about the dead men outside, surrounding the two of you?" he asked with a disbelieving smirk.

"The leaders of the whole thing were in talks with new buyers when Marcus and I came in," I said. "We'd meant to simply collect evidence and information to bring to law enforcement, but the buyers were there to take the women, and we couldn't let that happen. After we released the women, the buyers accused the leaders of setting them up and stealing their money, so a fight broke out in the courtyard."

"Then why were you and Marcus just standing in the courtyard?" the passenger asked.

"We had evidence for you. And also, I was trying to bring in the skip, Clarisse, but she died. You'll find her body in the house, I believe." I knew us being outside and Clarisse being inside the house didn't fully make sense. But I hoped it was enough to mention the skip and her body's location. A bounty hunter wouldn't just let a skip die if they possibly could save them. I didn't make money on dead bodies. I got paid when I brought them in alive.

"That's not where her body was found," the passenger told the driver.

Shit.

The driver turned away from me and opened his door. "Welp, that doesn't check out. Where's the other evidence you had for us?" he shut his door and walked around to the back side door where I sat. He opened the door and waited for my answer.

I lowered my head. Ailani never gave me the thumb drive. "I don't have it," I said, defeated.

The officer pulled me from the car, gruffly, like he'd treat someone who'd murdered a whole group of people and burned down their building to hide the evidence. Despite the women's testimony, I had no proof I was there to help rather than to kill. And once they saw the bark on my back they'd peg me as a killer, I knew it.

He led me toward the rear of the building, through a separate entrance from the one the public used, the same type of entrance I'd bring a skip through, or a cop would bring a suspect. "Of course you don't have proof of your story." He scoffed. "Why am I not surprised?"

THIRTY-FOUR

THE DRIVER LED the way as his partner, the other police officer, walked behind me, directing my steps and holding my arm. The Burnsville police department reminded me of a quaint building out of an old movie, a place where the worst crimes committed had more to do with petty theft than human trafficking and mass murder.

"I'm a witness, not a suspect," I repeated, dreading the physical portion of being processed, when the humans would know for sure I wasn't one of them. With only moments left to change their minds, my tone grew more stern and less begging. "You should be taking my statement, not processing me to book like a criminal."

They both ignored me. I couldn't blame them. How many times had I heard my skips repeating the same crap? Nearly every bail-runner insisted they were innocent and I was mistreating them, nothing implicating them was their fault. Surely these two cops heard the same excuses more than daily.

"Officer Lankle," the driver said to the cop behind the desk. "I need this suspect, Faline Frey, processed and then in the interrogation room for questioning."

Officer Lankle, who stood behind the desk, nodded. "Will do,

Officer Gains," she said. She went to work gathering paperwork, intake forms I assumed, and stashed them into a file.

"Meet you at the door," she said without looking at her coworkers, as though it was just another day, another criminal.

Officer Gains led the way as his partner escorted me through the steel door and back to the processing area. I'd never been past the door back at home at the police stations I'd dropped skips off. I'd gone through enough school to know the law and to keep my nose clean as a bounty hunter, but this part of the process was foreign to me, outside of what I'd seen on TV. And from what my limited experiences taught me, in most everything, TV got it all wrong.

"We'll need two females to search her," Officer Gains said as we neared another door down a hallway.

A narrow bench was bolted to the wall opposite the door. Officer Lankle motioned to it as she said, "Yup." and tossed the file she held onto the wood to go in search of some help.

My huldra sensed the fear bubbling up in me and nudged to take over. I calmed her as much as I could.

As I sat on the hard wooden bench, my back against the white cement wall, I knew this was it. I was surrounded by humans who would soon know I was not one of them, who would soon connect me to the monstrous stories the Hunters circulated about my kind. These humans would figure it out in enough time to label me an evil huldra, killer of men. After all this, after everything I'd done, everything Marcus and so many others had done on our behalf, the Hunters would win. In the end, the Hunters' history would override truth and plunge folkloric women into hiding, fearing for their lives even more than before. I would be the poster child for bucking the system and used to teach young Wilds to submit to their Hunter protectors. They would say, "After all, look what'll happen when you release yourself from the Hunters' protection."

Another woman followed Officer Lankle down the hall toward me and the two male officers. The women carried latex gloves, ready to begin their search of my body.

I stretched my fingers, willing my huldra to keep silent, willing my vines to stay inside my hands. I refused to use my abilities against these humans. They were only doing their jobs, and I would only prove the Hunters' lies correct if I lived up to the expectations they'd set out for us.

Funny thing, oppression. Long after the act is over, after the brain has been washed in lies and half-truths, the victim still lives in a bubble of it. Like an earthquake, the affects resonate far and wide, as she fights herself and others to prove her strength, her independence, and her endurance. How long can she oppose the cards stacked against her until her legs give out and she tumbles into the very pit of lies created by her oppressors to trap her?

I ran my fingers along the smooth wooden bench beneath me. No, I would not give up. I would not fold. I would allow life and hardships to sand me down, to smooth out my rough edges, but at my core, I was still me, a Wild Woman, capable of handling anything thrown my way. The Goddess had breathed her life into my ancestors. And I intended to honor her gifts, in whichever way she wished me to.

Officer Lankle unlocked the door across from the bench and directed me to stand and follow the women into the white, nearly empty room. The women snapped latex gloves on. The door shut, leaving the three of us alone.

Officer Lankle removed my handcuffs. "Go ahead and remove your clothing please, all of it," she said, adjusting her gloves.

"Okay," I breathed. I wished I'd worn shoes and socks to draw out the process, but my bare and dirty feet gave nothing to uncover. I unbuttoned my jeans and began to push them, hesitantly, down my legs. I spotted my right thigh where my identification tattoo had been and realized I hadn't seen the spot since Avera healed it. The light, discolored skin looked as though someone had tried to use an editing application to smear my pigment and got a little too zealous.

Before I shimmied my ankles out of my worn, torn jeans, someone knocked on the door. "Bring Ms. Frey out," Officer Gains requested urgently. "Now."

I looked to the women for an indication of what to do.

"You heard him," Officer Lankle said. "Put your clothes back on."

I nearly cried with gratitude. *Thank you, Freyja.*

My hands shook with frayed nerves and unreleased adrenaline as I buttoned my jeans. Blood. For the first time, I noticed the dried blood cracked along the skin of my fingers and under my nails. Of course I looked guilty of multiple homicides. I peered down to my chest. Blood splatter stained my shirt with spots of reddish-brown.

One of the cops in the room opened the door and motioned for me to go through it. "This way," Officer Gains directed.

No one placed cuffs back on me or surrounded me to make sure I didn't run.

"Sorry 'bout that," Officer Gains started as he slowed to walk beside me, in step with me. "It's just this way." He pointed to the right and we turned at the end of one hall into another. We were buzzed through another steel door and found ourselves in a more decorated hallway with paint and trimming and even art hanging on the walls, most depicting the towns near Mt. Mitchell. "You have to admit, you two looked pretty damn guilty."

I tried to give a sound of understanding, a way to brush it all off, but it wasn't in me. I swallowed to wet my throat enough to speak. "What changed?"

"Officer Marcus Garcia's statement," he answered. "Backed up by a phone call from an investigator with the Mill Creek precinct in Washington State, corroborating it all."

"Rod," I thought aloud.

Officer Gains stopped to look at me. "Yeah. Said he'd been forced to take an early retirement and go into hiding after he'd refused to ask a Seattle investigator to cover up a case with strong evidence linking Paul Garcia to the human trafficking ring as its real leader." He gave a shrug and kept talking as we walked. "There'd been a complaint formed by a potential victim's parents against the Samuel Woodry you'd mentioned, but that complaint was only the tip of the iceberg as far as what they'd wanted covered up. That Seattle investigator committed suicide three weeks ago. His file is lost."

I managed to make an affirmative noise as if this didn't shock me overly much.

He shook his head. "And that's not the most damning evidence I'm told you've helped to uncover. Minutes ago, a woman dropped off a thumb drive. Accord to Officer Garcia, it's digital evidence of the transactions of women for money, and names of the sellers and the buyers. The organization behind this all, the men, goes up into law enforcement and government...way up. It's too soon to see any reports about what's on there exactly, but if Officer Garcia's hunch is correct, Chief is likely to give you a medal or something. Hell, the president herself may even hold a dinner in your honor."

My head spun as we walked another twenty feet. We stopped in front of yet another door. Officer Gains turned the knob. I peered in, able to see an older man sitting at a table, with a basket of snacks and plastic cups beside a pitcher of water.

"Here she is, Chief," Officer Gains said, directing me into the room.

I spotted my male sitting at the other side of the table from the chief. Tears sprang to my eyes and wound their way down my cheeks. "Marcus," I uttered.

Marcus stood quickly enough to send his chair tumbling backwards. He closed the distance between us and pulled me into his chest. I cried, my nerves unwinding, my fear of being found out and demonized and tortured dissipating in his presence.

"It's okay, Faline," my love assured me. "It's over. It's all over. We got them."

My legs gave out and he held me up, pressing me into his chest. I sobbed with relief.

"We did it," was all I could get out past the sobs. "We did it."

Marcus pulled my face away from his chest to stare into my eyes. "*You* did it, Faline. You saved them, you saved them all."

EPILOGUE

JOURNAL ENTRY ONE

I'VE DECIDED to write down all that has happened, for future generations and so our stories don't get lost. I'll start at the end, because really, it's just another type of beginning.

It didn't take long to fix the damage to our coterie's tree homes and communal house caused by the Hunters. Marcus and I shared my room, while my mother finally occupied her own bed. My worries of living with her as adults dissipated within our first night at home. We'd spent our remaining time in North Carolina catching up, between cooking and cleaning for the healers who used their Wild abilities to close dagger wounds, calm anxiety, reset bones, and weave together re-balanced energies.

Once each of our allies had healed enough to travel home, we said our goodbyes and went our separate ways. Marcus and I stayed in the old bootlegger house for weeks after the others had left, to offer insight on the Hunter case as new details of the North Carolina complex unfolded. Of course, before we left town, we had to see Eonza's baby, Kyanite. My aunt had been right. Kyanite's greenish-blue feathers covered her body in soft fluff. Eonza allowed me to kiss her daughter's smooth forehead as she'd explained the meaning of her daughter's name. "It is a stone helpful in aligning energy," Eonza had said, gazing lovingly at her newborn. "For she is the first Wild Woman born to an aligned people. She is first to be born in a time of peace and freedom."

I carried the expanse of Eonza's words with me during my trip home. At first, I had set out on this trek to save my sister, then it was to save my coterie and my mother. Quickly, my mission had morphed into something greater than myself, no doubt reaching further than I will possibly ever know. At the end, I sought to save all daughters and mothers from the Hunters, all people, even the Hunters themselves.

The rusalki returned to Maine healthy and happy. It didn't take long for them to reach out to their sisters in New Zealand, where they now spend most of their time, appreciating their sisters' much more luxurious inground homes. They have plans to expand their family very soon.

The incubi and succubi returned to Portland and opened a free energy healing center. The center was so successful, they opened another one in Seattle, run by Marie near the home she shares with Celeste, and sometimes Olivia, in a small bedroom community outside the city.

Aleksander bought a luxurious cabin close to my property—near enough to keep from going crazy and far enough to keep Marcus from going crazy. He still leads the incubi hoard in Portland, but until his whole mate issue is sorted out, he has no choice but to leave his second in command in charge whenever he's up visiting Washington.

After the mermaids parted ways, I haven't heard of them coming back together yet, but I hope to. Elaine and Sarah joined a handful of their sisters in moving to Crete to live with the echidna. I've heard gossip, though, that a few mermaids set out to rejoin their long-lost siren sisters all over the globe. Something about a conversation they'd shared with the kelpies after winning the battle.

The foreign Wild Women returned to their homes with the comfort of knowing the American Hunters' organization had been snuffed out, thanks to their help and bravery. They no longer had to worry for their daughters' freedom. Of course, they still weren't so sure a harpy wouldn't accidentally expose the existence of supernatural females.

And as for Marcus and me, our war is done, but our life together has just begun. We're currently expecting our first child, and I'm pretty sure Wilds on this continent and others have bets going to guess the gender and kind of our little one. Our mothers, though, have made their wishes clear enough. My mother hopes for a little huldra girl. Marcus's mother hopes for a little xana girl. Marcus and I just want a healthy baby, no matter the gender, who'll embrace their abilities, thankful to be whoever Freyja, Danu, and Marcus's God made them to be.

Shortly after returning home, Marcus was offered a promotion to investigator with the Everett Police Department. He took it. We asked to remain anonymous when it came to breaking news about the human trafficking case, so we weren't given those awards Officer Gains thought we deserved. And in the Wild area of things, Marcus has proven a quick study in the ways of a xana. Showers with the man have never been more delightful.

The chief of the Everett PD suggested I apply to work with them, too, but I turned down the offer. I prefer the freedom of bounty hunting and the fulfillment I get when bringing in a predator skip.

My mother and I have a trip planned to visit our ancestor living within a tree, the ancestor who taught her our true history and instructed her to teach it to me. Hopefully, our ancestor will gift us with wisdom to pass down to my own child, because oppression helps no one and hurts everyone. This is why Wild Women were created. And this is why we will continue to thrive, for the delight of our Goddesses and the good of all kinds.

THE END

Thank you for reading! Did you enjoy?

Please Add Your Review! And don't miss more paranormal novels like, MIDNIGHT DESIRE. Turn the page for a sneak peek!

SNEAK PEEK OF MIDNIGHT DESIRE

A ball of dread unfurled in Willow McCray's stomach and pricked along her skin. The sensation confirmed her earlier premonition of death.

Willow trolled through Fusion, the dimly lit heavy metal bar, while all around her a colorful mix of otherworldly beings gyrated to the thump of the seductive beat. Emotions of the crowd swam high and swirled through her head in a sea of lust and euphoria.

Tonight she came here with three objectives: find her best friend, get the bloodstone amulet, and walk out the door alive. She tried to scope out the place for her quarry, affectionately known as Maeve the Metallurgist.

She shielded her eyes from a strobe light as she pushed her way through the mass of sweaty bodies. Willow scanned the room, but she couldn't spot her elusive friend anywhere. She glanced at her watch and frowned. It was already past midnight and there was still no sign of her. As much as she appreciated Maeve's ability to work under pressure, Willow didn't have time to screw around.

Her hand shook as she pulled out her cell and dialed Maeve's number. *No service.* She moved past the dance floor toward the line of barstools, and something crunched under her boot. She glanced at the floor and noticed a broken syringe. Wincing, she swallowed hard and kept on walking.

Considering her choice of meeting spots, apparently Maeve still liked to party, hard. She claimed smack took the edge off the brutal confines of her job. Forging charmed metal in dark, sweltering conditions couldn't exactly be a picnic. But did she have to turn to drugs? They'd agreed to meet here, but from the loud buzzing in her ears, Willow sensed trouble was on its way. She'd been calling and texting Maeve all day, and she still couldn't get ahold of her.

Guilt tightened around Willow's gut like an iron fist. When this mess was over, she vowed to get Maeve clean. Even if Maeve refused, she would haul her ass back to rehab. Not that Willow was one to talk. She'd never touched a drug in her life, and yet she'd done plenty to regret. In fact, she feared the darkness she may have permanently etched on her soul. *If I can save Maeve, maybe I can save myself.*

When Willow opened her mind to the crowd around her, the hairs on the back of her neck prickled. A ball of heat circled her head and tingled down her spine as her magick responded to the crowd.

The vision of a tall, dark-haired man with a strip of gold around his wrist swam in her head. She blinked and the image disappeared. *Could he be one of the demons trying to kill me?*

She pushed the vision to the back of her mind and glanced across the bar at a group of gorgeous incubi huddled together. *Sex incarnate* was all her mind could register as her gaze locked on the tallest of the three. He flashed a sultry smile, the promise of sin written all over his chiseled face. According to legend, incubi magick, if wielded at full force, was like catnip to most women and could enslave even the strongest female with sex. He waved and she caught a glimpse of a gold string around his wrist.

Hmm. She usually gave their kind a wide berth, but in this case, she'd make an exception. She plastered a smile on her face and waved back. The male tilted his head to the side and his red, watery eyes zeroed in on her boobs. She'd raided a bag of Maeve's old clothes and managed to squish her breasts into a black leather bustier—at least two sizes too small. She sucked air in through her nose, finding it hard to breathe. She just hoped she didn't pass out before closing. Willow pushed out her chest as he sauntered over to her side of the bar. *Showtime.*

The acrid stench of sweat clung to his clothing, along with a hint of ether, which usually came from cooking meth. "What's up, beautiful? Why don't you have a drink with us?" he slurred and motioned to his spot at the bar.

She moved a little closer to him and purposely let her fingers graze the string at his wrist so she could peek inside his head. Even if he didn't recall what he'd done five minutes ago, he might have a clue about Maeve stored somewhere in his junkie brain. *Nothing.* "Thanks anyway, but I'm meeting someone."

As she turned to walk away, he caught her by the arm and pulled. His thoughts screamed, *Screw you, bitch.*

Her hands balled into fists. She drew up her other arm, ready to counter with a thrust to his chin, when a deep male voice, as smooth as single malt scotch, murmured, "I've been looking all over for you."

The incubus let go of her and she spun around. A towering figure stood next to her. The stilettos she wore added four inches to her already tall frame, and she still craned her neck to gaze up at his face.

Eyes the color of obsidian locked on hers. His lush, dark hair matched the color of his eyes and a short-cropped beard accentuated the hard planes of his face. He wasn't only classically gorgeous, but his features were undeniably unique. "You looked as if you might need some backup," he murmured close to her ear.

"Thanks, but I'm a lady who can handle herself." *Maybe a bit of an understatement.* She let her gaze trail over his wide, muscled chest. His black suit jacket hugged tightly to his broad shoulders. She pegged it for Armani.

In a sleazy place like this, he was either a dealer or a demon. Both were notorious show-offs. Either way, she wanted to check him out and not just for his looks. She hadn't come here to flirt, but she'd play her part to the hilt if it meant getting info.

The stranger slid onto a barstool and arched his eyebrow. "I don't doubt it. But from what I've heard, their kind doesn't understand the meaning of the word no."

She glanced over her shoulder at the incubus. He scowled at her before skulking back to his place at the bar. "I think he finally got the hint. They must be slumming tonight. This isn't their typical hangout."

"Nor mine. Were you just trying to get away from that guy or are you really meeting someone? In which case, I'd be seriously disappointed." Heat flared in his eyes, and she sensed the passion burning beneath the surface.

"Oh? And here I thought you were being a Good Samaritan," she said in her best seductive voice.

His big, dark eyes trailed over her like a soft caress and lingered on the swell of her breasts, crushed against the top of her bustier. "Maybe I have an ulterior motive." He leaned into her, his voice low near her ear. "I'm in Jersey for business and I don't know anyone in Raven's Hollow. Would you consider showing me around town?"

"Are you propositioning me? Maybe you're one of those guys into the whole damsel in distress thing." Antsy, she glanced at the door again and her gut tightened. There was still no sign of Maeve. Without the amulet, Willow was as good as dead. Tonight she'd been forced to use a glamour to fake out her enemy, but the magick wouldn't last long, less than twenty-four hours at best.

Her light-green eyes were now a deep chocolate-brown and her wavy, auburn hair was blue-black and flowed down her back like a waterfall. At least her black leather trench added some coverage. Not that it protected her from the frigid temperatures outside, but it matched the outfit and concealed the two-foot long, solid steel, twin *athames* sheathed in her hip belt. A metal choker completed the ensemble.

He glanced at her collar. "The only distress you look like you're into makes me think of whips and chains." His eyes were dark and edgy, full of sinful promises. "I'm Alexandros. Call me Alex."

Most demons don't have names like Alexandros. Or dark, golden tans in the dead of winter for that matter. Reddish skin and horns were pretty much the norm. Although some, rare breeds, like the Hymara, appeared to be human but were no less deadly than their full-blooded counterparts.

Under the lights, Alex's skin glowed to a warm, toasty brown and reminded her of hot buttered rum. "I'm Willow." He offered his hand to shake, and her heart spiked when she caught a glimpse of his gold Patek Phillippe watch. Could he be the man from her vision? The moment her hand slid into his, she opened herself to his emotions. Turmoil and anger swirled all around him. She suppressed a shiver and hoped her expression didn't make him suspicious.

"A pleasure." The deep, sensual way he said the word *pleasure* made her shiver

"Well, maybe if you buy me a drink I might forget who I was supposed to meet." She held onto his hand and zeroed in on his thoughts, but he kept his mind shut tighter than the zipper on Maeve's leather pants—now digging into her skin. Apparently, Alex could block a mind probe. Intrigued, she released his hand and plastered a smile on her face.

If he was sent to kill her, she didn't want to risk getting jumped the moment she tried to walk out the door. She'd stall him in the meantime and try to figure out a way to get the upper hand.

His smile revealed a flash of straight white teeth. "I wouldn't want to get accused of plying you with alcohol and piss off the guy who shows up. He might try to kick my ass."

"Why? You look like you can handle yourself." Willow licked her lips and let her gaze trail over two hundred plus pounds of muscle. "Besides, how do you know I'm meeting a guy?"

His slack-jawed response made her chuckle. Some witches loved the idea of threesomes, choosing polyamorous relationships over monogamous ones. She just wasn't one of them. The more she pushed Alex off kilter, the better. Maybe he might even let his shields down. Most males toyed with some sort of twisted lesbian fantasy. She'd have to find a way to get him to talk. Not that she'd act on the fantasy, but who knows, if he thought there was even a remote chance, it might get him to talk.

He leaned in to her and whispered close to her ear, "Since he, or she, isn't here and you are, I guess it's their loss." Willow caught a whiff of his clean, male scent and fought the urge to sigh. The man oozed sexual prowess. Funny, the only males she attracted always ended up turning into major losers. After the last one, she'd sworn off men for good.

Her gaze rested on his face. She'd imprint every gorgeous inch of him to memory and burn out the batteries in her vibrator later. Then she realized she was fantasizing about someone who might be trying to kill her. *What does that say about the state of my personal life?* She seriously needed to get laid. "About that drink—"

"What will the lady have?" He waved his hand in the air, flashing his expensive watch, and the bartender appeared. Alex turned back to face her and smiled, a sensual curve of his lips.

"Patrón margarita on the rocks." At least the good stuff didn't give her a hangover. She tossed her small black clutch on the bar and leaned her hip against the hard, cold edge.

She glanced over at the bartender, a rangy werewolf with black, beady eyes. She couldn't question him about Maeve, not with Alex by her side. She cringed as he poured a generous amount of tequila into her glass and then added a shot on the side. She didn't plan on getting hammered during this little foray. Her telepathy worked better without the fog from booze, but what choice did she have?

"I'll have a Glenfiddich, neat," Alex said, taking a seat on a barstool. After a few minutes, the bartender placed their drinks on the bar along with the shot, a slice of lemon, and a salt shaker. Alex touched his glass to hers and smiled. "To welcome surprises."

"To welcome surprises." *If he was sent by the Agares, he was about to get one he'd never forget.* She tried checking him out more closely over the rim of her glass. But with his mass of dark, wavy hair, she couldn't make out even the slightest hint of horns. The way he mysteriously showed up here tonight and sought her out couldn't be a coincidence. Even more reason to think the Agares sent him.

When he set his drink on the bar, she contemplated slipping a potion into his glass. She kept one in the pocket of her trench, a special concoction made from licorice root and wolfsbane. The potion acted like a truth serum. A couple of drops and Alex would be forced to reveal his deepest, darkest secrets in a heartbeat. But his steady gaze never left hers.

"That's an interesting tattoo." He reached for her hand and caressed her pentagram with his thumb. Heat emanated off him like the flame of a match. She suppressed a shiver. Alex's touch contrasted with his size and dangerous looks. The man could just be a player, a master seducer lulling her into a sexual trance with his sexy voice and pillow-soft touch before he attacked.

"It's a pentagram, a sacred Wiccan symbol, and these," she said, touching each one of the five points, "represent the elements and the spirit." She shrugged, hoping to sound noncommittal. She didn't want to get into the differences between Wicca, an earth-based religion, and hereditary witchcraft. "The guy at the tattoo shop had it in his book. He rambled on about it while he inked me. I was pretty wasted at the time."

His dark eyes lingered on her mouth as she lifted the glass to her lips. She took a sip of her margarita and glanced down at his big hands, tanned and sprinkled with a smattering of hair. Funny, she never found a man's hands sexy. Suddenly her mind filled with images of Alex trailing those big, masculine hands over her body. She wondered if he fit the stereotype. Big hands, big...

"Are you considering taking me up on my offer?" The deep timbre of his voice pulled her from a host of fantasies. Willow dug her nails into her palm to get her head back in the game. She shouldn't be thinking about this man in such a raw, sexual way.

"Why not? My car's parked in the back." She probed through the nearby crowd to check if Alex came here with bodyguards. A virtual cacophony of conversations invaded her thoughts, but nothing about protection for Alex. Once she got him alone, she'd take her chances and pray she wouldn't be outnumbered.

"Then let's get out of here, unless I've got some competition." He motioned over her shoulder to the incubus whose head now lolled forward over the bar.

"I think you're flying solo." She had set her trap and let the consequences be damned. Willow rubbed her finger along the rim of the glass and licked off the salt.

She was savoring the tangy flavor of margarita mix along with the zing of tequila as it slid down her throat. *Headrush*. No surprise there. She couldn't remember the last time she'd slept or eaten in the past forty-eight hours, existing on a combination of raw nerves and pure adrenaline.

"You missed a spot." He ran his thumb along the seam of her lip. He put it to his mouth and licked. "Mmm, sweet." Her plan didn't involve foreplay...but *damn* he was hot. In another time and another place she'd be seriously into this guy. *Too bad I might have to kill him.*

"I do like my tequila, but every now and then a girl needs something a little stronger."

"Oh? What did you have in mind?"

Now she had his attention. Willow decided to play it up for the final *coup de grâce* and offered the bait. She leaned over, allowing him to get a glimpse of the rolled-up wad of hundreds, a bonus from her last job, now tucked in her cleavage and held by her black, strapless demibra. "I'll show you mine if you show me yours," she purred.

From the way his eyes widened with a mixture of shock and pure lust as they locked on her breasts, he clearly liked the view. Good. She'd be sure to use it to her advantage. "What are we waiting for?" When Alex reached into his pocket to pull out his cash, a pack of matches slipped out and fell on the floor. He shoved some bills at the bartender and waited for his change. Willow bent to pick up the matchbook, ready to hand it back, but when her fingers closed over the cover, she caught a glimpse of Maeve's face contorted in pain.

The image changed like a haze of smoke. Crouched next to Maeve's lifeless body, a shadow of a man hovered nearby. Willow's heart thudded in her chest as the shadow turned into form.

Alex?

Breath whooshed from her lips. The matches slipped from her grasp onto the floor. No wonder Maeve never showed up.

"Hey, are you okay? You look as if you've seen a ghost." Alex placed a hand on her shoulder.

Goddess, she hoped not. "F-fine," she lied.

The bartender appeared and Alex made small talk with him as he cleared their glasses off the bar. At least it gave her a minute to think. If Alex was the one following her, maybe he'd been following Maeve as well. Panic edged around her throat and made a tight fist in her stomach. What if he tried to sell Maeve a bad batch of heroin to get her to talk, then left her to OD?

She gritted her teeth and forced her fear into cold resolve. After years of practice, she'd become adept at pushing through her pain. Shaking, she picked up her drink to take a sip and calm her nerves, when she noticed her white-knuckled grip around the glass. *Don't break it. Don't break it.* A moment later, it shattered in her hands.

"Damn," she groaned as a broken piece sank into her index finger. Blood gushed from her hand and dripped onto the bar.

"Shit. You're bleeding." Alex grabbed a handful of bar napkins, wrapped them around her finger and squeezed. "Hold on. Let me try to find a real bandage." He signaled the bartender as she squeezed at her makeshift bandage until the bleeding stopped.

When Alex turned back to face her, he removed the napkin and ripped open the wrapper of a bandage with his teeth. "I would never peg such a slender lady like yourself for crushing a bar glass. Remind me not to piss you off."

Too late. "I can't believe how clumsy I am sometimes." She couldn't deny a part of her was attracted to him. But if Alex had harmed Maeve in any way, tonight he'd pay for his sins. Did he take advantage of the situation by playing on her weakness? "It's not fair, a man as attractive as you who's also funny." He lifted her hand to kiss her bandaged finger, and she forced herself not to cringe.

"Are you ready?"

"Absolutely." Through the corner of her eye, she noticed Alex glance across the bar at a hulking male nursing a beer by himself. She sucked in a breath when she caught a glimpse of the holstered side arm under his suit jacket. *Hmm, demon bodyguard?*

Alex inclined his head toward him and winked. Did he actually think he'd make a sale and get laid? *A real multitasking, drug-dealing sleaze bag*. There could be no witnesses for what she had in mind. He wrapped his arm around her waist. "I'll follow you."

"Good, because I like to take the lead." She grabbed his hand and guided him to the side entrance of the club, used for delivery only. Once they were outside, no one would notice them, not at this time of night. They passed through the crowd to the other side of the bar and exited the building.

When the heavy door closed behind them, she froze. She stared over the railing to the ten foot drop below and her stomach dipped. Goddess, she hated heights.

Her mind reeled as she peered out into the darkness in search of stairs or something to grab onto, but only found a steep ramp covered in ice and snow. Her heart pounded in her ears...in her throat.

"Willow?" Alex's voice whispered to her from somewhere far away.

The urge to throw herself flush against the building and squeeze her eyes shut became overwhelming. *Get it together*. She bit down hard on her lip instead and forced her legs down the ramp. When her boots touched the sidewalk, she breathed a sigh of relief. "S-sorry, I forgot where I parked." She waited until his footsteps crunched behind her, then spun around.

A flicker of moonlight danced across his handsome face. Cold air filled her lungs and pebbled along her skin. "First, I'd like to get a taste of what you're offering." Willow took a step closer to him. Puffs of icy breath slipped from her lips like white smoke in the frigid night air.

"Willow, wait. There's something you should know."

"Later," she murmured and grabbed him by his collar. She tilted her head to the side and opened her mouth. She cracked an eye open and waited for him to lean into her, close enough to catch a whiff of scotch and peppermint on his warm breath, then she head-butted him.

Alex howled in pain and stumbled backward. Willow didn't give him time to right himself. Instead, she thrust out her leg to the side and hit him with a roundhouse kick under the chin. His head smashed onto the pavement with a sickening thud. Pity, the big ones always did go down hard.

She glanced at his crumbled body and then pressed her boot to his neck. At least the stilettos had come in handy.

His eyes widened in shock. A gurgling sound erupted from his throat. She pulled one of her *athames* from her hip belt and pointed it straight at his groin. "Tell me, Alex," she said with a smile. "Are you fond of your dick?"

* * *

Don't stop now. Keep reading with your copy of MIDNIGHT DESIRE available now.

Want even more paranormal fun? Try the Ravens Hollow Coven books by City Owl Author, Shari Nichols!

And discover more from Rachel Sullivan at www.rachelsullivan.net

* * *

Danger and desire collide to form an unlikely alliance between a witch with a sordid past and a special agent who might be her future.

While trying to escape her past, kick-ass witch Willow McCray dispenses her own brand of justice swiftly andwithout mercy, until she crosses paths with sexy Magickal Bureau of Investigations Agent, Alex Denopoulos. Now, she must use her powers for good if she wants to stay out of Hellios, the mage prison for those who have broken the Wiccan Rede of 'Harm ye None.'

Alex will stop at nothing to catch a killer, including recruiting notorious felon, Willow McCray, to work for the agency. While under his guard, the lines between duty and passion become blurred the more time he spends with the red-haired beauty. His penchant for justice and deep-seated hatred of witches makes a future together seem impossible. But he's not ready to let her go. Now he'll risk more than his badge to keep her alive.

If only Willow can vanquish the evil surrounding them and give Alex what he wants—before she loses her heart and even her very soul in the process.

* * *

Please sign up for the City Owl Press newsletter for chances to win special subscriber-only contests and giveaways as well as receiving information on upcoming releases and special excerpts.

All reviews are **welcome** and **appreciated**. Please consider leaving one on your favorite social media and book buying sites.

For books in the world of romance and speculative fiction that embody Innovation, Creativity, and Affordability, check out City Owl Press at www.cityowlpress.com.

ACKNOWLEDGMENTS

As Faline's story comes to a close (for now?) I want to thank my agent, Jacquie Flynn, and my editor, Heather McCorkle. You ladies have helped to bring Faline and the other Wilds out of hiding and into this world. I will be forever grateful.

To my coterie—my family—words, even from this writer, cannot express my absolute love and appreciation for you. Kisses and hugs from now to eternity.

Thank you to my Wild friends who advise me and champion my work: Amanda Lynn, Rayna Stiner, Rachel Spillane, Sara Wilkerson, Alli Roerden, Lynn Moddejonge, Samantha Heuwagen, Cass Morris, Jody Holford, and Sarah Glenn Marsh.

And to my readers. I am overfilled with appreciation at your willingness to spend time in the world of Wild Women, and your eagerness to make it your own. Your messages to me of your favorite Wild groups, your most beloved characters, and your favorite scenes, make me smile. With this book, as well as my others, I hope that you're entertained and empowered.

ABOUT THE AUTHOR

RACHEL SULLIVAN is a dog-hugger and tree-lover. Growing up with three sisters sparked her passion for both women's history and women's advocacy, which led to her career as a birth doula and childbirth educator. These days she channels those passions into researching and writing fiction, concentrating on birthing books rather than babies.

When she's not writing, Rachel works in reference and circulation services at a public library. She enjoys exploring nature, learning, wine tasting, attempting to grow her own food, and reading. She lives near Seattle, Washington.

www.rachelsullivan.net

facebook.com/AuthorRachelSullivan

twitter.com/RachelSulli3

instagram.com/rachel_sullivanbooks

ABOUT THE PUBLISHER

City Owl Press is a cutting edge indie publishing company, bringing the world of romance and speculative fiction to discerning readers.

www.cityowlpress.com

Made in the USA
Lexington, KY
22 July 2019